JOURNEYS BEYOND THE PEAKS

Far *from* Magnolia Drive

A NOVEL

M.F. ERLER

Praise for Magnolia Drive...

"If you've ever had the feeling that life has given you more than you can handle, you'll really appreciate this book. It's a woman's journey through difficulties many of us experience, to find acceptance and self-transformation in the end."

—RICHARD BARTLETT, M.A., Ph.D.

"Far from Magnolia Drive" is a book that shares one woman's struggle through her emotional and spiritual journey. Author MF Erler tells the story of a brave woman, Mary Anna, who faces several issues that affect many people today. She talks about how parenting a child with special needs (Tourette's Syndrome) . . . The grief of loss in leaving behind a home you love, physical separation from family, and the death of her parents are covered with honesty. I felt inspired and hopeful for Mary Anna, and even for myself.

Erler writes with a voice of authenticity. It is very relatable. I found it to be a page turner – I didn't want to put it down!"

—KATHLEEN MCCAFFERTY
Ordained Minister, United Methodist Church

"FAR FROM MAGNOLIA DRIVE is an intimate and captivating story of a seeker who traveled through bouts of hopelessness and despair. The telling of Mary Anna Parker's journey is written brilliantly and compassionately by M.F. ERLER. This fictional character was totally believable and real as she traveled through her journey familiar to many. As a reader, Erler led me, with her descriptive writing, to seek along with Mary Anna for a return of hope and trust in her life. This is a must read for anyone who seeks for a return of trust and hope in their lives... "how to convince herself that life had been worthwhile". I was captured and felt the struggle right along with Mary Anna.."

— MARY M. SCHMIDT
Retired Teacher

JOURNEYS BEYOND THE PEAKS

Standalones

VOICES IN THE PAST
LAUREN'S DARK PASSAGE
FAR FROM MAGNOLIA DRIVE

THE PEAKS SAGA

Series

PEAKS AT THE EDGE
OF THE WORLD ~ *Finding the Light*
SEARCHING FOR MAIA
MOUNTAINTOPS AND VALLEYS
WHEN THE WORLD GROWS COLD
THE FOUNTAIN AND THE DESERT
BEYOND THE WORLD
WHERE ALL WORLDS END

JOURNEYS BEYOND THE PEAKS

Far *from* Magnolia Drive

A NOVEL

M.F. ERLER

FAR FROM MAGNOLIA DRIVE, *Journeys Beyond the Peaks*
by M.F. Erler

First Edition 2023

 FIRST STEPS PUBLISHING
Gleneden Beach, Oregon
FirstStepsPublishing.com

ISBN:
   978-1-944072-83-4 (hc)
   978-1-944072-82-7 (pb)
   978-1-944072-84-1 (epub)

All Scripture references are from the New International Version "Scripture taken from Holy Bible, New International Version (Registered Trademark) Copyright 1973, 1978, 1984 by International Bible Society. Used by permission of Zondervan Publishing House. All rights reserved."

All hymn texts quoted are public domain.
An asterisk * in the text refers to works cited in the References list

Cover photo by Robert H. Feser
Cover design and formatting by Suzanne Fyhrie Parrott

Please provide feedback
10 9 8 7 6 5 4 3 2 1
Printed in U.S.A.

DEDICATION

This book is dedicated to my father,
Robert Philip Feser
1919-2010

Although he was born and raised in Texas, he spent most of
his adult life living in other states. But he showed me —
You can take the man out of Texas,
But you can't take Texas out of the man.

GAMES
by Robert P. Feser
In bridge or stud poker
You play the cards you're dealt.
'Tis also true in the game of life:
Some are better players,
Stay in the game longer.
Others drop out early.
But no matter how you play,
All
Will
Lose
The Game.
But what the heck,
It's a good game
And worth the playing.
Life!

ACKNOWLEDGEMENTS

Heartfelt thanks to all the people who have read the many, many drafts of this book. You have been invaluable, and I want to thank each of you from the bottom of my heart:

Mary Schmidt, Colleen St. Pierre, Lammi Veitengruber, Richard Bartlett, Janice M. Goodison, Sierra Zemke, Mark Leichliter, Paul, Jon, and Emilie Erler, Delphia Blumenthal, Diane Bokor, Kathleen McCafferty, Rose Ottosen, Bonnie Smith, and Dan Feser.

Special thanks to Glenn Schiffman and his amazing class on "Writing Autobiographical Fiction."

Thanks also to the *Montana Women Writers Group* of Kalispell and the *Footprints Christian Writers Group* for such great moral support and openness in sharing their assistance.

AUTHOR'S FOREWORD

Magnolia Drive. It has a nice sound to it. For me, it represents a happy and innocent childhood. My parents built the small three-bedroom, two-bath ranch house on Magnolia Drive when I was almost five years old. I remember wandering through the stud-work once, as we looked at where our new house was going to be. We'd been in a rental on the other side of town since I was born. I remember some of that house, though my younger brothers don't.

After we moved to the new house, I can remember standing in the backyard, looking at the huge oak tree behind the house across the street. Everything looked so big to me then. When I revisited this place some thirty years later, all the neighborhood seemed to have shrunk.

Before, I saw it with a child's eyes. Age has reduced my vision. That seems to be the problem with life. As we get older, things that meant a lot diminish. But I'm not just talking about houses, trees, and streets. People diminish, too. Along with hopes and dreams. Perhaps even faith. That's what this book is about. An attempt to regain the faith I had as a child—back there on Magnolia Drive.

After all, didn't Jesus say that we need to become as little children to enter the Kingdom of Heaven?

Unfortunately, many of us are more likely to find ourselves feeling like Nicodemus, who visited Jesus by night and was told (in answer to his questions), "You must be born again." His response: "How can a man be born when he is old? Can he enter a second time into his mother's womb and be born?"

I often want to ask God this question, too.

When I'd just turned 11 and was told we had to leave Magnolia Drive and move north to Illinois, I felt like I was being ripped from my roots and sent into exile. For the rest of my life, I've had this longing for a place to truly call home.

Sometimes the mountains of the American West have filled that need. Other times, I've found it on the shores of the Great Lakes. Yet if I look deeply into my heart, I see that nothing can replace the original home. You may go back to the place, but it's never the same. Still, the need is there, so perhaps home is more than just a place.

This book stems from my need to look back on my own life as I try to determine if it's been worthwhile. The psychologist Erik Erikson* has divided life into eight psychosocial stages, ranging from infancy to adulthood. (See *Author's References* for further information on Erikson and others referred to in this book.)

Erikson's eighth stage is Late Adulthood, age 60 and above, when a person reflects on his or her life, trying to see if that life had meaning or not. Erikson calls this the Retrospection Stage. I can certainly relate to his theories as I've lived through all of his life stages. Now that I'm in my 70s, I often look back over my life and ask his key question, "Is it okay to have been me?"

This book is necessary to help me answer that question. It also answers my need to pass something along to those who come after me.

Since the characters in this book have been derived from people in my life, it is autobiographical fiction. I am not Mary

Anna, though many of her feelings are drawn from my own experiences. The book's settings and scenes are drawn from my imagination, too.

A prime example is that the place they live is Texas. Why did I make Mary Anna's home in Texas instead of where I was raised? Though I've visited often and have several Texan relatives, I never lived there myself. But I remember my father talking about Texas often, and singing songs like, *Deep in the Heart of Texas.* Is there some force in my DNA that's called me there?

In addition, there are literary reasons. My original fictional Parker family has nearly all its roots in Texas. They initially appeared in *Peaks at the Edge of the World*, my first book. When I created those first characters, Danny and Ginna Parker, many years ago, I really had no idea they would become so enwrapped with my own story. They are nearly real to me now, but I think that's common for authors, who live with characters in their minds constantly.

I decided to remain true to my initial ideas about the Parkers and to carry their stories forward and back in time. The first book in *The Journeys Saga, Voices in the Past,* is based in part on stories I heard about my ancestors that I have transferred into the fictional Parker family, making it a work of historical fiction. This book, *Far from Magnolia Drive* I consider another *Journeys Saga* offering, as it's an offshoot of just one branch of the family tree, that of Mary Anna Parker Evans. (See the fictional *Parker/Evans Family Tree* in the following pages.)

Tim Parker and his family are entirely fictional, including his parents John and Emilia. Tim and his wife Lauren are mentioned briefly in some of the *Peaks Saga* books. They were created long before this book was even the germ of an idea.

Lauren Parker has evolved into a main character in another *Journeys Saga* book, *Lauren's Dark Passage*, which is entirely fictional.

Some of my fellow authors have termed this book "fictionalized memoir" while others call it "autobiographical fiction". In other words, the feelings and thoughts are built on reality, but names and places have been changed. If any readers want to see a more detailed (but perhaps boring) account of my *real* life for comparison, I have included this in the *Appendix* of this book, along with a few photos, used with permission of those pictured.

There has been catharsis for me in writing *Magnolia Drive*. As Mary Anna works through her problems, I've been working through some of my own. I hope and pray this book may be a help to others who are going through trials. In many ways, my writing is therapeutic for me, but I hope it's also a way to reach out.

Even more than this, it's a story from within that needs to be told. All of us live in the present, but we're who we are because of our pasts, and also because of our hopes and dreams for the future—some of which may come to pass before we die.

*AUTHOR'S REFERENCES

Because this book refers to some other works, especially ones recommended by my counselor, I have included this list of books that have been of help to me. However, I make no claims to be an expert in mental health, and am only giving these references if anyone is curious. Not all the views expressed in these books are necessarily my own.

Chapman, Gary. *The Five Love Languages*, 1992, 2004, Northfield Publishing, Chicago, IL.

Harris, Russ. *The Happiness Trap: How to Stop Struggling and Start Living*, 2007-08, Trumpeter Books, Boston, MA.

Hayes, Steven, Ph.D. *Get Out of Your Mind and Into Your Life: The New Acceptance and Commitment Therapy*, 2005, New Harbinger Publishing, Inc. Oakland, CA.

May, Gerald G., M.D. *The Dark Night of the Soul*, 2004, Harper Collins, New York City, NY.

Erikson's Stages of Psychosocial Development, Accessed 2022, https://www.verywellmind.com/ erik-eriksons-stages-of-psychosocial-development-2795740

Spirit of God, descend upon my heart:
Wean it from earth, through all its pulses move.
Stoop to my weakness, mighty as Thou art,
And help me love Thee as I ought to love.

Teach me to know that Thou art always nigh;
Teach me the struggles of the soul to bear—
To check the rising doubt, the rebel sigh;
Teach me the patience of unanswered prayer.

George Croly (1780-1860)
Hymn text – public domain

The Parker / Evans Family Tree *(fictional)*

Robert John Parker +
(1914-2010)   m. 1946   **Anna Lee Harrison +**
(1924-2017)

Mary Anna Parker *   **Richard Evans ***
(1949-2029)
m. 1975

Roberta Lee *(1950-1950)*   **Jay Richard *** *(b. 1980)*
Daniel James *** *(1957-2030)*   **Amy Elizabeth *** *(b. 1983)*

John Henry Parker *   **Emilia Rene Haas ***
(1951-2032) bp Texas   *(1952-2032)*
m. 1970

Timothy John Parker *,**   **Lauren Graves ****
(1971-2036)   *(1972-2015)*
m. 1990 / divorced 2002

Ginna Rene Parker **
(b. 1991)

Annemarie **
(b. 2008)

Sandra Crawford **
(1994-2055)   **Daniel Trebor Parker ****
(1994-2044)
m. 2015

Dain Sven Parker **
(b. 2028)

Lucinda Pardis+
(b. 2033)   **Evin Trebor Parker **+**
(b. 2031) bp Colorado
m. 2058

Cinda Marie +   **Ian Daniel +**
(b. 2064)   *(b. 2071)*

Characters are in:

** Far from Magnolia Drive*

*** The Peaks Saga books*

+ Voices in the Past

CHAPTER 1
Walking in the Dark – 1994

My first big mistake was asking God for patience. He sent our son Jay fourteen years ago, and I'm still trying to learn to be patient.

The moon was barely peeping through the East Texas piney woods as I walked on our dark country road. Stalking along the grassy shoulder, I rubbed at the tears streaming from my eyes.

Today Jay stormed into the house after school screaming, "I hate the school bus!"

"What happened?" I asked, and kept my voice as calm as I could.

He slammed his backpack onto the entry's slate floor. "They kicked me off the bus for standing while it was moving."

"But why? Doesn't your driver know where you get off?"

"She was a sub. I was only trying to tell her where my stop was, and she gave me a ticket."

"A ticket?"

"Yeah, I can't ride the bus for a week, and you have to talk to the school principal."

This wasn't the first time Jay had trouble at school because of his Tourette's Syndrome and Obsessive-Compulsive Disorder. If things got out of *his* view of what the world should be, he exploded.

I stared at him, lost for words. *What am I supposed to do,*

God? When Jay got like this, nothing could stop the outburst, nothing I said would help.

He didn't wait for any reply, just stormed into his bedroom and slammed the door. I'd learned the hard way over the years not to open that door. He always needed time to calm before he could focus on anything.

God, why are you doing this to me? I cried to the empty night as I continued to trudge the lonely road.

No answer.

I wanted to shout at God, or whoever might be listening, *Can't you ever give me a break? And what about Jay? Why does he have so many difficulties in school? Rick and I try hard to help him, but nothing seems to work.*

Again, the silence of the night replied.

As I dashed away more tears, I wondered if Jay inherited this from me.

My husband Rick often said, "You're just as bad, just as emotional as he is, Mary Anna." He was probably right.

A cold wind slammed into my face as I turned the corner onto our rural road. Taking a walk was the only thing to do when tempers were boiling over in our house, even in this unseasonable chill for a Texas November. If only there was somewhere I could run. I didn't really want to go home, but we'd just moved here a few months ago, and I didn't have any friends I could turn to.

Rick had tried to listen when I explained Jay's problem this evening at dinner, but sometimes he was as caring as a porcupine. Get too close and the quills would get you.

"He needs to get out here and join us for supper," he snapped, as I served the meatloaf I'd pulled from the oven.

"There's no point when he gets angry like this." I glanced

over at our daughter Amy, who was deeply focused on eating as quickly as possible.

"I need to give him a good talking to." Rick rose and strode to Jay's bedroom door before I could speak again. Soon shouting echoed throughout our small house.

Amy seized her dinner plate and headed for her bedroom in silence. I sat down and tried to eat a bite or two, but the food stuck in my throat. Coughing, I grabbed my jacket and headed for the front door.

Rick and I had tried many times over the years to come to grips with how to raise Jay, but seldom agreed. He wanted to use tough love, but I feared this would fuel our son's frustrations and lack of self-confidence.

We'd tried counseling with our minister a few years ago when we were living out in West Texas, but he was one of those conservatives who equated self-confidence with pride. In my mind these weren't the same at all.

Maybe he and Rick are right though. Perhaps I was too lenient with Jay. *I just don't know*, I sighed into the chill dark sky looming above the road I walked.

Life with Jay was like a constant walk on T-Rex eggs. One wrong step, and a ferocious creature rose up and raged. His jerking tics often caused him painful muscle spasms, and his involuntary noises made people wonder if he was crazy.

Who wouldn't have a short temper, if they had to live with this all the time? *Jay tries to cope the best he can. He wants so much to be normal like his peers.* Again, my heart was asking, *God why?*

The tics and facial grimaces began when our son was small. We tried neurologists, counselors, and medications. Moving around for Rick's job hadn't helped, either. There hadn't been enough consistency, for either Jay or me.

Ever since we married, Rick had worked as a geologist for an oil company, so we followed the oil fields of the Overthrust Belt. Jay was born in Wyoming, a brown-eyed boy with my dark coloring. Daughter Amy was born in Montana. She was my blonde, blue-eyed baby, taking after Rick. Like her father, though, Amy's hair darkened to golden brown with the years.

Leaving Montana was hard for Rick. He loved the mountains close-by and the wide-open spaces. I'd grown up in East Texas, though, so I hoped we could get more settled here, especially now that the kids were in their turbulent teens.

The moon had climbed above the treetops. Nearly full. If only something or someone would shed more light into *my* life

For the past couple of years, we'd moved among many small West Texas towns like gypsies, following the oil explorers. I wished we lived closer to a city like San Antonio or Dallas, where there would be resources to help with Jay. But driving two hours, plus traffic, was too great a cost to join a Tourette's support group. And the good counselors were just as far away. There had been days when I thought about packing myself and Jay off to Dallas so I could take him to a good neurologist or counselor, maybe even live there on our own.

As this thought entered my mind, I said aloud to the night's emptiness, "The time has come to take action. I need to get off my butt and do something."

Yet, when I faced the idea of actually doing this, my heart cringed in fear. *You're too indecisive and cowardly, girl.*

This past year, it was as though my life had drained into a hot and parched desert. *Where is the living water you promised, God?*

Having a diagnosis for Jay's problems was a relief at first, but Jay hated going to the neurologist almost as much as he hated taking his medication. Sometimes the meds seemed to help, but he still had a lot of tics and jerky movements. His short-fused temper was the worst part, though.

Soon I approached our driveway. The wind was cold, and there was nowhere else to go, so I forced my feet toward the front door. An owl hooted in the distance. Off in the neighbor's woods a couple of coyotes began howling and yipping. Were they talking to the moon, or was God out there somewhere listening, even to them?

I stared up at the silvery orb suspended above our front yard. "If only someone would answer me," I said aloud.

The only reply was the owl.

Climbing the wooden steps to our trailer's front door, I took hold of the handle. The hinges creaked as I pushed it open. Then I heard the loud, throbbing music coming through Jay's bedroom door.

"So, you finally came back, Mary Anna," said my husband's voice from the family room. He was watching TV as usual.

"Where else could I go?"

"Any great new thoughts?"

I made no reply to this. Instead, I stalked down the carpeted hallway to our daughter's bedroom.

As expected, eleven-year-old Amy was sprawled on her bed doing homework. Every night was the same. Three hours or more. I knew she was trying her best, but she isn't a fast reader. That year her teachers piled on more work, probably because she had a different one for each subject, instead of one general classroom teacher. None of them seemed to pay attention to how much homework the others gave. I didn't tell Amy this, afraid it would only increase her frustration.

I seated myself on a desk chair next to the bed. "Anything I can help with?"

Amy looked up and shrugged. "No, Mom. Thanks, but I'm almost finished. Maybe tomorrow we can take turns reading my English assignment, though."

"Sure, I like reading with you."

"I'm glad, Mom."

Her blue eyes shone into mine. Some days I was so tired and drained from dealing with Jay that I had nothing left for Amy. This bothered me, but all I could do was my best.

***

Later, lying sleepless in bed, I listened to Rick snore softly. The sound didn't bother me, but I envied that he was asleep. My mind whirled around as I tried to pray, but my thoughts kept wandering.

Turning onto my right side produced an angry meow.

"Sorry, Tiglet," I whispered. "Didn't know you were there."

The tiger-striped cat we'd been given last year curled up between my knees and arms, in the hollow made by lying on my side. We'd always been cat people, so after Rick's first cat Tiger died, all of us longed to have another brown-striped cat. Since this one was a kitten when we got him from new neighbors here in our mobile home park near Corsicana, the name Tiglet came naturally. He felt warm and cuddly, and the sound of his purring began to relax me. Still the thoughts kept flowing:

I remembered when we first noticed Jay squinting his eyes and blinking almost constantly in kindergarten. Sometimes his mouth twitched, too. When we took him to the eye doctor, we learned he did need glasses, but glasses didn't stop the blinking. When we asked our pediatrician about it, she said he'd outgrow it.

The next thing that came along was the constant throat clearing, with clicking and hooting sounds interrupting his speech. About this time, I saw a feature about Tourette's on one of those news shows, probably *Sixty Minutes.* That's when I began to wonder, but no one else noticed. *Maybe I'm being paranoid,* I told myself at the time.

When we took Jay to an Ear, Nose, and Throat specialist, she said his noises weren't caused by allergies, and maybe he was becoming a stutterer. This turned out to be another dead end. I decided God was making me work too hard at learning patience.

How I wished I could go to sleep, to keep those thoughts from carrying me away. They just wouldn't stop—like a dam had burst in my mind. All kinds of old suppressed feelings flooded out. I kept petting the cat. He purred, but my mind reeled on.

By second grade, Jay's vocal noises were a disruption in class. The teacher sent him to the school counselor, who suggested getting a full psychological evaluation. The nearest child psychologist was over sixty miles from where we lived then. Though our health insurance didn't pay for any of this, we went through with it, wanting to help Jay as much as we could.

After the psychologist's long session with Jay, he sent us to a neurologist. When were we going to get any answers? The neurologist did a battery of tests, too, including an EEG. We had to drive over an hour to the doctor's office for each test.

Jay was deathly afraid of needles, and by the end, he didn't like doctors either. After all that, the neurologist said Jay probably had Tourette's Syndrome.

If only they'd explained beforehand that there's no definitive test for Tourette's. All they could do was rule out every other possibility.

What an ordeal! I'm not sure who it was harder on, Jay, or Rick and me. I still hadn't learned enough patience apparently, for this was only the beginning. The neurologist said we had to wait a year before trying any medication. I guess the doctors were waiting to see if anything else showed up.

I'd hoped for some miracle drug that would make everything better. But there never was one for Jay.

Denial set in, especially on Jay's part. He wouldn't even let us use the word Tourette's around him. Rick and I had to meet with his teachers every year to explain Jay's condition, to let them know that Jay wasn't being intentionally disruptive.

There are many misconceptions about Tourette's, and few people have firsthand experience with it. I noticed it was barely even mentioned in the psychology courses I took for my teaching certificate.

Still stroking Tiglet's head behind the ears where he liked it best, I mumbled aloud, "I wish I was a cat. My life would be so much simpler—just eat and sleep."

Almost as though he agreed, Tiglet put a paw on my hand. But nothing could stop my mind-train.

You need to stop being such a coward. If you think taking Jay to Dallas will help, then just do it.

My eyes scanned the dark ceiling above me. Sleep wasn't going to come until I made a decision about this. I wanted the best for Jay, but what *was* best? And if I did leave, what would happen to Amy? Or Rick? Or our marriage? These thoughts loomed before me like roadblocks barring my way. They bounced around in my mind like popcorn flying out of an open pan. Somehow, I needed to corral them, maybe put them on a string, like the popcorn garlands we used to make for the Christmas tree, when Amy and Jay were young.

CHAPTER 2
Jay in High School - 1998

Rick and I were with Mr. Martin, the high school principal, in his office—again. This was the second time this year I'd had to get a sub for the geology classes I taught, just so he could tell us what problem Jay had now.

"What's happened this time?" I managed to ask.

"Jay was shoved into a locker in the boys' dressing room," the man replied. "Of course, it wasn't his fault, but the substitute gym teacher sent both the boys to the office for fighting."

Rick was clenching his fists by this time. "You realize Jay isn't aggressive. Every year we meet with his teachers to explain the ramifications of Tourette's."

"It's one of the most misunderstood ailments," I added. "Too many people only hear of the stereotypes like cursing and ticing."

"I know," the principal nodded. "But we can't meet with every possible substitute teacher, too. I just want you to be in the loop in case this happens again."

"Well, thanks for that anyway," groaned Rick.

What did we ever do to deserve all this burden, Lord? It's just not fair. I guess it's not right to think this way, but I can't help it.

Well-meaning friends sometimes told me, "Life isn't fair." Whenever I heard this, I cringed inside because Jay freaked out if we ever said this around him.

Why can't life give us a break and be fairer? Some days I

wanted to shout this from a mountaintop. None were available in East Texas, though.

Mr. Martin's voice broke into my thoughts:

"Jay has never acted out his anger here at school, so I'm assured that he didn't start this fight." (Rick glanced at me with relief.) "In fact, he was in tears when I called them in individually."

There it was again. Jay's emotional nature. Some people would say he acted more like a girl. Rick hated to hear that. I preferred to think Jay was just thin-skinned, which made him an easy target for bullies who fed on that sort of thing. As early as kindergarten, he'd had trouble with bullies on the school bus, until an older boy from down the road noticed and started to sit with him. We used to take that boy and his little sister to church with us. I was glad a seed of caring was planted in this boy—by one small thing we did for them.

In sixth grade, Jay was bullied by a girl—a very sly and aggressive one, adept at making her transgressions look like Jay's fault. Even changing his homeroom teacher didn't help much. Once the girl got wind of it, she demanded that her parents move her to the other class, too. Fortunately, the principal of that middle school didn't bend to her parents' request.

After all these years, I was exhausted from the weight of raising Jay. As Rick and Mr. Martin talked, my mind continued on its own path, again thinking how difficult it was for Jay to be like his peers. The Tourette's complicated things, of course, but our frequent moves hadn't helped the situation.

Then I realized both the men had stopped talking. Rick had risen from his metal chair and was shaking Mr. Martin's hand.

"Thank you for your help," he said, as I stood, too.

Walking out of the office in silence, I knew there wasn't anything to say that would help. We'd talked this over for many years, and never came to any conclusions. Both of us hungered for answers—perhaps even solutions—but there never seemed to be any. Jay's doctors had experimented with various medications, with mixed results and unpleasant side effects. Now Jay was digging in his heels about meds.

As long as he's under our roof, we can enforce this regime, I thought. *He probably won't be living at home in a few short years.*

Lately, he had episodes where his eyes would roll back into his head. "I can't look at anything but the ceiling!" he'd cry. Then his tics would go wild.

Perhaps this was a side effect of the newest medication, pimozide. More to talk to the doctor about. All I could do as we walked out of the school was stare at the gray tile floor, wishing Rick would take my hand. My husband wasn't one to show affection in public, though.

Just last fall, we'd been in a class at church studying *The Five Love Languages**, a helpful book by Gary Chapman. I'd learned that my 'love language' was Physical Signs of Affection, but Rick's was Acts of Service. At least, now we knew better what to expect of each other. I remember telling Rick one day after church, "Now I see that we're just different. I will try to let you know I appreciate all the times you help with household chores."

"Okay, and I'll try to hold your hand once in a while," he nodded.

As weeks passed after that class, I discovered it was hard work to put these ideas into practice daily. It was all too easy to fall back into the old habits.

This day, I just let the hand-holding idea pass. My thoughts were too fixed on Jay: *If only we could have hope that Jay will get better. The doctors say fifty percent of Tourette's patients outgrow the symptoms. But will Jay ever change?*

I couldn't get this gloom out of my mind as we drove home in silence, and I was in no condition to go back to my classroom.

***

After moving to Texas from Montana, where the kids had gone through grade school, we'd lived all over the Texas oil fields, first in West Texas and then on the east side of the state. Since Amy and Jay were in middle and high school now, it was nice to be back in the eastern piney woods, where I grew up. We'd finally bought a house in a small town called Eureka. I was thankful to be out of the mobile home we'd dragged all over the west. Luckily, we'd stayed in a few places long enough for me to get a teaching job.

My brothers, Dan and John, lived in nearby towns. Dan was the one I felt closest to. We could talk about almost anything. John was quieter, so communication with him didn't flow quite as freely, but I enjoyed living close enough now to go shopping with John's wife Emilia. Since I didn't have a sister, I treasured Emilia's company. For one thing, we had very similar tastes, especially in clothes. One of our favorite things was to go Black Friday shopping at 6 a.m. on the day after Thanksgiving.

Sometimes, standing in long holiday checkout lines at our favorite clothing store, I'd talk to Emilia about my self-doubts.

"They seem to rise out of nowhere, like some of the bayou mists in the nearby swamps. I feel like I'm so clumsy, or not as talented as you and John."

She reached over and patted my arm. "No, Mary Anna, you're a great teacher. You've touched a lot of lives in your work. And what do I do? Just write reports and sell insurance."

"Don't be silly. You've done so well in your company, rising from a clerk-typist to a project leader."

"Oh, well, thanks for saying so."

"No, I mean it. Maybe part of my problem is an old saying I used to hear from my parents."

"What's that, Mary Anna?"

"They'd say, 'Those who can do, but those who can't teach.'"

"Oh, that's dumb! Nobody thinks that nowadays."

"I don't know. I still wonder if some of the disgruntled parents at teacher conferences are thinking it."

"No way. Teaching is one of the most difficult jobs in our modern world. People should appreciate teachers more."

"I definitely wish that," I sighed. "And for better pay, too."

"Try not to let yourself be ruled by those old ideas your parents had. I'm sure they have learned better since then, now that they've seen you and your brothers grow up. Dan is a teacher, too, like you."

I nodded. We were almost to the cashier now. "I've had this inferiority complex most of my life. I wish I knew how to overcome it. I see this lack of self-confidence in my children, too. Maybe it's just my nature, and they inherited it. Not what I wanted to pass on."

She patted my back, then stepped to the checkout. "Just let it be, Mary Anna. Like that old song."

It was good to have these talks with Emilia, but there were still times I asked God, "Why did you make me like this?" Then one Sunday, our pastor preached a sermon on a verse in the Bible that says, "Can the pottery ask the potter, 'Why did you make me this way?' "

Oh boy, I'm not supposed to ask God such questions, am I? Yet my mind does it anyway.

There were so many days when Jay's personality quirks overwhelmed me. He had a way of painting me into a corner, with no logical way out. Just as one example, he refused to eat bread that was stored in the freezer or refrigerator. But if the bread out on the kitchen counter got moldy, he freaked out.

I usually called my brothers on Sunday, just to chat and catch up. Today, Dan wasn't answering his phone, so I left a voicemail and called John.

"Oh hi, Mary Anna," he said before I could speak.

My family members still used my full name, since they'd always lived in the South, where double names were more common. I'd been shortened to 'Mary' when we lived in the northern states. This sounded so ordinary, and I wanted to be different, but learned to live with it.

"How's it going?" John asked into my tangential thoughts.

"Only so-so. We were at the high school principal's office again. Jay was in a fight in the boys' locker room. Fortunately, they knew he hadn't started it."

"He's a target for bullies, isn't he?"

"Yeah. Always has been. But what can we do to help him?"

"We've been in the same boat with Tim."

"Really? I never knew." Tim was John and Emilia's older son, now twenty-seven years old and married, with two young children. Even though John was a couple of years younger than me, he'd married soon after high school and started a family right away. I hadn't met Rick until college, giving my family a later start.

John's voice continued, "Tim had some of the same problems in high school. He wasn't very coordinated or athletic. People called him 'sissy' a lot. Now that he and Lauren are married, things are getting better."

"Hopefully once Jay gets older, things will improve for him. It's all I have to cling to."

"Well, don't give up hope, Sis. God has a plan for Jay."

"I sure hope so."

From there we rambled about our recent warm weather and whether rain was in the forecast. I didn't usually get into deep discussions with John. Dan and I had more in common, including our teaching experiences and reading the same kind of books, especially science fiction. For me, sci-fi was a good escape from reality, which I seemed to need often.

***

Even though Rick wasn't as happy in Texas, he was managing. Being a Midwesterner, he said he felt like a stranger in the South. When Jay was in high school, we'd bought a house in Eureka, a small town near Corsicana. Rick had an office job, which kept him closer to home. I was thankful we didn't have to follow the geologists all over the country, seeking out new oil supplies. Hopefully the kids would be able to graduate from the school system they were in now. What a relief that would be after moving so much when they were young. I'd already lost count of how many schools they'd attended.

Rick went to meetings in Dallas about once a month, but I didn't mind at all. It was nice to be on my own at times.

Thinking about this, I sometimes regretted marrying right out of college. I'd gone straight from being under my parents' care to being under Rick's. There were days when I wondered if I could ever really stand on my own two feet. Part of me wanted to, but another part was afraid of failure.

That fear of failure must be what had grown into my feelings of inferiority. My mother was very self-consciousness, and striving for perfectionism had ruled our family life. Her house was the most immaculate of any house I'd ever seen. Sometimes I chastised myself for not being the kind of housekeeper my mother was. Yes, Emilia was right. I had a lot of things I needed to let go.

Amid all those thoughts one evening, I sat on our back porch with a cat on my lap, as I often did. Amy and Jay were at a youth group meeting, and Rick was in Dallas all week. I loved it when I didn't have to worry about what to fix for dinner. A can of soup would do.

As I watched the sunset with our new cat Tigger, I thought of how he—our third cat—adopted us soon after we moved to Eureka. Tiglet had died just before that move, and Amy was disconsolate. When this striped cat kept showing up on the porch, Amy begged until we agreed to take him in.

We had a vet check him out, once we decided to adopt. He confirmed his sex, but said he'd already been neutered.

"How old is he?" I remembered asking.

"We can't tell," he replied, looking into Tigger's mouth. "He has no teeth."

"None?" I was flabbergasted. "But he eats dry cat food, and apparently managed as a stray for who knows how long."

"Well, he must just gulp it," said the vet.

"Why does he have that enlarged belly?"

"He appears to be malnourished. How long have you been feeding him?"

"Only a couple of weeks."

"He'll recover in a few more weeks. He's a lucky cat to have you."

"He's so friendly for a stray. Guess he just stole our hearts."

As I remembered that conversation, I idly stroked Tigger. Amy insisted on this name, to carry on the tradition of our tiger-tabbies. Tigger butted his head against my hand, as if to say, 'Pet me more'—like he could never get enough loving.

What a reminder to keep on loving my children and my husband. Love had made this cat's life take a turn for the better. Maybe love would do the same for Jay. Still, I knew it was never going to be an easy road.

***

Then something even more painful happened just a couple of weeks later. If Jay hadn't been afraid to talk to Rick, it would have saved all of us much pain and turmoil.

One morning, I woke to Rick's voice shouting at the other end of the house, "What's this stranger doing here, sleeping on my couch?"

I made my way to the kitchen, but stopped short of the family room. Around the corner from the sliding door to the patio, I saw Jay standing in front of our blue hide-a-bed.

"It's just my friend Greg," he began. "He was—"

"What are we? A homeless shelter?" roared Rick.

I could see the fear in Jay's eyes as he stepped back from his dad. "You just don't get it, Dad. You never will."

As Jay turned his back on Rick, my husband picked up a plate from the nearby breakfast-bar.

"Stop," I cried. "Don't throw that!"

Before I could say anything else, Rick whirled to face me. "Are you plotting against me, too?"

"What? I just woke up and heard you shouting."

"You always take his side, covering for him. Why is he letting people in my house in the dead of night without permission? Just tell me that."

I stepped back from the anger flashing in his eyes. "I don't know. Can't we talk about this rationally?"

Instead of replying, Rick threw the plate on the floor, grabbed his keys, and stomped toward the door. "I have to go to work."

As his car roared away, I crossed into the family room, stepping around the shards of plate. Jay and his friend had fled out the sliding door. Soon I heard my son's car crunching down the gravel driveway.

Once I'd swept up the broken stoneware, I poured myself a cup of coffee, hoping it would settle my churning stomach. Caffeine was the wrong choice right then, but the thought of eating something left me queasy.

Amy had already caught the school bus before any of this happened, so I was alone. When my hands stopped trembling, I headed out to the garage and drove myself to work. That day of teaching went from bad to worse, though. Being so tense to begin with, every little quirk of the students' behavior ramped me up more. I started snapping at them for minor infractions that I should have overlooked.

After lunch break, the principal took me aside in the faculty lounge.

"Are you okay? You seem really wired today."

"Oh, it's no big deal. Just some stress at home."

"Well, if you need to go home early, let me know. It's better if you don't bring baggage to school."

"You know I seldom do. This was just one of those mornings." I hoped the look in my boss's eyes was just concern and not displeasure. That would be all I needed right now.

By the time I got home that afternoon, I was on the verge of a full-blown panic attack. I'd had a couple of them before, but this one was the worst.

When Jay and Amy got home from school, I was sitting on the toilet with a wastebasket in my hands, the room whirling around me. I had the dry heaves, since I'd eaten little all day. I felt like I was being tossed around on a small boat in the midst of a stormy sea.

"Mom where are you?" Amy called.

"In my bathroom," I managed to reply.

She appeared through the dizziness. "Are you okay? What's wrong?"

"I've got vertigo. The room won't stop spinning."

"Here, let me help you to the bed."

"Thanks, Honey." Somehow I managed to stand as Amy took my arm and guided me to the four-poster bed in the master bedroom. The whirling began to slow down.

"Can I bring you anything, Mom?"

"Yeah, the pill bottle with the blue cap that's on the bathroom counter. And a glass of water."

"Okay."

I'd meant to take an extra Xanax as soon as I got home. The vertigo came on so suddenly that I couldn't, because getting off the toilet was impossible. My muscles had frozen in panic as the dizziness kept rising.

After taking two of the orange pills, I lay back on the bed's headboard, hoping I wouldn't vomit them into the wastebasket beside the nightstand.

Amy was the one who got dinner ready that evening. She came to check on me periodically and insisted I eat some of the tomato soup and grilled cheese sandwich she brought.

As dusk fell, Rick came in to wish me good-night. "I'll sleep in the guest bed so I won't disturb you."

His voice had its usual calm again, as though nothing out of the ordinary had happened. Did he even remember his outbursts this morning? He'd done this before, seeming to forget such events. I decided there was no point in bringing it up.

I took another Xanax after finishing the soup, and soon drifted into blessed sleep.

The next morning, though, I woke with a flaming migraine and called in sick.

Jay finally came to see me when he got home from school that next day. Amy had stayed behind for track practice, and Rick was going to pick her up.

"I'm sorry, Mom, I just can't handle Dad when he's mad."

Leaning against the pillows I'd piled behind me, I sighed, "What was all this about, anyway?"

"Greg and his father had an argument, so he needed some place to go. I told him to come to our back door."

"Well, that's ironic. His parent problems led to yours. Why didn't you just tell Dad this?"

"You know I can't talk to him. Not when he's boiling over like that."

"I wish you'd tried."

His eyes blinked, and he jerked his head to the left. Seeing his most common tics flare up, I knew this discussion had to end. He was too stressed.

"There's no point in rehashing it now. What's done is done. Next time, include me in the loop. That might help."

"Okay, Mom. I didn't want you to be caught in the middle."

"Thanks for thinking of me, but I'm always stuck in the middle anyway."

***

The next Sunday after we got home from church, I asked Rick if he would come with me to talk to our pastor about the incident.

He stood in front of his closet, rehanging dress pants and getting out a pair of faded blue jeans. "Why should we do that?" he snapped.

I took a deep breath and stared at myself in the mirror on my closet door. "Well, I just think we need a little advice on how to communicate better with Jay, so he's not afraid to open up to you."

"Well, I don't deny there's some miscommunication, but I don't feel comfortable telling Pastor Stan about it."

"I just don't know who else we can go to. Jay has doctors to talk to about meds, but we don't have any resources for us as parents of a Tourette's son. The support groups in Dallas are too far away. I'm feeling lost and alone in all this."

"Don't take it so seriously. If you just lighten up, things will get better." He closed his closet door and headed for the bedroom doorway. "I'm hungry. What's for lunch?"

As he left the room, I heard Jay and Amy's voices down the hall. Short of grabbing him, there was no way to get Rick to talk more about it alone at this point. I gave a deep sigh.

The next morning after Rick went to work, and before I had to be at school, I called the church office and made an appointment to see Pastor Stan by myself.

Over the years of our many moves, I'd talked to other pastors when things got rough at home. It was the only resource I had, but this time I'd hoped Rick would come with me.

When Pastor Stan came into the hallway to escort me to his office, I did my best not to wring my sweaty hands. Once we were seated on opposite sides of a long wooden table in his office, I tried to make small talk.

He appeared to want to get right to the nitty gritty, for he started with, "How can I help you, Mary Anna?"

"I don't know where to start," I murmured. "Jay and Rick had a big blow-up last week. When I tried to talk to them later, Rick acted like he didn't remember it, and Jay admitted he finds it hard to talk to his dad."

"Sounds like they're the ones I need to talk with."

I looked down at the dark brown tabletop. "I tried to get Rick to come with me, but he wouldn't. Jay has school, and I'm afraid to ask him. The last time we talked to a pastor, it didn't go well, and he won't have anything to do with counseling anymore."

"What happened? It wasn't here, was it?"

"Oh, no. It was when we were in West Texas, near Odessa. I know part of Jay's problem is we've had to move a lot for Rick's job. Jay doesn't handle change too well, because of his Tourette's and Obsessive-Compulsive Disorder."

"I see. I'm familiar with OCD, but haven't had much experience with Tourette's."

"Neither have most of his teachers through the years."

"So tell me, what happened to turn him off to counseling?"

"The pastor we talked with back then said Jay was just being selfish, that he was too prideful and needed to learn humility."

"All of us have those problems from time to time."

"Yes, but Jay's biggest problem is lack of self-confidence, not pride. I'm not sure how this pastor got off on it."

"Maybe it was one of his pet peeves."

"Perhaps. One time when Jay was being teased during Sunday School, he'd gone into the Boys' Room to cool off. When he does that, he often talks to himself. The pastor thought he was crying, and told Jay he was being childish."

"Some men have problems with tears, you know."

"I think Rick does, too."

"Why didn't Rick want to come with you?"

"He said he'd be embarrassed to tell you our problems, that he felt like you'd be up there in the pulpit judging us every Sunday."

"I'd never do that." His voice was full of surprise.

"I know. Rick has always had trouble accepting how Jay is. He thinks there's some way to overcome it all and make Jay normal. Maybe he thinks we just need to believe harder."

"What do you feel about that?"

Again, I stared at the wooden tabletop for a while before I answered. "I've prayed for God to perform a miracle and heal Jay, but He never answers."

"God always answers, but sometimes his answer is 'Not yet.'"

"Yeah, I guess. After so many years, it's hard to just keep asking the same questions over and over, or praying the same prayers all the time."

Pastor Stan reached across the table and held one of my hands in his, which took me by surprise. "God still hears you, even if it doesn't seem like it."

"I guess so, Pastor."

"Is there anything specific I can do to help you?"

Now I drew a blank. What could anyone do? "I suppose just pray for us," I said at last.

He did. Still holding my hand, he said a prayer asking God to touch our family with His love and peace, and to give Jay relief in his struggles.

After we both said "Amen," he looked into my eyes. "Mary Anna, do you feel like you're always caught in the middle?"

"I sure do."

"It's a difficult place to be. You sound like you're a 'pleaser' to me, trying to make everyone else happy at your own expense."

"Maybe so." I stared at the blue carpet under my feet.

"If I can make a suggestion, set down some boundaries for yourself. Make a list of things you won't tolerate from Jay or Rick, and let them know what these are."

"That sounds really hard."

"You need to find ways to protect yourself, so you don't get trampled in between them."

My heart pounded as I tried to picture myself confronting either of them with such a list. "I don't know if I'm strong enough," I sighed.

"Ask the Lord to help you. He's strong enough, even when we're weak."

"Okay."

He rose from his chair, and I followed him toward his office door. "Call me if I can help with anything else."

I nodded, but by now my voice had lodged in my throat. He shook my hand as I stepped out of the room.

When I got to my car, tears flooded my eyes as I thought of what I might put on that list. It was a good suggestion, but that night when I tried to write ideas on a notepad at the kitchen counter, my hands started to tremble. I sat there for almost half an hour, the paper still blank. Rick was in the other room watching TV, and the kids were in their rooms doing homework.

At last, I crumpled the piece of paper and tossed it in the trash. I couldn't bring myself to write on it, let alone show it to anyone.

CHAPTER 3
College and Crisis – 2000

I sat at the kitchen table, the phone to my ear, and my heart racing. Jay had just said he wanted to jump out of his third-floor dormitory window. He was a hundred miles away in his freshman year of college.

What am I supposed to say or do? God help me!

And what had brought this on? According to Jay, it was a phone calling card that didn't work. Perhaps we should have gotten him the cell phone he'd begged for. They were still a new thing and expensive, so Rick wondered if it was worth the money.

"What if Jay runs up a huge bill? He'll expect us to pay it," he'd said just the other day.

Neither of us had anticipated a problem like this, though perhaps we should have. It appeared we still had false hope that things would get better for Jay someday.

"Jay, are you taking your meds?" It was a question I knew I shouldn't ask, but I always did.

"I keep forgetting."

"Why can't you just go take it whenever you remember?"

"When I do, it's night, so I have to wait until the next day."

When he forgets again. It must be the OCD that makes him think he has to take it at a certain time. Or is it just denial, thinking that he doesn't need it?

"It's not my fault, Mom. There's too much stuff to remember here."

"I know." I tried to sound encouraging. "This is a big transition, being in a dorm on your own."

If only we had a junior college here. He could take classes and still live at home, but this town of Eureka is too small. One of the many things beyond my control.

"Mom, my RA wants to talk to you."

"Hello?" Before I had time to think, a kind-sounding female voice spoke on the line. "I'm Rachel."

"Hi, Rachel, uh—"

"Jay talked to me a long time tonight. I hope I've been some help. My boyfriend has OCD, too. It's a tricky beast to deal with."

"You can say that again."

"Anyway, since I know about him now, I can try to keep an eye out."

"Thanks."

"I'm available anytime he needs to talk."

I had no idea what else to say. We chatted for a few minutes longer, but later I couldn't even remember what we said. Perhaps my mind had lapsed into shock mode.

"Well, thank you, Rachel," I said at last. "Can I talk to Jay again?"

"He's gone back to his room."

Another wave of uncertainty washed over me. *Should I call him back or not? Will it help or just make matters worse?* Why was I being so indecisive? I felt lost.

I was still sitting at the table debating, head in my hands, when Rick got home from a meeting at church.

"What's up?" he asked as he closed the front door.

"Oh, I was just talking to Jay."

"Is he okay?"

"I don't know. He was upset, but he talked to his RA, and that seemed to help." I was afraid to say anything else. Somehow, I needed to get my scattered wits collected first. Maybe that was the reason I didn't call Jay back, either.

Someone stronger than me would know what to do. But I couldn't get my mind to function. I stared at the tabletop and then the walls for a long time, then finally went down the hall, changed into pj's, and crawled into bed. Rick was already asleep.

***

Jay's college years continued in the same pattern of highs and lows, and he usually called me at his lows. Besides classes he had trouble passing—and one he had to retake—the living situation never worked quite right. One year, he lived alone in an off-campus apartment, but he got depressed coming home to an empty place.

The times he tried having a roommate, his frustration mounted from the stress of living with someone else. As I thought about it, I remembered having an easier time living with roommates who weren't close friends. So, was this another poor trait he inherited from me?

"He just can't look at things from someone else's viewpoint," I told Amy one evening while I helped her with high school homework. I was glad I could help with the reading and language arts, but Amy was way ahead of me in math by this time. She never used her desk—just sprawled on her bed. I remembered doing this myself when I was in high school and college.

Amy shook her head at my remark about Jay. "Maybe it's his OCD that makes him so moody."

"I suppose so. I wish I could help him, but nothing seems to work. He won't take his meds like he's supposed to."

Our newest cat, Callie was curled up on the bed, nestled close to Amy. This cat loved to be with people. Maybe she thought they'd disappear like her former owners, since she was another stray that adopted us, soon after Tigger's demise. She kept hanging around, and we started calling her 'the calico cat'. When Rick finally gave in and accepted her adoption overtures, the name became just Callie.

"I wish Jay could learn to put himself in other people's shoes," I sighed, petting Callie's black and orange head.

"That's hard for any of us to do—even when we're more normal than Jay."

Listening to my teen-aged daughter, I marveled at her insight. *Why can't Jay be more like her? Why can't I?*

"How did you become so wise, Amy?"

"I don't know. Maybe from living with Jay all my life?" she shrugged.

"That must be it. I'm so lucky to have you for a daughter."

"Oh, Mom—"

As Amy matured into early womanhood, her natural love for working with children emerged. As early as age twelve, she'd begun earning extra money babysitting. Soon her summer jobs were at nearby daycare centers and preschools.

That was helpful when Amy's tastes in clothing changed. No longer did she want her mother choosing her clothes, so it was nice that she had money of her own to spend. As time went on, the two of us began shopping together, each for our own preferences. I loved the opportunity to relate to my daughter woman-to-woman. It got to where I valued Amy's opinion highly when it came to stylish dressing—similar to how I enjoyed shopping with my sister-in-law Emilia. It was easier to decide on purchases with some advice from one of them.

As high school graduation neared for Amy, she began talking with me about her career goals.

"I think I'd like to be a teacher, Mom."

"You are very good with children."

"I feel better with the younger ones, so I think elementary teaching would be best for me. Besides that, I can do crafts and art projects with them, too."

"Like you've done when you help at the preschool, right?"

"Also where I'm helping in a first-grade class now."

This was during Amy's senior year, when she was able to be in a work-study program at the nearby grade school, as part of her final classes.

"My first choice would probably be kindergarten," she added.

I knew that once my daughter had a goal, she pursued it thoroughly, so it was no surprise when Amy majored in elementary education in college. The university with the best reputation in our area was the same one Jay was going to, only a couple of hours from home. This helped me with the transition of becoming an empty-nester.

***

We always knew Jay would do something with maps as a career. He used to come home from school with pencil-drawn maps all over the edges of his papers. Many times, those papers didn't have good grades, but the maps were amazing. By the time he was in high school, he could draw an accurate outline of the United States freehand. I'd never known anyone else who could do that.

Thus, it was no surprise when he opted to major in geography at East-Texas University. Unfortunately, we still got those unsettling, panic calls from him.

One day in his third or fourth year of college, our house phone rang. I was home for lunch then because my school had an early release that day. My stomach tightened and I cringed when I heard the phone, a common reaction I'd developed since Jay went away to college. Almost every time the phone rang, he was in another crisis.

Not long after the phone card episode, he called to say he'd lost his wallet. With his credit card, driver's license—everything. I was beyond frustrated. How was I supposed to fix things from a hundred miles away? Once we got all the cards replaced, he found the old wallet a month later. It had fallen behind his dresser, but his room was such a mess that he hadn't thought to look there.

As I hurried to answer the phone that noon, I wondered what disaster I was expected to take care of this time. My heart began to slow a bit, however, when I heard his tone of voice: "Hi, Mom. Guess what?"

"Uh—what now?"

"I started my World Geography class today."

"And—?"

"I think I'm going to like it."

"Well, that's good."

"Yeah, the professor began the class by putting an unlabeled map on the projector screen. Then he asked if anyone knew where this was. I looked at it for a couple of minutes and then raised my hand. He asked what my guess was, and I said 'It's the border of Kazakhstan and Uzbekistan.' He stared at me for a few seconds and then turned to the rest of the class. 'No one has ever gotten that right before. How did you know?' 'By the shape of that mountain range, and those rivers,' I said."

"Wow, Jay. That's awesome."

Knowing my son as I did, I wasn't surprised. On family trips, he had gotten so absorbed in the road maps that he could name the route of every Interstate highway across the U.S., state by state.

Not all of his classes went this well. Even though he spent a lot of time on his computer, computer programming and math weren't his best subjects. Still, he managed to graduate with a 3.2 grade-point. It wasn't long before he found a cartography job, either. A non-profit called the Tip of the Mitt Watershed Council in Petoskey, Michigan hired him to make environmental impact maps.

I remembered asking, "Why do they call it 'Tip of the Mitt'?"

"Hold up your left hand. That's the shape of Lower Michigan—a mitten. See where your ring finger is?"

"Yeah."

"Well that's where Petoskey is, near the tip of the mitten. People in Michigan always talk with their hands."

All I could do was smile.

For several years, our son was a Michigander, as they called themselves. As usual for Jay, it was never a smooth ride. He often called to say it had snowed another foot. There I was in Texas, where it hardly ever snowed. What was I supposed to do?

"I can sympathize," I said, more often than I cared to remember. "Just try to drive carefully."

"At least they plow and salt the roads up here, but I'm still not used to driving in all this stuff."

Of course, he was hundreds of miles away, instead of an hour or two away at college. My panic attacks when the phone rang continued. Whenever I came home from work and saw the blinking light on the phone that meant we had a voicemail, my stomach would tighten and flip over.

One morning—so early it was still dark—the phone woke me.

Oh, no, what now?

The first thing I did almost every morning was take a Xanax to calm my nerves. That day I hadn't taken one yet.

"Mom," Jay's voice moaned.

"What?" I managed not to add 'now'.

"It froze last night, and my car is stuck to the ground."

"Stuck?"

"Yeah, the snow blew under it. Things warmed up enough to melt it, and then we had a cold front. Now it's all ice, and the frame of my car is frozen down."

I was still groggy, so my next question was, "What day is it?"

"Uh, Mom, it's Easter Sunday. I was planning to go to the sunrise service."

"Oh." I was glad to hear him say he'd wanted to go to church. But how had I forgotten Easter? Was this a new impact of Jay's troubles on my state of mind?

Still, when sunrise came to Petoskey, Michigan that day, he did manage to get his car free by using a hair-dryer to melt the worst of the ice. Then he went to a later church service.

Another call of Jay's troubled me even more. Early on a Saturday morning, the phone woke me again.

"Motorola sure makes good phones," said his familiar voice.

"What?" I was too sleepy to think.

"I just threw mine at a guy's car. It bounced off his passenger window and landed in my back seat."

"You what? Why?" I was wide awake now.

"The way people drive here makes me crazy."

I could barely believe what I was hearing, but then recognized this was a typical Jay tantrum. When was he going to outgrow this?

"Jay, you need to think before you act, please."

"Oh, stop it, Mom." He hung up on me.

At least he called back later to apologize after he calmed down. As for me, I kept on taking Xanax, and tried to make do with the panic attacks.

After five years in Petoskey, Jay's job ended, but he wanted to spend one more summer in Michigan. The year before, he'd become acquainted with a church camp called Fortune Lake, and he was able to get a counselor job for that summer. It was near a small town in the Upper Peninsula called Crystal Falls. He enjoyed working with teens, and fell in love with the open lakes and forests of the UP, as Michiganders called it.

He even began to text me now and then, sending photos of what he was doing and the new sights in Upper Michigan. One of his favorite tasks was setting up orienteering courses, which used his map skills well.

"I want to become a Yooper," he texted one day.

"What's that?" I asked, mystified.

"It's what we call people who live in the UP."

When camp ended that year, he moved into a friend's house in Crystal Falls and got himself on the substitute teaching lists for area schools. This earned barely enough to pay his rent, though.

After another summer at the camp, he finally faced the fact that he couldn't earn a living as just a substitute teacher and camp counselor, so he came to our new home in Palestine Texas, the one we'd built when Rick was about to retire in 2008.

CHAPTER 4
Reset 2010

Both our children were out of college by this time. Amy had landed a job teaching kindergarten in a town close to ours, and was renting her own place. We'd just settled into enjoying our empty nest, when Jay moved back home. At least Rick had agreed to build and settle in Palestine, Texas, so we'd be closer to my family.

Jay set up his computer in our extra upstairs bedroom, spending almost all day on the Internet.

"I wish he would take more responsibility," Rick said often.

"Me, too. He says he's searching for new jobs, but he doesn't want to go back to a cold climate—unless it's in Upper Michigan—so the openings are more limited."

"There you go, making excuses for him again," came Rick's usual reply.

"Hey, I don't know what to do. Do you want me to stand over him? He's an adult, but you know he's always had mental issues."

"Maybe we should start charging him rent."

I shrugged. "You'll have to talk to him about that, I guess. At least he buys most of his own food, and usually cooks for himself."

"Yeah, except for when he comes down the stairs, right after we've gone to bed, and eats all the leftovers we'd planned for tomorrow's dinner."

Again, I couldn't think of a quick comeback. "Hopefully he'll get settled into a job soon," I finally said.

"Just so he doesn't settle in too much here."

After a year, Jay reestablished his Texas residency, and decided to go back to college and earn a teaching certificate.

Rick and I agreed that this time the college bills were entirely Jay's responsibility, and he stepped up and took care of arranging his own student loans. These new signs of maturity made me feel better.

"I can teach geography and history," he told me. "I've always liked working with kids. If I get a good job, it will be much better than subbing. I'll be able to have my own classroom and connect better with the students."

I had seen how much he enjoyed helping with the youth group at church when he was in high school. During summers in college, he'd worked as a counselor at local youth camps, not to mention his experiences in Michigan.

Hopefully, things would come together for him this time, for a change. I'd prayed about his future every morning for so many years, and by now I wondered if God was ever going to answer. Did He even hear my feeble prayers?

Jay enrolled in the local community college, which had a partnership with University of Texas—Tyler. Thus, he was able to get the courses he lacked for the teacher certification requirements. To save money, he continued to live at home. In some ways, this arrangement meant less stress than having him living several states away. But then other complications rose unexpectedly.

***

Shortly after Jay had moved home, my brother Dan called. "Hi Mary Anna. We have a problem."

"Uh-oh. What?"

"Dad is in the hospital. We think he had a stroke."

"Which hospital?" My heart was racing.

"In Palestine. But they may have to move him to Tyler."

"Can he have visitors?"

"Yes, but he lost his hearing aids, so he can't communicate very well. I'm here right now."

"What's the room number?"

I was already halfway out the door when he gave it to me.

Dan met me in the hospital lobby and filled me in as we took the elevator to the second-floor ward of Mother Frances Hospital.

"According to Mom, she heard him fall during the night. She tried to help him up, but then she fell and bumped her head."

"Oh, no. Is she okay?"

"Yeah. She just got a small lump on the back of her skull."

"Who's taking care of her?"

Mon had Alzheimer's and by then had progressed to where she couldn't be left alone. She didn't remember how to feed herself or anything. If she tried to cook, she'd probably burn the house down. Dad was her primary caregiver.

"I know. That's why I'm staying with her."

I stopped and grabbed Dan's arm. "But who's there right now?"

"I was able to get hold of the Home Care Service they have. The helper usually comes once a week, to give Dad a break for a couple of hours. They sent someone for the morning, so I could be here."

Dad was sitting up in bed, looking alert, when we walked in. This helped me relax a bit.

"Hi, Kiddo," he said hoarsely. "Good to see you. I wish it was under better circumstances."

Ouch, I thought. I hadn't been going to Mom and Dad's house as often as I used to. My hands were full getting Jay settled in.

This turned out to be Dad's best day in the hospital. The next night, he had another stroke.

When I entered his room the next morning, he was staring at the ceiling, with a feeding tube going down one nostril. The nurse who stopped by told me that he couldn't swallow anymore without choking.

"Dad, it's Mary Anna. How are you today?" I felt self-conscious having to shout so he could hear. As a result, I didn't talk to him much—just sat beside his bed for an hour or so, before heading to teachers' meetings at my school. We always had a lot of these at the beginning of the school year.

In two days, I was scheduled to attend a teacher training event in Colorado. It was my first chance, since beginning teaching several years ago, to attend an Environmental Education Workshop. I didn't want to miss it, and Dan insisted I go. He understood how much it meant to me.

After five days at the workshop, held at the Jefferson County Outdoor Education Center, I was wishing my school district could afford a facility like this one. The session's facilitators told us Jefferson County was the 'Cadillac' of outdoor education centers, and it didn't take me long to be convinced this was true.

The final session ended after lunch on Friday. While I

was packing the last of my stuff into my compact car, the cell phone rang. My pulse raced when John's number appeared on the screen.

"What's up, John?"

"Uh, I have bad news, Sis."

"Dad?"

"Yes, he died early this morning."

"Another stroke?"

"Probably. The doctors aren't sure. One of the nurses found him on the floor in his room. He was disoriented, mumbling about having a lot to do today. By the time they got him back to bed, he was unresponsive. He didn't linger long after that. Time of death was around ten this morning."

Right when I was wrapping up this workshop. My heart suddenly felt like a lead weight. Tears welled up, and my voice left me.

"Are you okay, Sis?"

"Yeah. Just in shock. I shouldn't have left for this training session. I wish I could have told him good-bye."

"None of us got to."

"When will we have the funeral?"

"Don't worry about that, I'll take care of it. Dan and I are going to the monument place to choose a head stone in a couple of days. Do you want to come?"

"If you can wait until I get back from Colorado."

"Sure. Why don't you text me when you get home? Then we can compare schedules."

"Okay." I got into my car and raced home, as fast as the Colorado and Texas roads would allow.

***

That was how my mother, Anna Lee, ended up living at our house. Both Dan and John had full-time jobs and couldn't fit her into their houses or their schedules. Dad was the one who carried most of the burden of caring for her, and that option was gone.

Fortunately, Rick and I had two spare bedrooms in our new house, so we had room to accommodate both Jay and Mom. After the move to Palestine, I'd found a part-time teaching position. The science classes I taught were only in the morning that year, so Rick arranged his schedule to start work after I got home for lunch. In another year, he would be retiring from Exxon-Mobil, anyway.

Both of us were phasing into this new adventure of retirement, but I wasn't quite ready to fully stop working. Besides, we had a new home loan to pay off.

Standing at the kitchen sink early one afternoon, preparing yet another meal, I realized how tired I was getting. Jay took care of most of his own needs, even doing his own laundry. Mom was the one who woke early and wanted breakfast by eight. Lunch had to be right at noon, dinner at 4:30. These were the times Dad had used, and Mom was resistant to changing.

Jay was a night owl, which shouldn't bother me, except that I was a light sleeper and often heard his computer's sounds coming through the ceiling of our bedroom.

Cleaning up seemed a never-ending job with Mom around. I rinsed dishes and put them in the dishwasher almost all the time, either loading or unloading. She had many toilet 'accidents' too, so there was always laundry to wash for her.

There were nights when I felt like Mama Walton on the old TV show. *Good-night, Grandma. Good-night, Jon-boy.*

After a couple of years of this full house, I realized I'd bitten off more than I could chew. (One of Dad's favorite old adages.) Once again, Callie-cat became a refuge. When things got too much for me to handle, I gathered the cat into bed and tried to relax. I was still dependent on Xanax, though.

CHAPTER 5
Even Older Memories

Mom living with us began to stir many memories of my parents, especially Dad. The tasks of care-giving kept me from having the time to really mourn for Dad, though. Sometimes the memories were disturbing, too.

Dad was one of those people who believed that if you gave too many compliments to anyone, they'd get conceited. Sort of like people who equate self-esteem with the sin of pride. It was how he was raised, I suppose. Still, he'd made me so self-conscious that I often had no confidence. He was quick to point out areas I needed to improve, but he forgot to give any compliments when I did something right.

For example, when I was about six, joining the children's choir at church, I'd heard him say to the director, "I hope you can do something with her. She can't carry a tune in a bucket."

Even though I liked to sing, Dad often said he didn't like my voice because it was too high.

One of my clearest memories from childhood was his drilling me on math facts:

In third grade, we were supposed to do a sheet full of random addition or subtraction problems in a minute or less. I never got through all those problems in sixty seconds. One night's memory was still vivid in my mind—standing with my back pressed against the closet door, with Dad firing math facts shotgun style.

"Come on, Mary Anna, what's four plus eight?"

When I couldn't answer in a split second, his face clouded, and he stepped closer. I pressed harder against the wooden door, wishing I could disappear inside the grain. He stood over me, putting out more problems rapid-fire. "Don't be so slow," he snapped.

I think this may be why I developed a phobia for doing math in my head. Even now, a page full of numbers can trigger anxiety in me. The one thing I've known since childhood is to never volunteer to be treasurer of anything.

Still, there were many things I was thankful for. One of the biggest was that our parents took all three of us to Sunday School when we were young. I have vivid memories of Bible stories told and special activities at summer Bible School. We attended a large Methodist church in Palestine, Texas. There was a choir for every age group, so I'd worked my way up from Angelus Choir (first through third graders) to the Carol Choir (fourth through sixth grade.)

Unfortunately, when I was starting sixth grade our family moved to Nebraska. The church there was much smaller and had only an adult choir. For some reason, my parents gradually stopped attending church after the move, though my brothers and I kept going to Sunday School and youth group meetings. Whether they planned it or not, our parents had given us a good foundation. It took me a long time to begin building on that base, though. All the way into college. But it was good the early basis was there.

Another memory was more common in the South. Because of Mom, it had a great deal of significance.

When I was about seven or eight, my parents hired an African American maid named Linnie to watch us kids after school while Mom was at her bridge club. Linnie also did the ironing while at our house. I remembered her running the hot iron over a *Colonial Bread* wrapper, to melt the wax on it.

"This smooths out the wrinkles in the clothes," Linnie said. "Better than starch."

Linnie was to my childhood eyes an older woman, with maybe a little gray in her hair. She was soft-spoken, but a kind and loving person. If John and I talked to her, Linnie listened, though she didn't tend to start conversations.

Both of our grandmothers lived in other towns, so for those years, Linnie became a surrogate grandma. I never felt uncomfortable around her, like I sometimes was with my real grandmas. Maybe this was because I didn't see Nanny or Nana enough to know them well.

One evening, Linnie stayed late and made supper. Perhaps it was the night our youngest brother Daniel was born. She warmed a can of cream of chicken soup, using water to dilute it. Mom always used milk, so I wondered if it would taste strange. But it was fine. *Now I realize that every time I make a can of condensed soup with water, I think of Linnie.*

We weren't sure who brought Linnie to our house. Maybe Mom went to pick her up while we were at school. It's odd the things you don't notice when you're a child. She was just there when we got home, and then she went home somehow when her work day was over.

Once, though, she needed Mom to drive her home, so we rode along. That was the only time I saw where Linnie lived. It was in a shabby part of town with only dirt streets, and little rundown wooden houses. It looked rather sad.

After we'd dropped Linnie off at her house, I asked Mom, "Why do the colored people live in such poor places?" (The N-word was forbidden in our family, even in the 1950s.)

"It's not their fault, Mary Anna," said Mom quietly. "People who are poorer than we are in things are still good people. Always remember that."

I can still picture this entire scene, even though it happened at least 60 years ago. The words my mother had said took on more and more meaning for me as the years went by. She had gone out of her way to make sure I didn't look down on any of the poorer people who lived in town, regardless of the color of their skin.. I never knew, until many years later that Mom's childhood had been lived in poverty, too. Out of it, she must have forged an understanding of all people less fortunate, and compassion for them. It was one of the best legacies Mom left—tolerance. Even though we lived in a segregated world then, I knew my parents didn't think it was right.

It's strange at times the bits and pieces remembered from childhood—the valuable and the seemingly trivial reside side-by-side in our adult minds. Another memory dates from before I turned ten, because we still had the old 1950 Packard, a big 'boat' of a car. John and I called it that because it rocked and swayed down the road like a boat on a quiet pond.

Back then, our 1950s house in Palestine had a flat-roofed carport instead of a garage. One day, Dad backed the Packard half-way out and climbed onto the car's roof.

"Come on up, kids," he said to John and me. "Climb up the back bumper to the trunk lid."

Once he'd helped us onto the groaning car roof, he proceeded to boost each of us on top of the carport.

"Wow," I said. "We're up so high." Apparently, I hadn't developed my fear of heights yet. John stood close to me and watched as Dad joined us.

"Now, you kids are never to do this without me," he said. "Never, never!"

We nodded solemnly. Of course we couldn't have anyway, since neither of us could back the car out.

Next, we walked carefully across the gravel and tar roof of the carport to the edge of the sloping roof of the main house. Here, Dad helped us up again.

"Be careful now. The shingles can be slippery."

Soon we stood right at the peak of the roof and surveyed our entire yard, plus the neighbors' rooftops and trees. It was like being on top of the world.

I'm sure Mom never knew about this adventure Dad took us on, and I don't remember how often it happened. But there was at least one more time, for I have a memory of standing up there after dark one night, watching Fourth of July fireworks in the distance. I held tightly to Dad's hand. As long as he was there, I wasn't afraid.

Both my parents were somewhat introverted and awkward socially, so it's no surprise that I was, too. Throughout my growing years, especially my teens, I saw them adapt to socializing with the lubricant of alcohol. I got this habit, too, especially in college. Though it helped that 3.2 percent beer was legal for 18-year-olds in Colorado when I attended Colorado State University. Later, I was fortunate to find friends who were more interested in Bible studies than beer—who helped get my faith back on track.

***

In 2010 I was in my twentieth year as an earth science and geology teacher. Many evenings I sat at the rolltop desk in the corner of my bedroom, and prepared lesson plans for my high school classes. One night, as I looked through my rock and mineral samples, it hit me where my interest in geology came from. Dad.

Yes, there were times when I'd felt over-corrected, but when it came to reading and science, he was always encouraging. Before I was old enough to read, he started reading his favorite childhood books to me, *The Hollow Tree*, by Albert Bigelow Paine.

"I remember my grandpa reading these to me, Kiddo," he'd say.

As I got older, he read me books about archeology, geology and botany. I loved this special time with him, and learned a lot of things beyond my years.

For my tenth birthday, Dad got me a small microscope. This literally opened a new world. He showed me how to prepare slides of everything from onion skins to blood. This new hobby paid off years later when I took biology in college. That microscope (which I still own) opened the world of rocks, minerals, and crystals to me, too.

It's strange how so many thoughts can flash through a mind almost at light speed. These recollections came much faster than it's taken to tell them. Picking up a large quartz crystal Dad gave me long ago, my mind flowed through more memories.

Ironically, it was while we lived in the barely-rolling, hyper-cultivated cornfields of Nebraska that Dad turned into a rock-hound. Maybe, like me, he missed the rolling hills and piney woods of East Texas. Anyway, he started taking all three of us kids trekking through gravel pits and along streambeds, where the cornfields ended in little remnants of nature.

After two or three hours, we'd come trooping home with our rocky treasures and washed them in the kitchen sink. When I thought about it later, I was surprised Mom didn't object. She probably slipped in and scrubbed it well with cleanser after we'd left. Maybe it helped that Dad bought a diamond saw and grinding wheel, and made jewelry for her from some of the semi-precious stones he found.

The part I liked best about this rock-hound stage of our lives was the vacations to the mountains. We got to see all kinds of geologic wonders, especially the Rockies. I think this was when the mountains started calling to me, almost like voices from heaven.

On every trip, we'd stop at each rock shop we passed, and my rock collection kept growing. I still had most of those specimens, some displayed in baskets and bowls in our family room.

My mind refocused from those memories as I looked at a sample of sulfur crystals I'd bought at one of those rock shops. Yes, Dad's legacy to me was science.

The lesson plans were completed now, but I continued to sit and reminisce.

The first Earth Day in 1970 was a watershed event in my life. I was already halfway through college, majoring in journalism and hoping to be a writer or reporter. I'd been editor of my high school newspaper and fell in love with the work. Yet when Earth Day came along with so much talk about the threats to earth's environment, I felt a strong urge to get involved. The late 1960s and early 1970s were heady days of optimism, idealism, and dreams of changing the world, which flowed naturally into me. In fact, that day of April 22, 1970 grabbed me and turned me around.

A conversation with a classmate still comes to mind: "This is just a flash in the pan," he said. "Nothing is going to change."

"No way," I'd replied. "I'm going to go out and change things somehow."

At first, continuing in journalism seemed like a good contribution to saving the environment, but my early interest in geology moved me to change majors to Geology and Environmental Sciences, a brand-new major that emerged as one of Colorado State's responses to environmental awareness.

My life would have been entirely different without Earth Day. I was twenty, seeking my place in the world, a place to have an impact and make a difference. With that changed major came changes in my social life, too. That's how I met Rick, at a gathering of geology majors called The Rockchucks.

When I joined the group one morning before my first class, I found myself sitting across from a handsome blond.

"Hello, you look new here," he said. "Are you a Rockchuck, too?"

I smiled and nodded a reply, "Just joining."

A strange inaudible voice in my mind said, *He's the one I've chosen for you.* Was God actually talking to me? It almost felt like He tapped me on the shoulder.

Maybe Rick felt the same urge, for he invited me out for a study break just a few days later. From then on, we became a couple. After only a year, we were married.

Those last two years of college were when my childhood faith was resurrected and began to mature, mostly because Rick was a Christian, too.

For the first few years of our marriage, things were naturally falling into place—before Jay came along. That's when the ground beneath our feet began to tremor, like the rumbling prelude to an earthquake.

I didn't realize it then, but that was just the beginning of trials to come. It was time to learn faith must be refined like precious metals, in fire.

***

Over the years, Jay became a contradiction of emotions. He wore his heart on his sleeve. It happened most often when it would have been better for him to keep his cool, like that boy's locker room incident in high school. But other times he'd withdraw into himself and become impossible to read.

This was when I'd often find him high up in one of the pine trees in our backyard. (Seems like we usually found a house with good climbing trees.) It reminded me of how I used to climb the mimosas in the neighbor's yard when I was a child. Their smooth bark and low branches made them perfect to climb for a child less than five feet tall. They were my favorite place to go when I needed to think. I don't remember anyone else up there with me, as I smelled the fresh scents of the tiny green leaflets and the fluffy pink flowers. If I touched the doubly compound leaves, the leaflets would shrink back, looking more like the pinnate feathers they were named for.

Up in one of those trees, I could leave the common world behind, looking out at the neighborhood through a world of green and shadows, a place where elves and gnomes might peep out from behind a shrub. Perching in a tree became my magical place, where I went to be alone with my thoughts.

Jay really does take after me, I guess.

I was a tomboy growing up, and preferred boys' games and sports to girly things, while Jay went back and forth between acting girlish to being all-boy. When I took a child psychology course to update my teaching certificate, I learned that psychologists called this androgenous—a mix of male and female traits.

Perhaps, Jay's androgyny developed because he didn't have many guy friends growing up. We moved so often because of Rick's job that his main playmate was his sister. *Maybe if he'd had a brother.*

Many times, I overheard the two of them playing. Their favorite room was the one beneath a laundry chute leading from the bathroom to the basement. This was in our Billings, Montana house, where we'd stayed put long enough to put a basement under our trailer.

Jay would build elaborate cityscapes with all kinds of blocks, which Amy populated with her plastic toy ponies. Then both of them would dive-bomb this city with block-missiles thrown through the laundry chute. Sometimes, there were even paratroopers floating down from the chute's opening in the ceiling, attached to handkerchiefs with string.

Whenever I asked what they were playing, one of them would reply, "It's Pony Wars, Mom. Our favorite game."

As I remembered my children's early years, some of my dominant memories were spurred by things that took place while we were living near Billings, Montana in the early 1990s:

"Dad, please come play catch with me," said Jay.

"Sorry, I can't," Rick replied. "I have to clean out the garage and then wash the car. You could help me, you know."

"But, Dad, my Little League coach says I need to practice my fielding."

"Work is more important."

There were times that Rick played with the kids, but not as often as I would have liked. I wasn't much better, though, I have to admit. One thing I liked to do, however, was teach them how to cook. *This is probably why they're both good cooks now.*

Then there was fishing. At first, Amy was the one who brought that up most, "Can we *please* go fishing this Saturday?" she'd ask.

"Sorry, I have to do some maintenance work on the church building. I don't have time to go get a fishing license," Rick often replied. His father must have been a worker, because work was often foremost in my husband's mind.

It was nearly the same when Jay said, "Dad, why can't we go deer or antelope hunting like my friends and their dads?"

"We don't have the money to spend on guns, ammo, and hunting licenses," Rick would say. I knew his family weren't hunters—it wasn't part of his upbringing, so I couldn't fault him for that.

Later, though, Rick changed his mind and bought the kids ice-fishing poles. Sitting over a hole drilled in freezing water wasn't my idea of fun, so I stayed home when he took Jay and Amy to a nearby frozen-over lake.

They came home with a few perch and very cold hands and feet. This was when Amy decided winter fishing wasn't for her.

"It was cool to look down through the ice and see the fish," said Jay. "I'd go again."

The next expedition was two or three weeks later. Amy stayed home and helped me bake chocolate-chip cookies.

Both the guys came home that day with bright red cheeks and numb toes because of a stiff wind on the lake. They proudly displayed two small fish.

"Maybe we should get an ice house," said Rick.

"That's what my friends have," Jay added.

Somehow, Rick never got around to checking out the ice houses at the local sporting goods store, though. The fishing rods were neglected for the next several months.

Once summer came, Rick borrowed a buddy's boat and took the whole family out on the same lake, now thawed. He even got longer rods and reels for each of us.

As we sat in the small aluminum boat, my mind drifted to the first time Dad took me fishing back in East Texas.

"Hey, kids," I said, "You want to hear about my very first fishing trip?"

"Sure," Jay nodded. "It'll help pass the time. We're just downing nightcrawlers today."

"Yes, please," added Amy. "We're not catching anything."

"Okay," I began, "I was probably nine years old, for I know my youngest brother—we called him Danny then—was a fearless toddler. Mom put him on a leash to keep him from jumping into the roiling brown water that flowed by the muddy shores.

"We were somewhere in the piney woods, but I doubt I could find it on a map. I only knew we drove a long time to get to this place Dad called Lock Eight. I had no idea then that a lock was a way for boats to get around a dam. But I do remember seeing the frothy water rushing over the dam there. Dad said the foam was from soap in the water and not to touch it."

"It was polluted, wasn't it?" said Jay.

"Yeah, most likely. Dad helped us get our bamboo poles set up with baited hooks, lead sinkers, and round bobbers of red and white plastic.

"'When the bobber goes under, a fish has the bait,' he said. 'So pull your line in.'

"For a while, I sat on a stump watching my bobber half-submerged in the brown water. A skinny reptilian head broke the water's surface nearby.

"'Daddy, is that a snake?' I called.

"He came to my side. 'Looks more like a mud turtle,' he said. 'No need to worry. If it's a water moccasin, you'd see more of its long body and its white cotton mouth.'

"I hadn't been worried about snakes before that, but now I started watching for a cottonmouth like a scared bird."

"Are there lots of snakes in Texas?" Amy asked.

"Well, maybe a few more than here in Montana. We had rattlesnakes like here, but we also had cottonmouths and copperheads."

"Ugh!" she cried. "Go on with the story, Mom. I hope there aren't any more snakes in it."

"No, there aren't, Amy. Dad walked over to check on John, who sat close by. I turned back to watch the muddy water, and soon my attention was diverted when my bobber suddenly disappeared. I pulled on my pole as hard as I could, until a pale brown fish lay flopping at my feet.

"'Whatcha got, Kiddo?' Dad called.

"'It's a fish!'

"'Yes, indeed,' he laughed, coming over. 'Looks like a drum-fish.'

"'Can we eat it?' my brother John asked, laying down his pole and running over.

"'No, they're not good eating,' said Dad. "Specially in this water.'

"'So what do we do? Throw it back?'

"Meanwhile, Dad was taking the hook from the fish's small mouth. A big black hog was eyeing him from the pines behind us, where our old Packard was parked. Dad didn't say anything, just tossed the fish toward the hog. In a quick gulp or two, the fish was gone. Another hog arrived too late for the last bite.

"'Daddy, whose hogs are those?'

"'Could be anyone's, Kiddo. They're running wild around here.'

"'Will they hurt us?' They looked big and fierce to me.

"'No, just don't throw things at them, except fish,' Dad chuckled.

"That's what we did the rest of the day. John and I caught several of the drum-fish, and they all went to the wild hogs.

"Dad took us fishing about once a year for a while. But after this, Mom didn't want to go along anymore. As I got older, I would have liked to go again, but Dad tended to take my brothers, leaving me home with Mom. She taught me to make chocolate-chip cookies.

"So, Amy, I guess when we made cookies while the guys went fishing, I was inadvertently passing on a stereotype from my childhood."

"That's okay, Mom," she grinned. "We had fun."

"And *we* loved eating the cookies," added Rick.

All too soon, though, Rick's fishing trips became further apart. Jay began to prefer hanging out with friends. He and Rick managed to get a trip in once a year, but most of the time the rods and reels gathered dust in the garage. When we left Montana for Texas, I sold them in the moving sale.

CHAPTER 6
The Price of Memory – 2013

It was only ten-thirty a.m. and I was exhausted already, standing beside the toilet wiping Mom's bottom. Almost every day, she had what she euphemistically called 'loose bowels.' Because of Alzheimer's, she could no longer care for herself. Dad had been her only caregiver for almost seven years before he died. As the eldest and only daughter, I'd felt it was my job to step up, back in 2010 when Dad died. Rick agreed to the plan, but after almost three years had gone by, both of us saw our patience wearing thin.

Is this another of those lessons you've sent to teach me patience, God? Why can't you ever let up on me?

As I helped Mom undress and get onto the transfer bench in the shower, the image of Jesus washing his disciples' feet came to mind. This experience was definitely a lesson in humility. Lathering Mom's hair, I couldn't help wondering why I had more gray hair than this eighty-three year-old woman.

Even though my back ached once I had her dried off and dressed again, it was time to get lunch. Mom's usual fare was Jell-O and cookies, though I'd managed to get her interested in applesauce and mac-n-cheese. I would have joined her, too, but I was allergic to wheat and had to stick to the gluten-free versions of pasta.

As I served the food, it felt like I'd gone back to raising preschool children. Except this was my mother. Sometimes I caught myself saying I was the mother, instead of her daughter.

Today Mom was talkative, telling how their barn cats drank milk from their cow when she put it in a bowl for them.

As she finished her applesauce, she said, "My father took some kittens in a gunny sack to drown them, because we had too many cats. I was late for school one day because I had to bury my cat who died."

This was typical of her memories, just isolated bits and pieces. She seldom talked about her childhood. The cats were one of the few things she mentioned. They must have been special to her. I remembered the neurologist saying that the oldest and dearest memories were the last to go.

Once lunch was over, Mom moved to her favorite chair to read a library book. She'd always been an avid reader, though she didn't understand much of what she read these days. I got my love of reading from her, so I wondered if I'd end up paging through books like her, with no idea what I read yesterday, or even a few minutes ago. What a scary thought.

The next day, Mom went to the freezer to get ice—which she did about every twenty minutes—and the door handle broke. Unfortunately, Rick was home when it happened.

"Why can't she stop getting ice all the time? Now look what she's done! How much longer do we have to put up with her? She flushes the toilet every ten minutes, using expensive water we have to pump from our well. The septic system is probably overloaded already."

I tried to think of a calm reply, like, 'She doesn't remember she just went there.' But my voice disappeared while my tears rose. Rick stormed to the back door and stalked to his car. Then he was gone in a squealing of tires, taking his temper elsewhere. Still, I felt abandoned.

Mom sat in her rocking chair, unaware of the problem she'd caused.

Once my tears ebbed, I called my brother Dan.

"What can I do?" I blubbered into the phone.

"Maybe it's time to look into a memory-care facility," he said.

"Won't she feel I'm abandoning her? When we had her in one for just a week, so Rick and I could go camping last summer, she nearly had a fit."

"Mary Anna, you need to take care of yourself, too. Otherwise you won't be able to care for Mom. It's not a crime to get some help." His kind voice felt like a virtual hug.

"Still, I feel I'm responsible. What if they don't take good care of her?"

"You're expecting too much of yourself, Sis. You have to think of the rest of your family."

I knew he was right. Having Mom here had put a strain on our marriage. With Jay living here also, the stress had ramped up even more. "Yeah, I feel like I'm at the end of my rope," I sighed into the phone.

"Let me do some calling around," said Dan. "Maybe the Memory Gardens, where she stayed while you went camping, has some openings."

Only a day later, Dan called with news that Memory Gardens did have a single room open. We reserved it for Mom right away, even though it was more costly. We knew having a roommate wouldn't work for her. After Thanksgiving we relocated her, so we could have one more holiday with her at home.

Once we'd settled Mom with her own furniture, she adapted surprisingly quickly.

"In a way, I think her Alzheimer's is a blessing," I told Dan.

"She's living in the moment, since most of her memories are gone. She'll be okay now, and you will, too."

"I hope you're right." I leaned on his chest. "I can't help feeling guilty. I should probably visit her every day, but I can't seem to manage it. The best I can do is once or twice a week."

"Like I've said. All you can do is your best. Don't be hard on yourself. You still have a job to do at your school, and then there's Jay to deal with."

I stepped back from him, looking up into his face, since he was over six feet tall. His brown eyes were warm and caring. "Yeah, there's always something with Jay," I sighed.

On a hot summer day, a few months after we'd moved Mom to Memory Gardens, I sat in our air-conditioned sunroom. I knew I should go to see her, but it was getting hard to know what to say. She asked the same questions over and over, though I tried not to let it drive me nuts.

Instead of going to the home, I continued sitting with a cat on my lap, doing nothing productive except letting the memories flow:

Some of Mom's love for cats must have rubbed off on me, because as long as I could remember I'd wanted a cat for a pet. I begged over and over while growing up, but all Mom ever allowed was a goldfish. Later, my brother John got to have a turtle and Dan had a hamster, so Mom must have let up a little. Apparently, pets still had to be in cages or aquariums, though.

I'd always thought Mom's germaphobia and perfectionism about housekeeping were the reasons she didn't want pets in the house. There was probably some truth in that, but once she also said, "Having animals in the house is a sign of being poor. I was ashamed for my friends at school to come over, because I never knew if there would be chickens or even a pig in the house."

When I remembered Mom's story about burying her cat, I also wondered if she was trying to protect us from grief. Our parents never took us to wakes or funerals, even for our grandparents. The first time I saw a body in a coffin was at a wake for the father of a high school friend. I'd never met Sally's father, but the image of his face in that casket is still clear in my mind, even after all these years.

I was thankful love for cats was one thing Rick and I had in common. Our first cat, Tiger, was gifted to him shortly before our marriage. Rick had grown up in a house with pets, mostly cats and birds. Both of us thought a house felt empty without a cat.

Up to this year in our marriage, we'd had four cats, mostly brown tabbies—the first cat Tiger set the precedent. The majority were gifts like him, but the calico we currently owned had adopted us. For weeks, she kept coming to the front porch. One very frosty night, we finally gave up and let her in the house. She was arthritic and malnourished, so her life improved, and she thanked us by jumping into a lap every time someone sat down. Callie liked to sleep between us at night, just to make sure we didn't disappear—though sometimes Rick and I didn't sleep in the same bed anymore.

I didn't mind if the cats wanted to sleep with me, for the sound of their purrs and slight snores was relaxing. Sleeping cats were like sleeping babies, always cute. The one we got as a kitten, Tiglet, loved to curl up on my shoulder. So comforting.

As I sat and petted Callie, feeling her silky fur and hearing her contented purr, I thought, *At least I can cuddle the cat.*

Looking into her green eyes I murmured, "If only you could talk, Callie. What was your life before we adopted you?"

She looked up and meowed, as she often did when spoken to. Maybe Callie wished she could talk to us, too.

Closing my eyes, I imagined what it would be like to hear a cat speak. But then I realized perhaps it was better that Callie couldn't tell any of my dark secrets, the things I told her that I never wanted anyone else to hear—like how I envied my friends and my brother John, who had grandchildren. I was almost sixty-five, and the prospects looked bleak, but I kept it to myself. I didn't want to make Jay or Amy feel bad about being single.

Sitting with a cat had become like meditation for me. I could focus on the present and set my worries aside. Instead of fretting over the past or worrying about the future, I listened to their purrs, looked at the fur's patterns and colors, felt its texture—and began to relax.

Often I'd tell Callie, "I don't need a priest or a guru. All I need is you." This didn't always work, though. Sometimes I got so depressed that even the cat was no help. Depression had gotten much worse for me after menopause.

Along with serenity, our cats had taught me the ephemeral nature of life. The cat who seemed fine a few days or even hours ago turned up dead on the road—or lying on the floor in an awkward, paralyzed state. The hardest part of having pets is burying them. Perhaps Mom was right, after all.

Still, I was thankful we'd exposed our children to grief because it was an inevitable part of life. Rick and I took them to their grandparents' funerals—and shared grief with them, whether it was for a family member, a friend, or just a pet.

Thinking about it now, I didn't resent how I was raised. But I was thankful I could fill some of the gaps for our children, things that were missing in my own childhood. Sometimes I wondered if being over-protected from life's hard knocks had made me too sensitive, less able to cope. One day, when I was visiting with John and his wife over coffee at their house, he shed some light on this for me.

"I get so low sometimes," I sighed. "It seems like I'm falling into a dark pit."

"You know, our mother had depression issues, too," said John.

"I wondered about that. Did she talk to you about it? She never did with me."

"Your dad told us," said Emilia. "He also said that your mother's mother spent some time in a mental hospital."

"Oh, sounds like it runs in our family," I said. "Maybe that's why I get so moody and sensitive. Rick says I tend to dwell on the negative."

"I've seen you do that, too," said John. "Please don't be angry with me. From what I saw over the years, Mom was trying to self-medicate with alcohol."

Emilia nodded. "Once when we were visiting them, at about ten in the morning she was already pouring herself some bourbon."

"I never saw that, I guess," I said. "But I do remember on family vacations how when we settled in our motel room, out came the bottles of bourbon and ginger-ale."

"Right after Dad went down the hall to the ice machine to fill the plastic bucket," John added. He looked directly into my eyes. "Mary Anna, if you start feeling like you are hopeless, or want to hurt yourself, please call us."

I stared at my brother. This was really stepping out of his comfort zone.

Emilia rose from her chair at the kitchen table and pulled me into an unexpected hug. "Perhaps you should look into finding a good counselor, if it gets that bad."

"Yes, please," John nodded. I could tell he was thankful to his wife for stepping up and laying all this out for me. "We love you, and we know it's been hard with Mom and all. You've had to deal with some of the worst parts."

"There's no shame in admitting you need help," added Emilia.

Another morning in the sunroom, all this scene replayed in my mind. Again I was cuddling Callie.

"What do you think, cat?" I said aloud. "I'm trying to do better. Am I getting anywhere?"

Callie just looked up at me and meowed.

CHAPTER 7
Too Close for Comfort – 2014

One day in the middle of summer, I woke in the morning about to explode and didn't even know why. Was I trying to carry everyone else's problems on my shoulders again? Disturbances arose daily with Jay living at home. His obsessive thoughts and behaviors left me always on edge.

Even though Mom was at the memory care, there were still burdens—whether paying for prescriptions or making sure she had the right kind of protein drinks. She was getting most of her nutrition from those.

I took a walk, hoping to burn some excess energy and clear my mind before the heat of the day built up. Bluebirds and finches filled the air with their music, and I spotted a few of them flitting from tree to tree in the neighbor's field. When I reached the woodlot at the end of our road, I heard a woodpecker pounding away. I wasn't surprised that I couldn't see it, for they were often heard and not seen, the opposite of that old saying about children.

Just as I reached the thickest patch of pines, a flash of black and white with a banded red topknot flew overhead. My heart raced, not just in surprise. We lived within two hundred miles of the fabled Texas Big Thicket, where some think the rare Ivory-billed Woodpecker may still exist. I wasn't sure how long it was since there was a supposed sighting of one.

I didn't get a good look at this bird's bill and couldn't

remember offhand the differences in the white patterns they had on their wings. I just shrugged. It was most likely a Pileated Woodpecker, anyway.

Beyond the trees of the woodlot was an open meadow. Just as I reached this, a dark shape moved into my line of sight, soaring like a hawk. When I caught a glimpse of its almost translucent red-brown tail, I knew it was a red-tail. Usually a marsh hawk was flying low over this meadow, displaying its white rump-patch, harrying frightened field mice and voles. Maybe this red-tail had taken over its territory.

I gazed across the waving, green grass beneath the trees and saw the lupines beginning to bloom, what Texans call Bluebonnets. This meadow sported only scattered patches of their sky-blue shades. Not like the unbroken fields of blue found in the plains further west.

As I turned back toward the road home, a few Brown-eyed-Susans along the shoulder caught my eye. The contrast of their dark brown centers and bright yellow petals looked like spots of sunshine in the grass.

Seeing them always brought back the memory of the first time Dad pointed them out to me. I couldn't have been more than four years old, because it was one of the Sunday afternoons when we went to visit my younger sister's grave.

I wasn't exactly sure how I knew this. The memory was there long before I understood it. Now I realize how we as parents never know what will make a lasting impression on our children. Sometimes it's the smallest things that we probably thought insignificant, like Brown-eyed-Susans.

After my parents moved to the new house on Magnolia Drive, when I turned five, those Sunday cemetery visits stopped. My second brother, Daniel James, arrived three years later when I was in third grade. I was too young then to put this all together and didn't even know about our lost sister Roberta Lee, until I was around ten-years-old.

As soon as Dad told John and me about her, all those pieces of memories fell into place in my mind—the visits to that grassy place with carved gray stones arranged all around, my little feet dancing on a flat piece of stone with letters carved in it. And the Brown-eyed Susans. As years went on, those became my favorite flower, reminding me of the sister I'd never known.

Now as I walked by those brown and yellow flowers, I remembered all the times I questioned my birth order. Often, I wished for an older brother. Then perhaps some of his friends would have asked me on dates. Or maybe an older sister, who could help me learn how to attract the guys and be someone to confide in, to share clothes with, to teach me to use make-up. All things I never learned very well. I would have even been willing to share a bedroom.

Of course, all this wishing didn't change a thing.

By this time, I was walking up our gravel driveway. As I entered the back door, I was bombarded by the sound of Jay pounding on his desk and swearing at his computer. Obviously, something wasn't going his way. I hoped he was doing work for one of his college classes, not just playing games again.

Cringing at the noise, I slunk into my bedroom. The feeling of careening down a steep incline on a runaway sled threatened to overwhelm me, like my vertigo attacks a couple of years ago.

I hope he doesn't kick another hole in the wall, I thought. *When is he going to finally get settled in his own place? He keeps coming back like a boomerang. Why does he have to be so emotional—like me? Which of us has learned this from the other? Or is it something we both inherited?*

An even darker memory of Jay loomed in my mind as I crawled into my bed, even though I tried to block it. Just a week ago, I'd been in a rush to get dinner on the table in time for Rick to go to a meeting at church. Jay heard me banging around in the kitchen and came down the stairs in a huff.

"Why all the noise?" he demanded.

"I'm trying to get dinner for your dad—and you, if you're hungry—before someone loses their cool," I snapped, knowing I was the one losing control.

"Mom, stop it! You and Dad need to stop ticking me off. I can't help it that I have to stay here until I can afford to move out."

I was at a loss for words, wondering where the outburst came from.

Then he opened a drawer and grabbed one of my paring knives. Holding it above his wrist, he shouted, "Maybe you'd be better off without me. Should I just end all your suffering here and now?"

"Jay, please—no—" I calmed my voice as much as I could, though my heart was racing. "I love you. Don't hurt yourself—or me. Please, just hand me the knife."

My hands were shaking as I reached slowly toward him. He closed his eyes and slapped the knife down on the countertop. Then he took the beige-carpeted stairs two at a time, heading for his room.

I'm not sure how long I stood there in shock. Somehow, I finished the casserole and put it in the oven. When Rick came home about a half hour later, I felt calmer. But I was afraid to tell him what had happened. I couldn't face the thought of finding words, so I said nothing about the incident.

Here I am a week later, hugging a pillow in my bed.

Jay was still shouting and pounding on his desk. I wished I could crawl under the covers and fall asleep forever and not face dealing with Jay, or myself, anymore.

"It's not that difficult, you know," said a whispering voice in my head. "All you have to do is take the whole bottle of Xanax."

I lay there with that image in my mind for a long time, contemplating obeying. But I didn't get up. Then I heard a very different-sounding voice: "When all is said and done, remember Jesus loves you."

This wasn't an audible sound either, but the words were just as clear as if they were spoken. *Can this be God talking to me? Does He really do that?* I wasn't used to hearing voices in my head.

That second voice didn't speak again, but I didn't go to the medicine cabinet. Instead, I stayed in bed hugging a pillow and trying to calm down. At last, Jay stopped yelling.

A few tears finally came, dampening my pillow. Then a sudden jerk of the bed startled me, as one of the cats nestled against me and started purring as I stroked its soft fur. This was Muffin, one of two cats we recently adopted from the animal shelter. Seems we needed more than one cat these days. Muffin's personality was a lot like Callie, except for her coloring. She was a brown-striped tiger, with some of the mottled brown of a tortoise-shell. Her brother, Puffin, was a black and white tuxedo cat, named for birds who wear 'tuxedos', the Arctic puffins. I couldn't bear to separate them, so adopted both. When I brought them home, Rick rolled his eyes. Lately, though, he'd begun to bond with Puffin.

I must have fallen asleep with Muffin, because the next thing I heard was soft cat-snoring and the sound of Rick closing the back door and calling, "I'm home. What's for dinner?"

Groggy, I pulled myself up, while the cat opened one eye, glaring at me. "Sorry, Muffin. Duty calls."

I groped my way to the kitchen and I tried to look alert. "How about pizza? There's some in the freezer, or we can order out."

Now Rick began to glare.

"Sorry, I must have fallen asleep when I meant to lie down for just a few minutes."

"You do that a lot lately, you know."

"Yeah. Having Jay here takes the stuffing out of me, even though we've moved Mom to the memory care."

"Okay. There's never a dull moment when Jay's around, I know. I'll call in an order for an extra-large pepperoni."

"Thanks, Rick." I gave him a hug. "It's been a rough day."

You have no idea how bad, I said to myself. I was too ashamed to tell him about my suicidal thoughts.

CHAPTER 8
A Different Kind of Legacy – 2015

After that suicidal episode, I knew I needed help. With my sister-in-law's suggestion about counseling hovering in my mind, I went to see our family doctor, Dr. T, in hopes that he could prescribe something that would help with my anxiety and depression.

Instead, he told also me that I should consider counseling. At first, I was insulted, then hesitant. But he persisted, "What you need right now is beyond my expertise. Here's the name of someone I've heard is good." He handed me a slip of paper with a name written in ink. "Sorry all I have is a name, but please consider it. He comes highly recommended."

That paper sat on my desk for at least six weeks before I finally did something with it. I looked the name up on the Internet and after a few more days, called the phone number I found. A kind-sounding male voice answered. Right then, I didn't know how unusual it was to get him and not his voicemail. The voice assured me that he'd work with our insurance. This was a big worry, after the huge bills we'd had for Jay from the child psychologist. Still feeling shy, I made an appointment for three weeks out with this counselor, Dr. B.

My mind didn't register everything we talked about at our first session, but I noticed he was a good listener, not too ready to heap on the advice. The main thing I remembered was when he asked, "What is it that I can help you with the most?"

"Well, you can help me see there's still hope out there somewhere, that the best part of my life isn't over."

His reply? He nodded and said, "Okay."

Then I must have mentioned something about feeling God was far away and not answering my prayers, for he said, "I'm a Christian, too." This was when I realized God *did have* a hand in this. I hadn't purposely sought out a Christian counselor, but He led me to one anyway.

During our first year of weekly sessions, Dr. B asked one question several times, "What's your image of God? How do you picture Him?"

At first, my only answer was, "I don't know."

So I began to pay more attention to where my mind went when I prayed. After pondering for several weeks, I told Dr. B, "What I see is not sharp and clear when I think of God. It's a hazy picture of a huge white throne with a tall, glowing man seated on it. I think he's old, and I don't feel comfortable standing there in front of him. He's powerful, and he can see right through me, like I'm naked."

"Is he judging you?"

"Definitely."

"Do you feel anything drawing you to him?"

I shifted uncomfortably in his brown leather chair before I replied. "No, I want to stay at a safe distance."

"Do you ever picture Jesus when you pray?"

"Not really. I guess I can visualize paintings I've seen of him, like the one of him holding a lamb. My mother liked that one. But I mostly see the old man."

"Are your images of Jesus ever connected with the man on the throne?"

"No, they're separate things entirely."

"What about the Holy Spirit?"

"I can't picture him at all. He's just an invisible force, I guess."

"Like the Holy Ghost?"

"That's right. Maybe because it was the term I grew up with—Father, Son, and Holy Ghost."

"Have you seen God this way most of your life?"

A light clicked on in my mind when he said this. "For sure. I've never thought of it before, but I do. Why is that? I've matured, studied the Bible for years. I believe somewhere it says, 'God is love.' Why do I still see God like a stern father disciplining his child?"

"People's images of God the Father are strongly influenced by their relationships with their human fathers. It's normal."

"That's sure true for me. I picture a stern judge whenever I think of my own father, too. He's been dead four years now, but I still see him this way.

"Maybe we can work on that," Dr. B nodded.

"I don't know. If I've been like this for over 60 years, it's a lot to undo."

"It will take time, but don't give up hope, Mary Anna."

***

Only a month after this particular session, something else rocked my world. My brother John announced he and his family were moving to Alabama.

"Why?" was the first question I asked, when he called. My pulse jumped as he spoke again.

"Emilia's parents are there, you know."

"Yeah, I remember. But I depend on your being here." An empty feeling flowed through me as I stared at the gray ceramic tile of my kitchen floor.

"Hey, I'll only be a phone call away, Sis."

"That's not the same."

"Our dad is gone. Mom's in the memory care and doesn't even remember who we are."

"I know." By then, I was fighting back tears and was glad he couldn't see me.

"Our kids and grandkids deserve to be near some extended family."

"Okay." I swallowed hard to keep my voice calm. "I guess I'm being selfish, but don't we count as family?"

"Of course you do, but so does Emilia's side. I wish there was something else I could do to help you, but the time has come to follow my wife's wishes. She's given up a lot of her family time by staying in Texas."

"But your job is here." I grabbed this last lifeline. John worked for an investment company based in Houston.

"I'm doing a lot of my work from home now. In a few more years, I'll be eligible to retire, now that the economy is recovering from the Crash of '08."

"All right," I sighed. "When will you be moving?"

"As soon as our house sells here."

"So soon?" I collapsed on one of the kitchen stools, and my head began to spin. "What about buying a house there, wherever it is you're going?"

"We've already bought a house in a suburb north of Huntsville."

"What? You never told me that."

"We did some house-hunting the last time we went to visit Emilia's parents. I was afraid you'd be upset."

"I guess I am. Why are you dropping this on me all at once?"

"Apparently that was a bad idea, but you seem to be doing better since Mom's in the memory care."

"Yeah, sort of. We still have Jay living with us, you know."

"He's pretty high-maintenance, huh?"

"That's an understatement. Maybe when he finds his own place, things will calm down. At least Amy has her own house now, the one she bought last fall."

"Why can't Jay live with her?"

"John, I'd never consider loading Jay and all his issues on Amy."

"Oh yeah, I can see that."

Silence settled, and I switched the phone to my other ear. "Can I at least have a going-away party for you all?"

"Of course, if you want to. It'll have to be in the next week or two, though. Our house here is under contract. The buyers want to take possession in two weeks."

"What?" My heart sank all the way down to my shoes, and tears spilled down my cheeks.

***

A few days later, as I began planning the party, I realized this was one of the longest conversations I'd had with John in recent years. He'd always been the quiet, reserved one in our family, taking after our mother. Dan and I were more like Dad. This made John a good match with Emilia, for she had a dominant personality. She'd climbed the corporate ladder, working in the same firm as John. When she had a goal, she pursued it with passion. I envied this, wishing I was more like Emilia. I also admired her dedication to her family.

I should be happy that she will be closer to them now, I told myself. *She has shown a lot of devotion to them over the years.*

Emilia's family had always been close-knit. She and John often made the long trek to Alabama for holidays, and faithfully visited her parents twice a year.

John determined the best day for the party I hosted was right after the movers left with all their furniture. I prepared lasagna with tossed salad and garlic bread, knowing they were his favorites, and ordered a decorated cake from the bakery, since I wasn't much good at cake art.

Dan came, too. He and his wife had recently separated, so I knew why he came alone, and we all avoided that subject.

I didn't want John and Emilia to feel guilty about their plans. As we began to eat, I asked about their new house. "Is Huntsville a big city?"

"I don't think it's as big as Houston, but it's connected with NASA, too, so it's similar," John replied.

"Once I've checked out the stores, we can go shopping when you come to visit," smiled Emilia. "We could still get together at Thanksgiving and do our Black Friday thing."

"I'd love that. I know I'll miss our shopping trips here."

While I was serving dessert, Emilia was saying, "We're excited that our son Tony and his family are coming, too. He's already found a job near Huntsville. It's a growing area."

"Really?" Glancing at John, I saw him staring at the floor. Here was another thing he'd avoided telling me. "What about Tim?" I asked. He was their elder son.

John shook his head. "Tim's work is still in Texas. He— uh—lives in Jacksonville now, almost an hour from here. We don't get much communication from him."

I had a strong suspicion there was something they weren't saying about Tim. Even Emilia had gotten quiet. Trying to change the subject and cover up my *faux pas*, I grabbed a tub of ice cream from the freezer. "Who wants Neapolitan with their cake?"

"I do," Dan chimed in. "Mom and Dad always bought that kind."

"Yeah," John laughed. "You always ate the strawberry, and I ate the chocolate."

"Leaving me the vanilla." I hoped my laugh didn't sound too forced.

Later in the evening, when the dishes were done, the three of us sat on my back patio, watching the sunset. Emilia had gone to Tony's to help them pack for the movers, and Rick went downstairs to watch TV.

"We had a good childhood here in Palestine, didn't we?" said Dan.

"Yeah, typical 1950s," John added.

"Dad goes to work. Mom stays home and keeps the house."

"Right, Sis," nodded Dan. "Kids walk to school. Sometimes even walk home for lunch."

I smiled as these memories rose in my mind.

John's voice resumed, "Kids grow up, get married, and have kids of their own."

"Some do, anyway." The slight catch in Dan's voice startled me, before I remembered he didn't have any children of his own, and divorce was looming on his horizon. I could also sympathize with the no grandchildren aspect of his situation.

A nice cool breeze began to move across the patio, and I decided it was time to change the subject.

"You know, when Mom was in the hospital that time she got pneumonia, I'd drive Dad over to visit with her every day.

At first, she was too sick to realize he was there, but when she finally did, his smile was so radiant."

"Yeah, I remember that too, Mary Anna," said Dan. "And last year, when Dad was in the hospital, I'd take her over to see him. Even though she was old and bedraggled, not quite herself anymore because of the Alzheimer's, the looks he gave her were priceless."

"How do you mean?" John asked.

"Well, his eyes would light up like a young man's seeing the love of his life. He glowed when she came into the room."

"I remember that, too," I nodded. "Our parents gave us a great gift by just being so in love with each other, right up to the end."

"I need to tell you guys something," said John, his voice suddenly quiet.

I wondered if this was about Tim, so I was surprised when he said, "It's from the day Dad died. First, I have a question, though."

"What's that?" I stared down at the gray concrete of the patio.

"Did our parents have a baby girl that died?"

"Yes, they did. Dad told us when I was about ten, I think. He said she was a preemie and only lived a couple of hours."

"I vaguely remember you telling me some of your memories about this," said John. "My own are too fuzzy."

"I never knew about it at all," added Dan, turning to me.

"Well, when Dad told us, John was only six or seven, and you were just a baby. Why is this important now?"

"It has to do with something strange Dad said that last day. I guess I'd better tell you the whole story."

"Yes, please," said Dan.

"Okay, here goes," John began. "As soon as I entered Dad's room in the hospital's care center that morning, I could sense something was different." John looked toward the last of the sunset sky. "He was sitting up in bed, his brown eyes shining.

"When he spoke, his voice was much brighter than the day before. I even commented on how chipper he looked, as I sat in a chair near his bed. Right away, Dad reached over and took my hand, another thing out of the ordinary.

"He smiled and said, 'I had the most wonderful time yesterday.'

" 'Really?'

" 'Oh, yes. I spent the day with my daughter.'

" 'Mary Anna isn't here. She's still at a workshop in Colorado.' I said this before I realized Dad probably couldn't hear me. So I was even more surprised when he said, 'No, my other daughter. Roberta Lee has such beautiful blue eyes. Her life was too short.'

"My mind was blank, as I asked 'Uh—who's Roberta Lee?' After a moment, I remembered you telling me something about a sister with that name. There was a strange glow in Dad's eyes. His answer didn't seem to be addressed to me at all, when he went on:

" 'My sweet wife wanted to pretend nothing happened, but I just couldn't. I used to be angry with God about it. Now I know it was meant to be. Her life had meaning even though it was brief. Maybe that's also true for my brother George. Last night I got to have a long talk with him, as well.'

" 'I thought George was your father's name.' My heart began to pound.

" 'Oh, it was,' Dad nodded. 'My parents named their firstborn son after my dad.'

" 'Dad, you were an only child.'

" 'Only one who survived infancy, son.'

"By now, I'd forgotten to wonder why Dad could hear me so well. This conversation was taking such strange turns that my head was spinning.

"Then Dad mumbled, 'Mother and Dad never talked about it. Most people were like that back then. But I wonder if my mother would have been better off to have shared her grief. The same could be said for your mother, when we lost Roberta Lee.'

"Again, Dad was squeezing my hand. It was a strange feeling because he rarely touched us, you know. The room had an eerie feeling. I shook my head to try and clear it. Glancing around, I realized I was still seated beside Dad's bed. His eyes were closed, but he was breathing slowly.

" 'Dad,' I murmured.

"The brown eyes opened.

" 'Sorry, but I have to get to work now.'

" 'That's fine. I have work to do today, too. I'll see you bye and bye.'

"He squeezed my hand as I rose from the chair and murmured, 'Yes, I'll see you tomorrow.'

"But I was wrong. The call came when I'd been at my desk for a couple of hours. A nurse's voice on the line sent a chill into my bones.

" 'I'm sorry, Mister Parker,' she said. 'Your father is gone. We'd just checked on him within the last half-hour. He told the aide he had big plans today. The next time we went in, he was lying on the floor in the bathroom. I'm so sorry for your loss.'

" 'It's all right,' a voice was saying. Was it really my own? 'I know where he's gone.'"

"That's eerie," murmured Dan. "What do you think it means?"

"The only thing I can say is we don't know what lies beyond this world we're living in," John sighed. "I take some comfort that he thought he was going to be with his daughter and brother who had already died. Like he did believe in heaven, after all."

"I agree." Reaching over, I patted John's arm. "God and His ways are unfathomable, when you come right down to it. I believe He gave those visions to Dad for a reason."

John looked up in surprise, then nodded, "Thanks. This whole experience made me more aware of what God is doing in my life, which is why I wanted to share it with you two. For many years, I thought Dad was agnostic, maybe even atheist. He would never talk about God or how he was raised. After we grew to be teens, he stopped going to church. But that last day's conversation revealed a spiritual side of him I'd never known. It's also part of why I agree with Emilia. Our offspring need the experience only extended family can give. It's important for our children and the grandkids to live closer to her side of the family now."

I kept my hand on his arm, though my fingers were starting to tremble. "I wish my children could have those experiences, but it's too late now. Rick's parents both died several years ago. You should take the opportunities you have, John. I'm sorry I was trying to keep you here."

Dan shifted his weight and moved his chair closer to mine. "Well, I like how your story gives me a different view of Dad. He could be strict and intimidating sometimes."

John began to chuckle. "Yeah, like the time he told us he'd disown us if we ever bought a motorcycle."

"He said that to you boys? I never imagined such a thing. You know, sometimes he scared me. I always felt like I never measured up to his expectations."

"It was probably because you were the eldest," said Dan.

"And the only girl," John added. "That probably made him more protective of you—especially since our sister died."

We all fell silent for a moment, then I continued, "I wonder what she would have been like. I always wanted a sister."

"Hey," Dan gave me a playful shove with his elbow.

"Oh, but I do have the two best brothers in the world." I joined in the laughter.

The strangest thing happened at my next session with Dr. B. As soon as I walked in the door, I asked, "Is it acceptable for me to give you a hug?"

He looked puzzled for a second. "Sure, it's all right, if you want to." Then he stood and we gave each other a short embrace. "What's this for?"

"I think I've found a new side of my father." I sank into his big leather chair. "He wasn't only a judge, after all. My brother John told us a story which really opened my eyes."

"I'd like to hear it," he smiled.

CHAPTER 9
Winter Descends — 2017

As I got out of my car in the memory care facility's parking lot, I hoped I remembered the code to open the door and prayed the lock was functioning properly. Last week I'd waited almost ten minutes for someone to hear me knocking.

Also, there was Mildred, who always came to the door, trying to sneak out. She must've had a keener sense of hearing than the staff because she reached the door as soon as the code numbers were punched in. Or perhaps she was lurking right around the corner.

Today the code worked. The opening lock gave a loud click, and there came Mildred. I slipped in, managing to keep her away from the open door. The process reminded me of trying to keep our cats from sliding out the door at home. Carrying my guitar made things even more awkward. Fortunately, Rick had given me a new backpack case for Christmas this year.

When I stepped into her room, Mom's face lit up. "Hello," she smiled. "Are you going to sing to me?"

"I always do, Mom."

"That's nice."

She used to say my name but hadn't for almost three months, since before Christmas. I wondered if she remembered who I was. Her memory lapses were getting worse by the week. Last time Rick came with me for a visit, she thought *he* was her husband.

Another time, she said, "I don't have a husband. Can you find me one?"

"Okay, I'll try," was all I could think of to say.

After that, Mom had asked, "Could you take me to Oklahoma to see my parents?"

I didn't have the heart to tell her that they were long-gone and buried here in Texas, so I nodded and said, "We'll see about it later." At least I had the assurance Mom would forget she asked that in just a few minutes.

A couple of weeks ago when I walked into her room, I found her naked from the waist down. "What's going on, Mom?"

"Someone's going to get me ready to go soon."

"When are they coming?"

"Soon."

When I went into the hall to ask an aide about this, she told me, "She's been like this all morning. We're not sure what's going on in her mind. We can't keep her dressed."

I was glad Mom let me put her clothes back on that day, once I said I'd take her out sometime soon.

On days like this, visiting Mom depressed me.

Often I thought, *I hope I don't live much past 80 and get like this.* From what I'd seen in Mom, life had just become mere existence—a life of aches and pains, doctors and hospitals, lying in a nursing home waiting to die. What was the point of that? I'd just be a burden to our children.

When I talked to my counselor about that, he reassured me it was Depression talking, trying to drag me down. So I tried not to listen to those voices.

Some days, when Mom was more responsive, the visits went better, even though she always asked the same question: "I don't suppose I've ever shown this to you, have I?" Reaching to her nightstand, she got the yellowed newspaper clipping from 1943.

The irony was I had never seen this article until the Alzheimer's started. Now Mom was showing it to anyone and everyone constantly.

"Yes, Mom." I tried to sound patient. "You showed it to me last time I was here."

In spite of these words, Mom pushed the article into my hand.

"You know, I was valedictorian of my high school class."

The article had a black-and-white photo taken that year of a very good-looking young woman. "This is a nice picture of you." I always searched for something new to say, even though Mom would never know the difference.

"They took the photo at school." She pointed to the smiling picture. "My parents didn't own a camera, but even during the Depression, my dad always had a job and a car."

This was the same thing she repeated every time. It was a ritual of what memories she had left. Today, it occurred to me why Mom wanted everyone to see this article late in her life. It was probably the only memory she had of being truly valued and recognized for her achievements.

When I handed the article back, Mom slid it into a book sitting on the bedside table. The clipping had become so worn that one of the staff had laminated it. "She shows it to everyone," one of the aides said. "We didn't want it to get torn." I was thankful for their thoughtfulness.

By this time, I had the guitar out, already knowing which songs Mom liked to hear. First came *Jesus Loves Me*. Tears came to my eyes as I watched Mom's lips mouthing the words. Next we sang *Amazing Grace*.

After this, I moved on to the ones Mom had often sung to me as a child, *O Danny Boy* and *My Bonnie Lies Over the Ocean*. After a couple of others, I ended with a favorite of my own:

> *My hope is built on nothing less*
> *Than Jesus' blood and righteousness.*
> *No merit of my own I claim,*
> *But wholly lean on Jesus' name.*
> *On Christ the solid Rock I stand;*
> *All other ground is sinking sand.*

Rick had read the words of this hymn at Dad's funeral service. As I thought about plans for Mom's service, I definitely wanted to include that hymn.

Having to consider funeral plans was heart-wrenching. Dad died rather suddenly in 2010. It was hard to believe he'd already been gone over six years. There were still days when I thought of my Daddy fondly and wished I could give him a hug. Hugs hadn't happened often when he was alive, but I could remember times when he'd taken my hand as we were walking on some of our rock-hounding trips in Nebraska.

I'd been Mom's caregiver since he died. The move to Memory Gardens had taken some of the load off my shoulders now. Sometimes, though, I saw things that bothered me when I was there, like Mom's clothes getting mixed up with someone else's, even though her name was sewn into all of them. I often thought that if I had her at home I could bathe her more, keep her cleaner. But the costs of my anxiety and the stress on our marriage had been too high.

My brother Dan told me not to be so hard on myself. "You did your best. You couldn't keep carrying this weight alone."

I knew he was right, but it still didn't remove my guilty feelings. When Mom fell and broke her tailbone last fall, remorse had come crashing over me, even though it could have happened at home, too. In the middle of the night Mom had tried to go to the toilet and fallen. I kicked myself about it, and wondered if I would have been more careful with her.

Whenever Mom had been in the hospital, things got even tenser. The first day, the nurses said things like, "She's so sweet, such a good patient." By the second day, they'd moved her to a room closer to the nurses' station and strapped her to the bed. "She can't be trusted to stay in bed," they told me. "She insists she needs to go home. Or down the hall to the dining room. We keep telling her we'll bring her food to her, but she doesn't remember five minutes later."

"I know. It's the Alzheimer's."

Once when I was sitting next to her bed in the hospital, Mom kept asking for her shoes.

"Mom, you don't need your shoes."

"Yes, I do. I have to go down the hall."

"Why?"

"To play the piano."

"Huh?" First I was confused, but then remembered there was a piano in the common room at Memory Gardens. Mom used to walk down the hall and play two or three plunks on the keys, then go back to her room.

"Mom, there's no piano here. We're in the hospital."

"Oh." She settled down for a few minutes, but soon she repeated, "I need my shoes."

"No, Mom, you fell. Remember? You can't walk right now."

"But I need my shoes. Can't I at least have *one* of them?"

I couldn't help a chuckle. What good could one shoe possibly do? That's when I realized there was no point in reasoning with her.

Since that fall, Mom was bed-ridden. She used to get a little exercise walking down the hall, or going to the dining room for meals, but this was her second major fall in a couple of months. Based on her age and mental condition, the doctor said there was no point in sending her to rehabilitation. Besides, that facility didn't have any open beds.

A social worker from hospice came to meet with me while Mom was still in the hospital. She was very kind, and urged me to put her on hospice care. Especially appealing was the fact Mom could still go back to her old room at Memory Gardens.

"That's home to her now. It does seem like the right thing—for her to be as comfortable as possible," I said.

When I told John and Dan on a conference call, they agreed. "She has a living will that states no heroic measures are to be taken to prolong her life beyond what nature provides," John said.

"That's right," said Dan. "Do you have it on file, Mary Anna?"

"It's in the drawer where I keep her papers. I remember reading it just the other day. It does say, 'No heroic measures.' It's hard to think of just letting her die, though."

I held back tears. Apparently John could tell, for he said, "Hey, it's okay. Think how you'd feel if you were in her position someday."

"Thinking about that is really depressing. I wouldn't want to just linger on and on, and cause my loved ones unnecessary pain. Still, hospice seems so final."

"She's in the Good Shepherd's arms," said Dan. "We can trust her to His care."

I sighed and wiped at tears which were falling by then. "That reminds me of a painting Mom always had on her wall at home. It showed Jesus standing in a meadow, holding a lamb close to his chest. I think it's in one of the drawers of her dresser, still waiting for me to hang it on her wall at Memory Gardens. She's been there almost four years now. Why haven't I done it?"

"Don't blame yourself, Mary Anna," Dan murmured. "You're doing your best—remember."

It was a good thing we'd kept paying for her room at the home while she was in the hospital so she could return to it. One of the first things I did when I took her back was hang that picture of the Good Shepherd where Mom could see it.

Being bed-ridden meant Mom had to be on a catheter, which she periodically managed to pull out. Now that she wasn't getting any exercise, her mind and body went into rapid decline. She lost her appetite and began to shrivel down to mere skin and bones.

"People in this stage of Alzheimer's lose their appetite because they don't feel hunger anymore," the hospice nurse told me. "The body is gradually forgetting how to function as her brain deteriorates."

This took a huge toll on me as I watched Mom from day to day. My own emotions began a downhill slide, to the point where hope drained away.

***

The last day I saw my mother now dominates my memories. I'd been volunteering one Friday afternoon at Amy's school. It felt good to be back in a classroom without the responsibility of being the primary teacher. Instead, I could do whatever Amy needed help with and enjoy being with the children my daughter taught.

That day I was listening to each one read aloud, then letting them choose a sticker to put on the reading chart beside the door. Hearing them read and seeing the progress each was making gave me a great deal of admiration for Amy's teaching skills.

When I drove to the school that day, the skies were dark and threatening. By the time I left, snowflakes were filling the air—not your typical Texas weather. It was a slow, tense drive to Memory Gardens as the snow began to stick to the road.

Texas rarely got snow, so the highway departments had no equipment to deal with it. I took a brief breather from the traffic by stopping at a convenience store on the way, buying a cappuccino.

As soon as I opened the main door and walked into the dining room, one of the aides met me. "The hospice nurse, Janet, wants to talk to you."

Janet looked up from her laptop when I stepped into Mom's room. "What's wrong?" My heart was already beginning to pound.

"According to the staff, she's been unresponsive all day. It probably won't be much longer, maybe even tonight."

"So soon? Just like that?" My voice couldn't get past a whisper. I pulled a folding chair closer to the bed. Part of me wanted to say something, but the rest of me was afraid. "What should I do, Janet?"

"Do whatever is natural to you," she said as she adjusted the bandages on Mom's feet. "Normally she protests about the pain when I do this, but today she barely reacts. There are sores on her feet from pressing them against the foot of the hospital bed. She's tall, even for her age, and isn't used to a foot board, so she keeps pushing at it."

My guilty thoughts rose again: *Here was something else I could have done better at home. If only I had the courage and stamina to hang on, to care for her longer.*

"I've been saying good-bye to her for a long time," I sighed, finally finding something to say.

"Yes, Alzheimer's is a prolonged good-bye." Janet patted me gently on the shoulder as she headed for the door.

I sat for about half an hour by Mom's bed, sipping the coffee. When it was gone, I rose and put the dirty cup into a small waste basket nearby and left.

Later that evening, after the night nurse called to tell me that Mom was gone, I began to ask myself the same questions over and over:

Why didn't I hold her hand?

Why didn't I give her a kiss on the cheek like I always did before?

Why didn't I say, "Love you, Mom." ? She'd always reply, "Love you, too, Mary Anna." Was it because I knew she wouldn't be able to answer? That seems so selfish to me now.

Why didn't I at least tell her good-bye?

When Rick and I drove back to Memory Gardens in blowing, drifting snow, it was too late for any of those things. I hadn't seen many dead bodies before. Lying there, eyes closed and mouth hanging slightly open, Mom looked like a broken doll. Something that had been there before was missing. There was no life force—just emptiness.

I knew that image and my unanswered questions would haunt me for the rest of my life.

CHAPTER 10
Earthquake - 2017

Months slid by, though I barely noticed. Somehow, I couldn't keep count after Mom's funeral. Jay had finally moved to his own apartment, but he wasn't far away. He tended to bring over his laundry and drop by at meals.

One summer day after lunch, he joined me on the sunporch, while Rick went to work out at the gym. I was glad we lived in a large enough town to have a gym. We'd moved back here to Palestine, Texas in 2008—just before Jay came home from Michigan.

It was nice to be back in my hometown where my best memories were. We'd even added a third cat now, a male orange tabby. A neighbor gave him to us, soon after we'd finished building this home. Jay dubbed him Sir William of Orange, though mostly it got shortened to Orange-boy. Jay wanted to take this cat to his apartment, but that building didn't allow pets.

I did only a bit of private tutoring, thankful to be retired from classroom teaching. Jay had his teaching degree. He substitute taught whenever he could, while he applied for jobs across Texas. I prayed his years of indecision about a career were over, since he was well over thirty.

In a way, I was surprised both our children were teachers. Of course, I was a teacher, but I didn't start out with that goal. There were very few teachers in my family, just a cousin. One of Rick's sisters was a teacher, though, and several of his nieces.

"I think I've finally found myself," Jay said, as we sat on the sunporch after he'd come for lunch. "I had to break out of the mold the world was trying to force me into."

"Okay."

I'd learned that when Jay started talking in metaphors, it was better to just nod and listen. This had always been more difficult for Rick because he was so analytical. I'd worked at it for a long time in parenting Jay. At the same time I tried not to judge too quickly or let my own emotions get in the way.

Jay took a deep breath, looking over my head, and said, "I've been dating lots of people, and not all of them are women."

What? echoed in my mind. *Did I really hear that? Or is he joking? There's only been one other time he told me a deliberate lie to test me.*

Now he sat looking at the floor, as I tried to think of a reply. My world had instantly turned upside down. Not even the new cat was enough to de-stress me this time.

***

Later, when I tried to remember, there was no trace in my mind of what I said to him. Like the survivor of an earthquake, I was in shock. My whole world had changed in a flash. Nothing was how it used to be.

If only he was lying. Like the time he called from work to say he'd wrecked his car.

That time, after I'd gotten out of shock and asked how he was, he confessed, "I'm fine, Mom. I was just upset, and wanted to see how you'd react."

That whole experience was still a mystery in my mind, probably a symptom of his OCD. But this time, I could tell he'd meant what he told me about his dating.

The following afternoon, I took my cell phone, went for a walk, and called my counselor. His voice, instead of his voicemail, answered for a change. Perhaps that was a God-thing because he was usually with a client.

I'd swallowed my pride by going to a counselor, and still didn't talk to many of my friends about it. That day, even after talking to Dr. B, I didn't know what to say to Jay.

How can I tell any of my friends—risk their condemnation? This thought overwhelmed me with shame. *And what about Rick?* A dark pit began to swallow me up.

A couple of days later, when Rick was out of the house, I told Jay that I still loved him unconditionally, but after that, everything became a blur. I felt numb. Was it denial or anger? Dr. B had said the stages of grief weren't always consecutive, but tended to shift back and forth. Some days I wondered if I was feeling them all at once.

Jay's revelation required me to question everything I'd been taught in church and thought I believed. Was homosexuality inborn? Or was it a choice? Or worse—a grievous sin, as my church taught? I had no idea anymore. I wanted to talk to friends but couldn't, for fear Rick might find out second-hand. Jay made me promise not to tell Rick, saying he wanted to find a way to tell his dad himself. How long would that take?

As days, weeks, and then months dragged by, I often cried myself to sleep, mourning the loss of the son I'd thought I had. During those long sleepless nights, I began to remember possible warning signs I'd missed. For example, Jay's androgynous tendencies as a child. How he liked to grow his hair long was one example. Long hair was popular with many boys, so I didn't give it much thought. In college, he liked to dress up in what looked like kilts for Halloween.

Though once he told me, "It's just a skirt, Mom."

I still didn't get it, even when I started finding a few women's jeans in his laundry, thinking they were a friend's or something he'd bought at the thrift store, without realizing they were women's instead of men's. Once I jokingly told myself, "Maybe he's a cross-dresser." Not realizing he truly was.

Occasionally, when I folded laundry he'd brought home from college, I found a pink shirt. This set my mind flowing back to when I was in junior high. During the 50s and 60s, girls were expected to always wear dresses, at least according to my schools' dress codes. At home, though, I liked to try on my brothers' shirts, sweaters, and slacks. One time, I even put on one of John's ties.

Many times, I remember wanting to go to the Boy's Club with my brothers, where there were basketball courts and a trampoline. All we had at the Girl's Club were sewing and cooking classes. I tried hard, because Mom was an excellent cook and seamstress, but sewing and cooking weren't my talents.

As I sat sorting Jay's socks a few weeks after his shocking revelation, I wondered, *If I'd grown up in this time instead, would I have been convinced I was gay, too? Did Jay inherit this tendency from me?*

For several years, I had assumed Jay's interest in the Gay Community was because his good friend Susan had come out as a lesbian. They'd known each other all through high school. Once they'd even gone on a date, but the relationship had never been traditional. When Susan first came out, Jay was quite upset, though later they began to act like good buddies. It was hard not to blame her. *How much influence did Susan have on his thinking?*

One day, soon after this emotional earthquake, Amy and I went out to lunch at our favorite local bistro. After much debate, I decided to ask if *she* knew about Jay.

"Yes, Mom. I've known for a couple of years."

Again, I was in shock. "Wow, I guess you're good at keeping secrets." My eyes wandered around the restaurant, trying to find a place to rest my gaze.

"I'm sorry I couldn't tell you sooner. Jay made me promise."

"Yeah, I'm in the same boat now. Jay hasn't decided how to tell Dad, but he wants to do it himself."

"I'm glad Jay finally found a way to tell you. You know, he's always been different."

"Yeah, I see that now. I thought it was the OCD and Tourette's that made him act the way he did, especially around other guys. He was always socially awkward.

"I think he's had so much trouble finding the right girl that he decided to try the other."

"I suppose that could be true. I guess I still harbor a hope that he'll outgrow this or something."

"Maybe, Mom. But right now he believes it's who he really is."

After that exchange, we changed the subject. There was nothing more to say. Amy was in a rough patch, too. Jeff, the boyfriend she'd been dating the past three years, had just broken it off with her, so I was also in mourning over the son-in-law I'd been hoping for.

Once Tom, the bistro's waiter, brought our meals and walked away, I said, "Amy, I'm so sorry about what happened with Jeff. You two seemed so right for each other. We really liked him, and I know his parents liked you."

"Yeah, I've lost more than just a boyfriend. This past year, he started acting distant, and I wondered what I was doing wrong. I still don't understand what happened."

"Some men have trouble with committing these days." I saw the tears welling up in my daughter's eyes. "Would you go back to him, if he asked you?"

Turning to look out the window beside the table, Amy wiped at tears. "I'd have to really think about that. I'm not sure."

My stomach was starting to ache, something which often happened when I was stressed. "Amy, I'm sorry for the ways I failed you growing up. Jay took so much of my time and energy that you got neglected."

"No, Mom." She reached across the table and took my hand. "You gave me a lot, like all those nights you helped with homework and we read together. They're special memories for me. You even helped me over the phone when I was in college and needed help getting ideas for term papers."

Tears filled my eyes, too. "Thanks, that means a lot. If there's ever anything you need, please let me know. I want to be here for you now."

"Love you, Mom." Amy smiled and took a deep breath, "I've joined a singles group at my church."

"Really? That's great." Amy had been going to one of the new nondenominational churches in town that used contemporary music. Rick and I understood that she needed to have her own space, so we didn't expect her to attend our church.

"Now, don't get all excited, Mom. It's not one of those groups where everyone is looking for a mate. We all just like hanging out together."

"Okay," I said, glad to see her smile again. But I was still wondering what these modern young people meant by 'hanging out.' I didn't ask.

Nights continued to include tears for both of my children. Part of me wasn't sure I could keep on living like this, but each day the sun came peeking in my windows. Morning had arrived, with another day to face and get through. So I forced myself to get out of bed.

***

My younger brother Dan was the first person I told about Jay, after my counselor. Something held me back from telling John right away.

A day finally came when I knew it was time to talk to John. Just the day before, Rick and I had a nice visit with him on the phone. Now that they lived in Alabama, John had started doing a lot of hiking in the southern Appalachians. He was planning a backpacking trip with some friends and invited Rick to join them. It was nice that John and Rick had something new in common, even though we were living across the South from them now. The two of them were alike in many ways, especially in keeping their feelings to themselves.

It was getting close to noon when I called John, so I wasn't surprised to get his voicemail. I left a short message to call back if he had time, wondering if this was God's way of telling me today wasn't the right time.

Still, I was relieved when he called an hour later. "Just had to finish lunch. What's up?"

"Do you have a few minutes?"

"Sure."

I took a deep breath and blurted it all out. "Jay has told

me he dates men, that he thinks he's bisexual. Please don't tell Emilia yet. Rick doesn't know, and Jay needs to tell him. I'm still trying to get my head around it. It's even harder because he's started pulling away from us." I was breathless and my hands were shaking. *There, I've crossed the river of no return.*

"I understand. He's probably being distant because he fears Rick's reaction."

"I'm sure that's part of it. I hope you're not angry that I told Dan first. You're just as special to me, you know, and I love you."

"Love you, too, Sis." His voice was gentler than usual.

John didn't often express his emotions, unlike how I wore my heart on my sleeve. I was touched by the understanding in his voice.

"Thanks, John. I appreciate you and Emilia—your caring and support. I can't help wishing you lived closer sometimes, but I do understand why you needed to move."

"I'm glad you understand. We're never more than a phone call away."

"I know I shouldn't question God's plans for my kids, but I sure don't understand it. Amy's boyfriend, who was almost a fiancé, has broken up with her, too. Why can't a nice girl like Amy find the right guy? Is she just meant to be single?"

By this time tears streamed down my cheeks. I wondered if he could tell.

"It's hard to say," he murmured.

"Yeah, God's ways aren't ours, like the Bible says. This doesn't take away the pain, though. I'm still working on learning to accept."

"I can relate. You know it's been over ten years since Tim and Lauren divorced?"

"I'm sorry, John." For the first time in the call, I could hear pain in my brother's voice. "Do you get to see the grandchildren?"

"Not since Lauren moved them to Colorado. Fortunately, we have Tony and his wife and kids nearby."

We both went silent for a moment. I wished I could think of something comforting to say. Our pastor says all families have their troubles, but I didn't say this aloud to John. It sounded too trite.

"Off and on since the divorce Tim has hinted that he thinks he's gay." John's voice became tight with emotion. "Maybe I was too tough in my answers to him, because now he's not communicating with us at all."

"Oh, wow." *I see why he hasn't told me this before.* For some reason, I was staring at a photo of John, Dan and me that was sitting on the end table beside my chair. It was taken at the going away party I had for them when they moved. "I wish there was something I could say to help," I murmured at last.

"Lauren told Emilia soon after the divorce. We didn't believe her. We thought she was just being spiteful because she was hurting so much. Now we're unsure what to think."

"I guess I shouldn't have called to unload my problems. You guys have enough already."

"No, it's all right. Sometimes it helps to share our burdens. Maybe I should try to reconnect with Tim."

"Knowing you understand about Jay helps a lot. Be sure to tell Emilia hello for me. I'm hoping to come see your place out there soon, so I can tell her about Jay face-to-face."

John's tone of voice changed and I heard another voice in the room. "I need to go now, Sis. My wife's sister just got here to visit."

I tried not to feel envious because they were closer to Emilia's family now. *Our family used to be like that, but now we're the ones all scattered.*

"We'll be praying for you and your family," John ended the conversation. "Take care and God bless."

"I'll keep you guys on my prayer list, too." *Not that I'm praying like I should these days.* I swiped at more tears as I hung up the phone.

CHAPTER 11

Geysers Boiling Over - 2017

Over our years of marriage, I'd learned that certain things made Rick angry. Most of the time, he was very even-tempered, but once in a while, I'd misstep and he got upset over something I didn't expect—such as if I complained about the weather.

"Why are you never satisfied? You're either too hot or too cold," he'd say.

Other things that bothered him were when I worried about how we'd cope when we got old and senile like my mother, or if I mentioned wanting grandchildren. You'd think I'd know better, but sometimes I just needed to talk to someone and he was the only one around.

Gradually, though, my counselor helped me see life in a more positive light. When I caught myself griping or worrying, I'd try to stop, though I wasn't always successful. Old ingrained habits die hard. But Dr. B reminded me of the emotional and physical benefits if I tried to be more positive.

Lately, he was helping me learn how to disengage from an uncomfortable situation—let it pass on by, like water off a duck's back, as Dad used to say. (Seems like my dad had a proverb for every occasion.)

Yet, deep down my anger still lurked, and if something unexpected set it off, it was like a geyser. There was no stopping the eruption. All the pent-up, held-back frustrations boiled over and spewed out. And since it had been suppressed to the point where it was rotten and toxic, it was ugly. I hated myself when I let that happen.

There were days I considered suicide when I got this way, thinking myself a worthless person. *I'm poisoning the lives of those around me. Wouldn't the world be better off without me?*

What stopped me? So far, something had—I'd remember how much I loved my family and didn't want to hurt them. But there were times I wasn't even sure this was enough.

At one session when I told Dr. B this, he said, "Stop and think about it. Do you see that considering suicide is ultimately selfish? You would be ignoring the needs of the people around you who depend on you."

This surprised me, but as I processed his words, I saw he was right. "Okay, I suppose Jay might go right over the edge if I did such a thing. I am thinking only of myself, aren't I?"

He nodded, and went on, "Don't be too hard on yourself, though. You're only human. The world won't always look as dark as it does today. It's the depression talking to you right now. Remember, when you're down in the bottom of the dark pit and a voice is saying, 'There's no way out of here except dying,' that's a lie."

"I really want to push my raging negativity away," I moaned. "To focus on the positive—to be a good wife and mother, to be the person Rick and my children need me to be. Sometimes I don't think I'll ever be good enough, though. And when I'm really down, I think: *I don't care. I should just give up.*

I broke down into sobs when I saw the concern in his eyes. "I'm sorry, Dr. B. I don't want to let you down, either."

"Hey, you're still doing the work. We'll get through this. Don't give up."

After that session I began to think differently about how to prevent the explosive eruptions of my putrid geyser. There were no easy answers, but I was still alive because of Dr. B. He had given me some tools to begin working on, and he emphasized that it would take time and practice to make them into new habits.

Some of my Christian friends told me to pray more, to seek God's presence. Why did I feel so empty when I prayed? Sometimes it seemed like years since one of my prayers made it past the ceiling. I'd look at things I wrote in journals years ago and think, *I remember when I believed that.*

Then everything had caved in with Jay's revelation of his sexual orientation, his coming out of the closet. Nothing was the same anymore. The world had turned on its head, and I'd been trying to live upside-down ever since.

About this time, Dr. B was helping to stabilize my medications. I admitted I'd been taking Xanax for much too long, over ten years, in fact. When he found this out, he was concerned. "Xanax is a tranquilizer, and it's meant to be used short-term. I have a feeling it may be contributing to your depression instead of helping it."

"Okay. I like the way it calms the storms in my mind, though."

"I think it would be better if you switched to a good antidepressant, like Lexapro."

The word antidepressant hit me like a rogue wave, leaving me feeling weak and worthless. "I hate the idea that I can't cope without drugs," I muttered. "I guess I'm just a weakling." (It didn't occur to me until later how inconsistent this was, since I still depended on the tranquilizers.)

Dr. B made eye-contact with me as he spoke again. "No, Mary. This isn't something you caused. Depression is a physical problem, not just mental. I see you as one of the strong ones because you realize you need help. You're already doing the work."

"The work?"

He nodded and smiled. "You sought me out. You're trying to do the things I suggest. You show a lot of will power. I wish more of my patients were like you."

"Well, thanks," I managed to smile back.

"So, will you try this work of changing your medications?"

"Okay."

Counseling with Dr. B was the beginning of a long journey, like climbing mountains. Some days things were gradually getting better. We'd been working on my seeking hope for four years already in 2017. After a few weeks, the Lexapro seemed to help. When I woke each morning, I resisted the desire to spend all day in bed or to pop a Xanax. Maybe—just maybe—I could wean off it soon.

Other times, hope appeared like a distant light on the horizon, but as soon as I approached, it disappeared like a mirage. Maybe true hope was a thing that only existed beyond this world—'in the sweet by and by', as the old song said.

Some days were better than others. There had been times when I wished Rick would come with me to counseling, but he was reluctant. I guess he thought I was the one with problems—and he was probably right. At first, this really frustrated me. Now, with Dr. B's help, I was working on what I *could* change and learning to accept and live with the things I couldn't. A plaque on my wall summed this up well:

"Lord, grant me the serenity to accept the things I cannot change, the courage to change the things I can, and wisdom to know the difference."

Perhaps I needed to get one of these for Jay.

CHAPTER 12
Face to Face - 2018

The phone rang one January morning shortly after Rick had left for his daily workout. Caller ID showed Texas, so I answered, even though I didn't recognize the number. Too often, these were Robo-calls, but I could never be sure.

To my surprise, a male voice said tentatively, "Aunt Mary Anna? This is Tim Parker."

"Tim? Oh, John's son. Right?"

"Yes, ma'am. I hope I'm not disturbing you. I'm off work today."

"No, I don't have any plans. What can I do for you?"

"Well, maybe it's more what I might be able to do for you. My dad suggested I call and tell you why I divorced Lauren. To be honest, I was surprised he called me. He said it was because of something you told him recently."

I remembered John telling me they thought Tim was gay. Not sure what to say, I murmured, "Okay—"

"I live in Jacksonville right now," he continued. "I'll be moving to Tyler soon."

Does this move have something to do with a new relationship? I hesitated to ask.

When I didn't speak, he went on, "Anyway, I wondered if you'd like to meet me for coffee today. I like that bakery in downtown Palestine. Maybe we could meet there in an hour or so? That's about how long it takes me to drive there from here."

I'd already told him I didn't have any plans, so it was too late to make an excuse. Maybe this was one of those surprises God liked putting in my life these days.

"Yes, it would be nice to see you, Tim. I've been wondering how you are. I guess your dad told you about Jay."

"Yes, ma'am, he did."

"Well, okay. I guess we can meet at the Palestine Bakery. At about ten a.m.?"

"I'll be there. In case you don't recognize me, I'll be wearing a red plaid shirt and black jeans."

As I hung up the phone, I realized it *had* been a long time since I'd seen Tim, probably at his wedding over twenty years ago. He and his family had lived in Rusk, one of the small towns of East Texas. We hadn't communicated with them much, partly because of our nomadic existence back then.

Should I feel guilty about this? Maybe he was closer to his wife's family, or their problems kept them away from our family. My curiosity was piqued now.

An hour later, I was sitting at one of the metal bistro tables in the bakery, with a cup of cappuccino in front of me. A couple of times the bell on the door jingled, but when I looked up, I saw only women entering. Just as I began to wonder if Tim wasn't going to show, a young man in a red plaid shirt stepped into the bakery. His hair was golden-brown, wavy, and nearly down to his shoulders. He smiled shyly at me as he approached the table.

"Aunt Mary Anna?" He reached out his hand.

"Yes. You must be Tim. I'm glad you recognized me because I probably wouldn't have known it was you."

"It's okay. A lot has happened since I last saw you. May I sit down?"

"Of course."

He pulled out the gray metal chair across from me and seated himself with a slight sigh.

"Can I get you something, sir?" a waitress asked presently.

"I'll take a cappuccino. Oh, and one of those raspberry scones."

"I think I'll have a scone, too," I added. "Please make mine gluten-free."

"Very good, ma'am."

As the waitress walked away, I nodded to Tim, "I like how everyone uses 'ma'am' and 'sir' here in the south. When Rick and I lived in the north, we hardly ever heard it."

"I guess it's just part of the southern culture, isn't it?"

I smiled. At least we were off to a pleasant start.

Soon the waitress returned with Tim's coffee and two small plates with warm scones, shining with melted butter on top. Mine had a little flag on a toothpick with the letters "GF" on it.

"Mmm, they really do a good job here, don't they?" I smiled.

"For sure. It's worth the drive from Jacksonville," he said.

"Will it be worth a drive from Tyler?"

"I don't know. That's twice as far. Maybe I can get Sam hooked on this place, though."

"Sam?"

"He's my partner. We've been together a few years."

"Before your divorce from Lauren?"

He shook his head, concentrating on sipping from his coffee cup. "There was another back then, but now I think Sam is the right one. It's hard for everyone to understand where I'm coming from. They all just want to hide their heads in the sand. Maybe Dad is trying to wrap his head around it. I was surprised when he called me about you."

"I'm glad he suggested you talk to me. Our son Jay has told me he's bisexual. Is it the same thing?"

"Not exactly. Dad implied we had something in common, so I guess that's it. Frankly, I don't talk to my family much anymore. Not after what happened to Michael."

"Who's Michael?"

"He was my first partner, the one I left my wife for."

"I see. What happened?"

His eyes suddenly reddened with tears, and he looked down at the floor.

"I'm sorry. I shouldn't have asked if it's too painful."

He took a shuddering breath. "No, it's okay. I'm long overdue to tell someone about it—if you don't mind."

Looking across the table, I sensed hurt and anger flowing from him like some powerful aura. I reached over and patted his arm. "I'm told I can be a good listener. And I'm willing, even though you don't know me very well."

"Maybe it's easier this way."

We sat in silence for a few minutes. I glanced around and noticed only two other people were in the shop. *Good thing we're here before the lunch hour.*

After taking another bite of the scone, he looked into my eyes. "Michael was the truest friend I've ever known. The closer we got, the more I realized he meant the world to me, not just as a buddy, but as a true partner. I loved him in a way I'd never felt for anyone, not even Lauren."

He stared at his coffee and took a deep breath. I kept my hand on his arm, and he didn't pull away.

"We both realized we'd been different all our lives, but now that we had each other, we knew the truth. Of course,

Lauren went nuts when I told her. Michael didn't have a spouse because he still lived with his parents—"

A sudden catch came into his voice.

"Anyway, we moved in together, and after a few months, Michael finally told his father he was gay. That didn't go well."

"What happened?"

"The next day, when Michael went to get the last of his things, his dad had thrown them all out on the front lawn in the rain."

"Oh, my."

"As he tried to gather them up, his mother came out and handed him a loaf of homemade bread.

"'When will you be back?' she asked. Michael said he could tell by the look on her face that she had no clue what was happening."

"How sad!"

"That wasn't the end of it, though. A couple of days later his dad called and asked him to come get his bicycle. Michael told me his dad sounded really sorry, that he even apologized for losing his temper."

"Well, that was better."

Tim shook his head and I saw dark hatred flare in his eyes. "Not really. When Michael went over there, his father called the police."

"What?"

"He swore up and down that Michael was harassing him, and then had him arrested."

I was speechless.

Now Tim brushed angrily at a couple of tears. "I didn't know until the next day. I was sick with worry all night when he didn't come home. At last, he called in the morning from the county jail, asking me to bail him out."

Again, I couldn't think of anything to say, but held his quivering forearm.

"When we got home, he was an emotional wreck. I tried to help him calm down, and he finally did a little. He wouldn't tell my anything about the night in jail, but he seemed pretty traumatized. I asked why he hadn't called me sooner. He shook his head and muttered something about the nature of his father's charges.

"The morning was flying, and I needed to get to work, afraid I might lose my job. So I left him sitting at the kitchen table. He refused to go to bed or even sit on the couch."

"That's awful. How could a parent do such a thing to their own child?"

"I don't know. Now you can see why I don't talk much to my family. There's more, though."

"What?"

He made a gulping sound in his throat as though holding back a sob. "When I got home from work that afternoon, Michael was still at the table, lying in a pool of his own blood. He'd slashed his wrists and committed suicide."

Tim held his face in his hands, still trying not to sob. I wished I knew what to say, but no words came. I moved my hand from his arm and took his hand.

"I don't think your father—my brother—would ever do a thing like that," I murmured at last.

He finally looked up. "Well, things are looking a little better with my parents. But I'm afraid to try to see my kids. My ex-wife Lauren and my brother Tony detest me."

"Well, at least you've told *me*. I hope that helps a little."

"Me, too. Please don't tell anyone else, though."

"No, I won't break your confidence. But I think John might be ready to hear this story now. It's been years."

"Maybe. I think I need more time to get up my courage."

"I understand, Tim."

"Has Jay talked to *you* much about being gay?"

"Well, he told me, but now he's started acting distant, even though he's still living nearby. It's hard," I sighed.

"I'm sorry he can't talk to you yet."

"Not as sorry as I am."

"Hopefully he'll come around. It's taken me a long time to face everything, too."

"How long have you known?"

"That I was gay? Probably ever since junior high. All my friends were getting interested in girls, but I just couldn't manage it. I started noticing I was attracted to guys instead."

"That early?"

"Yeah. Did Jay ever say anything about this?"

"No, I guess he kept it to himself."

"So did I. I kept praying for God to change me, to heal me of this problem I had. I even went to meetings at our church— sort of a Gays Anonymous thing. Nothing helped. When I met Lauren, things got better for a while. I enjoyed talking to her, and we had a lot in common. We got to be good friends, so I decided marrying a close friend might be what I needed."

"Did it help?"

"For a while. We managed to have two children. By the time our son Danny was born, we both knew something was missing. There wasn't the passion my guy friends talked about in their marriages. I mean, I liked Lauren, but I began to realize what I felt wasn't real love."

"Did she love you?"

"Yeah, I'm pretty sure she did. She was devastated about our divorce, and really angry. I don't think she understands what I've been going through."

"I can relate to that."

"I know. Maybe that's why I felt this need to tell you everything. At least you're listening. No one else in my family has—so far," he sighed.

"I'm sorry, Tim. I know how it feels when people don't listen. But maybe my talking to John has opened a new door for him to listen to you."

"So how is your husband—Rick, is it? —taking things?"

"He doesn't know yet."

"Oh."

I needed to get the subject off Rick, so I asked, "When did you meet Sam?"

"About five years ago. It was a while after Michael. One day at the gym, I saw him. There was something about him calling to me. I don't know how to explain. It was a deep attraction. The sort of thing my high school friends kept saying about the girls.

"With Sam, the feelings I'd had for Michael reawakened. We started dating, and one thing led to another. I wanted to tell my kids, but I didn't have the courage. By this time, Lauren and I weren't communicating at all. They'd moved to Colorado, so it was a long trip I couldn't afford. Maybe I should have tried harder, but I felt unworthy as a father. I wasn't sure Lauren would allow it, anyway."

"I'm sorry. It must be hard." I took a deep breath, and again caught myself looking around at the nearby tables. An elderly couple sat about six feet away, so I moved my chair closer to Tim in order to talk more softly. There was probably no need, but this conversation was making me self-conscious.

The bell on the door chimed again as two women entered. I heard their laughing voices as they chose a table. To my relief, they picked one on the far side of the room. As a waitress came from the kitchen, the smell of fresh bread followed her. The scent was comforting, even though it reminded me that I could no longer eat wheat. Fortunately, this bakery had good gluten free choices.

Trying to bring my mind back into focus, I searched for words to say. "Tim, I hesitate to ask, since I don't really know you well, but as a mother I can't help it. Do you think being gay is part of who you are?"

"I've spent many years asking myself that same question and finally accepted that it *is* who I am."

Even though my heart started pounding, I heard the sincerity in his voice. "You sound sure about this."

"Absolutely. I have no doubts left now. It's such a relief."

"I wonder if I'll ever be able to reach the point of completely accepting Jay's choices."

"It's not a choice," Tim said, shaking his head. "It's learning to be who you are. Believe me, I tried everything else. I wanted to spare Lauren and my kids the pain, but I couldn't go on living a lie."

Tears welled into my eyes. Blinking them back, I stared at the wooden tabletop. The sound of clinking dishes reached my ears, as the older couple's table was cleared.

"Before the divorce, Lauren and I tried counseling."

"Did that help at all?"

"No, not really. I couldn't open up about the real problem."

"You mean you didn't tell him—"

"Her—"

"About your uh, desires?"

He looked down at his empty plate. "I was a coward, trying to hide behind the person I thought I should be. It was a lie. When I finally came out, it was too late to save our marriage because it wasn't based on what a true marriage should be."

"Do you think you'll marry Sam?" I wanted to keep the subject on Tim and Sam to keep from thinking about Jay and his dad.

"Not sure yet. There are still some things that need to be worked out. I guess I want to be really sure this time."

"Well, I can't blame you for being careful." My plate was empty now, though I barely remembered eating the scone. "I guess your parents aren't thrilled about you living with Sam."

"No, they say we're living in sin. I guess in their church's eyes, we are. But I've decided all I can do is be myself."

He kept coming back to this idea.

"I've heard Jay say that, too. He says he's pansexual."

"It's hard to say whether he's still questioning, you know."

"This is all so confusing. My world has been turned upside-down."

"I think the whole world is topsy-turvy."

"Where do I go from here?"

"All I can say is to keep on loving Jay. In spite of all my parents and the church think about me, I still believe God has a plan for me somewhere, somehow. Though I can't see it yet, I won't give up believing."

Looking into his light brown eyes, I felt warmth for this nephew I barely knew and wondered where it was coming from. Maybe it was because I sensed he understood like no one else could.

"I'm sorry. I need to get going. I have a job interview in Tyler." He rose from the table and pushed his chair in.

His voice sounded so sad, my heart went out to him. I stood with him and without thinking about it, pulled him into a hug. "Tim, I'll be praying for you—for whatever my feeble prayers are worth."

"I feel the same way about prayer sometimes, but I keep trying anyway."

I liked the way he hugged me back. It was the best hug I'd felt in a long time. Why was this? *It's not as though a man has to be gay to give good hugs.*

"I just want to thank you for being you, Tim."

He stepped back and smiled. "It means a lot to hear you say that."

"Well, I really mean it."

We stood in silence for a few seconds, feeling awkward. Finally, I patted him on the shoulder. "Stay in touch if you can."

"I'll try." He turned and walked out the door to the sidewalk.

The bell on the door chimed his departure, as I headed to the counter to pay the bill. There I discovered Tim had already paid for both orders. I was surprised I hadn't noticed, but I *was* preoccupied.

CHAPTER 13

Promise of Spring - 2018

One balmy spring day, I sat on our back porch, thinking how thankful I was to be back in Texas. Early spring in places like Wyoming and Montana had gotten me down. Just yesterday, I'd found something from a journal I'd kept shortly after Amy was born. I was probably dealing with post-partum depression at that time, but there were days, even now in Texas, when I sank back into those gloomy thoughts.

I forced myself to refocus, to leave the dark thoughts behind, and began to pray for Jay. It was hard to know what to say anymore. My mind wandered, as I thought of how different my two children were.

Amy was definitely a strong-willed child. Even as a baby, she vociferously demanded her way. When she was hungry, she wanted to be fed *now,* or maybe even yesterday. Yet she was a picky eater. For her first few years she lived on Cheerios.

Traveling with her was torture sometimes. Whenever she wanted out of her car-seat, she cried until we stopped, even on a remote logging road in Montana or the Texas Piney Woods.

She often fussed her way through Sunday services, but many times, our current church didn't have a nursery. I wanted to take a little container of Cheerios to occupy her, but Rick hesitated, saying he didn't believe in snacking during worship.

Another thing Amy was stubborn about was falling asleep. No matter how tired she was, she fought it right up to the end. I found the only lullaby that worked, *Silent Night,* when we flew to Chicago—on her first Christmas—to visit Rick's family. It worked so well that I sang the carol to Amy at bedtime all year round. Even as she got older.

In fact, *Silent Night* became a special ritual for the two of us. Once, when Amy was assigned to teach her class a song in sign language, it came naturally to teach her the ASL hand signs for this carol.

By the time Amy reached high school, this resistance to falling asleep manifested itself in her being a night owl. Ten or even eleven o'clock would roll around, but as Rick and I went to bed, Amy would be cleaning her room.

Mornings were the opposite. Her alarm would go off for what seemed like several minutes before she finally hit the snooze button. Ten minutes later, the whole process would repeat itself. We tried putting the alarm across the room so she had to get out of bed to turn it off. Somehow, she managed to accomplish this in her sleep. A couple of times, I even resorted to putting ice cubes in her bed to force her to get up. I lost count of how many times she missed the school bus. In fact, I gave up and started driving her to school myself. It was a relief when Amy got her driver's license and could take herself to school.

Being a typical worrier, though, I stood at the front window each day as she drove off, saying a prayer for her safety. I'd done the same for Jay when he began driving, and I also prayed each morning for Rick as he drove to work.

I smiled as I remembered that. Times like those were frustrating, but they became fond memories later. Amy was a college graduate now, so she must have managed to get herself to all those morning classes. I wondered if she still put the alarm clock across her room, so she could get up early to drive to the school where she taught now. Especially those extra-early mornings when she had bus duty.

Amy's strong-willed nature was also competitive. Combining this with Jay's rigid sense of what was fair and right in his mind caused some major confrontations. One of the most vivid situations I remembered was how they argued every night, during the countdown to Christmas, about whose turn it was to open the little window on the Advent Calendar. Those arguments often made holidays less than joyous.

"Mom, Jay's cheating again!" I heard this call much too often as they were growing up. The sound was so clear in my head at times that I went to see where they were playing—before I realized the kids were grown and gone from the house.

Our daughter's competitiveness plus our son's obsession with rules caused most of the problems. Jay loved to play games of all kinds, but board games were his favorite. Not just the ordinary Monopoly or Candyland, either. He liked to create his own games because, of course, he could make up all the rules. He had a talent for it, and some of his ideas were quite creative. Since his dad was a petroleum geologist, it was natural for him to invent games about oil exploration, refining, and distribution. His love for maps added some amazing graphics, but often the rules were so intricate that no one could follow them.

"You just do that so you can always win," Amy would accuse.

"I do not," he'd retort. "You just aren't smart enough."

Of course, I was the one who had to step in and mediate. Perhaps that's why I'm not a big fan of board games. (Another reason was my lack of talent for strategy. My brother John usually won most games as we were growing up.)

For Jay, gaming turned into a major pastime while he was in college. There was actually a board game fan club on his campus that specialized in finding and playing new and old rare, unique games—even some vintage ones from the early 50s and 60s. In a way, I was thankful he was into this instead of expensive video games, although some of the popular new board games were quite pricey, too. Someday, I hoped Jay would find a way to put this creativity and skill to good use, whether in designing new games or maybe using them as teaching tools.

I'd also seen some very positive sides to Amy's strong will. It helped her become a dedicated cross-country runner. In her senior year, she placed in the top ten at the state meet. Texas is a big state, so it was a great accomplishment.

Her determination also meant Amy's faith was firm, so she didn't bend to peer pressure. As she'd grown into womanhood, I admired her persistence and self-reliance. At times I prayed that I could be more like my daughter.

I knew it wasn't right to compare my children. Still, I wished sometimes that Jay could be more like his younger sister, too.

Ironically, there were times when Amy took on the role of older sibling, looking after her brother. When they were both in college in 2002, Amy walked all the way to his dorm because he'd called me to say he had a bad headache, but was out of aspirin. Like I was supposed to solve this from one hundred miles away? In desperation, I phoned Amy, who was living in another dorm on the same campus. She did have a bottle of acetaminophen and agreed to take him some. It was such a relief to have her help that evening.

Several years later, though, Jay returned the favor. In 2016, while he was living at home again, someone rear-ended Amy's car while she was on her way to work. That time, the panicked call came from her. Both Jay and I answered the extensions at once. (We still had a landline then.)

"Are you okay?" was my first question.

"Yeah. The back end of my car is crunched, and the rear window is broken. The guy was driving a pickup truck. He says the police are on their way."

I could hear her trying not to cry, and was at a loss about what to do.

"Don't worry, Amy," Jay spoke right up. "Tell me the street names, and I'll be right there. Something like this happened to me in Michigan."

Relief washed over me. My adult son was finally stepping up to the plate as the big brother.

A couple of months later, after a day of substitute teaching, Jay stopped in the kitchen where I was starting dinner. Usually he tromped upstairs without a word.

"Mom, remember my old boy scout leader, Mr. Baker?"

"Yes." *Of course, I remember.* The memories flashed across the screen of my mind as fast as lightning.

Boy Scouts had been yet another difficult time for Jay because of his androgyny. Most of the other boys either ignored him or teased him. Too many activities ended with him coming home in anger or tears. Rick and I tried talking to Mr. Baker, but nothing changed.

The scout leaders paid little attention to Jay's desire to work toward Eagle Scout. I lost faith in the organization when his troop-mate Tom became an Eagle. Tom had been expelled from high school for possession of drugs.

I wiped those thoughts out of my mind, though, when I saw a smile in Jay's eyes.

"So what about Mr. Baker?" I asked in my calmest voice.

"He's the principal of the middle school in Corsicana, where I subbed today."

"Really?"

"He popped into my class while I was doing a Texas history lesson. At first, he looked surprised to see me. I just kept on with the discussion I was leading. When class was over, he came up and shook my hand. I was sure surprised."

"What did he say?"

"He told me I was doing an exceptional job and said he wants me to sub there anytime."

The smile on Jay's face and in his voice spoke volumes. Another step forward for my maturing son.

Jay still had his bad days, because Tourette's is caused by a complicated brain chemical imbalance. Various medications work differently in each patient. There's no real standard treatment for a condition that shifts colors like a chameleon. Because of the side-effects he'd experienced over the years, Jay refused to take any meds when he went away to college.

Knowing that added to my stress. Sometimes I caught myself telling God, "You said you wouldn't send more than I could handle, but you did when you sent Jay."

One day, a voice in my head replied, "I only promised to send what you could handle with *my* help."

Oh, boy...

***

After I'd been going to counseling for several years, I told Dr. B, "I must be a slow learner. I've been coming to you for so long."

His reply was uplifting: "Don't look back and wonder why it's taking so long. Look ahead with hope. Step back from judging yourself, or seeing things through the eyes of others judging you. Yes, you've fallen down sometimes, but you've gotten back up."

"That's because you've helped me."

"Every step forward is a victory, even the baby steps. Don't belittle that. Just keep walking with the Lord. Let Him hold your hand."

"It's difficult for me to believe He wants to hold my hand."

"Why is that?"

"I guess I don't feel worthy."

"None of us are worthy, you know. Not really. Still, He wants to take your hand and lead you—because He cares."

CHAPTER 14
Alex — Summer 2019

Two years had slid by since my world flipped over. Time had folded in on itself, like a retractable telescope. Jay was still keeping his distance from both of us, but one day he called to say he'd decided to tell Rick about his sexual orientation. I was relieved, but also fearful. What if Jay got cold feet? I knew we were both fearful of his dad's reaction. Hadn't I been living in fear for twenty-four months already? *Lord, please don't let Rick disown him or something.* The story Tim Parker had told about his friend Michael haunted me.

For me, the past two years had turned into a blur. There were things that must have happened in that span of time, but I could barely remember many of them. Yet some things were blazed into my mind like a firebrand, such as the day Jay texted to tell me about his significant other, "Alex is gender-fluid, Mom. Sometimes he's more to the feminine, while I'm pansexual. I can feel attracted to any sex."

"Any? I thought there were two, male and female."

"Oh, Mom, your terminology is so out of date."

So bisexual must be passé, too. It's lucky I haven't said it to Jay. I wonder if Rick is ever going to wrap his mind around this.

A sick feeling rose in the pit of my stomach whenever I thought about that future revelation. When I tried to sort things out in my mind, all I knew was I wanted my children to be happy, that I loved them dearly. But could I really accept all this?

My feelings sank even more when Jay emailed me a picture of himself with Alex, their arms around each other's shoulders. With reality staring me in the face, I couldn't take refuge in denial anymore.

One day toward the end of summer, Jay's car pulled into the driveway. Two young men got out. At least, *I* thought of them as men. Jay's hair was much longer than I'd seen before, curlier, with blond highlights. Had he been coloring it? The other person was slender with long dark hair pulled back into a ponytail.

I stood in the kitchen as they came through the back door.

"Hi, Mom," Jay's voice called from the hallway. "This is Alex."

To him, it was so simple. Not to me. Feeling awkward, I reached out and shook Alex's extended hand where he stood in the mud room. *It's just a normal handshake,* I told myself.

"Do you want anything to eat or drink?" *What else am I supposed to say?* All I could do was fall back on being a mom.

"No, thanks," Jay said. "We just came to pick up some stuff out of my closet."

In preparing to finally move out, Jay had put most of his belongings into boxes and took what his little Subaru could carry, leaving the rest behind. He'd promised to come for it later, but a couple of years had passed. While I stood wondering what to say, he and Alex hurried upstairs and began carrying boxes down to his car. Alex was very quiet. *I guess I would be, too, in his position.*

After four trips, they stopped and sat at the breakfast bar. "That's all we have room for right now," said Jay. "Hope you don't mind that I'm still leaving some stuff."

"It's okay, I guess. No one's using that closet right now."

In the back of my mind, I wondered if they were moving in together, but I was afraid to ask.

"Where are you guys headed from here?" I hoped this question sounded casual.

"Oh, didn't I tell you? I got a teaching job in Phoenix."

"Phoenix, Arizona?" My heart began to pound, and the room took a spin around me. "Why didn't you tell me?" I glimpsed how much he'd been hiding from me. What else was there?

"Yeah, Mom. Sorry if I forgot."

"You forgot? What kind of explanation is that?"

He stared at the floor. "I said I was sorry."

I smiled bleakly. "Phoenix is a long way from here."

"But I have to go where the job is."

"Both of you?"

"Alex is looking for a tech job. There's plenty of those in a big city like Phoenix."

I wanted to say, 'This sounds pretty up-in-the-air to me.' But all I did was nod at them and mumble, "Well, good luck."

I guess my question about their living arrangement was answered. *Not that I really wanted to hear this.*

"Say, where's Sir William of Orange?" asked Jay.

"You mean Orange-boy? He's probably in my closet where he likes to sleep, curled up under my dresses that hang down to the floor. Why?"

"We found an apartment that allows cats. I think it's time he came out of the closet." He glanced over at Alex and grinned as he said this, and I suddenly saw the double meaning.

"So you're taking him. I'll miss that boy cat, but at least we still have Muffin. Puffin died a couple of years ago. We found him dead alongside the road."

While they gathered the cat and his necessities, I realized perhaps this was a good thing. Having a pet to care for and cuddle might help Jay with his emotions, the same way cats helped me.

I was going to need a lot of cuddles myself. I still felt like I'd lost my son. He'd been so distant emotionally, and soon he'd be distant physically, too.

Once the cat had been located and settled in their car, complete with food, water, and litter box, they were ready to leave. Suddenly, my heart physically ached as I wondered how long it might be before I saw my son again.

"Can I get you all anything for the road? A couple of sodas maybe?" It was all I could think of to say.

"That'd be great." It was the first time I'd heard Alex speak. He had a calm-sounding voice. Perhaps he would be good for Jay.

I got two cans of cola out of the fridge and handed one to each of them as they headed out the back door. In the driveway, Jay let me give him a hug—at least.

Feeling self-conscious, I turned to Alex and gave him a quick hug, too. "I look forward to getting to know you better," I murmured.

He smiled, and Jay nodded. "I'll email you guys soon, Mom."

"Is that how you'll tell Dad?" *Or is he backing out again?*

"Yeah, sure," he muttered.

They climbed into the gray Outback, Jay revved the engine, and they were off in a crunch of gravel and a cloud of dust. I stood with my hand in the air, trying to smile. After the car turned the first street corner, I went into the house, wiping at tears.

***

A couple of weeks later, an email with an attachment came to me from Jay. I'd had to set up a new email account after he came out, so we could communicate without Rick seeing any of the messages. His note said: "Mom, here's a letter explaining things to Dad. Will you give it to him, please?"

So, this was all the courage he could muster. Putting the burden on me, but it was something I'd had on my shoulders a long time already. At least I'd passed the stage when I put away all his photos from childhood and school, when seeing them brought too many sharp pangs of loss.

Because I was so nervous about Rick's reaction, I took the letter to Dr. B and let him read it first. I was relieved when he offered to let Rick read it in his counseling office. He wanted me to be there, though.

A few days later, I convinced Rick to come with me to my next appointment.

"Why?" he demanded. "Are you going to tell me you want a divorce?"

"No," I stumbled over the words. "It's not like that, but it's something we need to work on together."

Somehow I made it through the next twelve hours, until the appointment time finally arrived. I couldn't help worrying if Rick would be asking *me* for a divorce after this.

As we drove to the counseling office, I was still debating how to answer if Rick asked how long I'd known.

Many ideas floated through my mind—*A while—A few months—Over a year—*

While he parked the car, I took a deep breath and decided the truth was the best way to go.

I was thankful Dr. B went straight to the point and asked Rick to read the letter I handed to him. After he'd read Jay's letter, the room echoed with silence.

Then he turned to me, grimacing. "I sort of expected something like this. Though I didn't want to believe it. How long have you known?"

"Jay told me about two years ago."

This was where I expected Rick to explode, but he didn't. Instead, he said, "I'm sorry you had to bear this all alone for so long."

"It wasn't easy." Tears flooded my eyes as I searched for more words. "Amy knows, too." Meanwhile, I was thinking, *Please don't ask me how long she's known. Amy should be allowed to make her own decision about how to answer that.*

Many people say there's a numbness that sets in after an emotional shock. Just like on the first day Jay came out to me, my mind blanked out for a while.

Finally, my focus came back as Dr. B expressed his willingness to help the two of us any way he could, saying, "My door's always open."

I relaxed a bit into gratitude for him. The three of us began talking about the difference in attitudes between society and the church.

"The Bible says homosexuality is wrong," said Rick.

"As a Christian, I have to say I feel the same way," Dr. B said.

I couldn't resist adding, "Many doctors are saying there's evidence it's an inborn trait. Part of me has a hard time accepting this, but another part of me wants to. As I look back, I see all kinds of red flags in Jay's life that I missed or didn't want to see."

Rick shrugged. "I guess I can, too. Now I don't know what to think."

A little light bulb turned on in my brain. "You know, I remember in a Bible study on the Old Testament, how someone asked why God let Jacob and King David have more than one wife."

"Yeah, I remember that," Rick nodded. "Some of the kings and patriarchs had concubines, too. Does that mean God was saying polygamy is permitted?"

"What do you two think?" asked Dr. B.

I liked the way he guided us to keep talking.

"Well," Rick resumed, "I remember one Bible teacher who said polygamy wasn't God's true will or perfect plan, but He allowed it because of the culture of the time."

Now I had to speak my mind. "If that's true, then why can't we apply the same reasoning to the present? Our culture is moving toward accepting homosexuality, so does God 'allow it', like he did with polygamy in ancient times?"

Rick was shaking his head, and I shifted my gaze to Dr. B. He nodded and said, "Well, we're all sinners, aren't we? One sin is no worse than another. The Bible names a lot of sins, even including gossip."

"I can agree with that," I said.

"Still, we need to stand up for what's right," Rick added.

A lump rose in my throat. Dr. B must be able to tell, because he continued, "I'm glad I don't have to be the one walking into King David's throne room and telling him to get rid of all his wives."

"God never did that, did He?" I couldn't help adding this thought.

Rick glared at me, "Well, He did send a prophet to bawl him out when he took another man's wife, Bathsheba."

"I've always wondered why God let David marry her," I sighed, "He even made her son Solomon the next king, over all his other sons."

"There was an awful lot of heartbreak and bloodshed in David's family after that, though."

"That's true, Rick," said Dr. B. Our hour was running out, and I knew he was looking for a good way to end the session. "Our best example of how to act is Jesus. He didn't condemn people, just called them to Himself in love."

Rick turned his gaze down and looked at the floor. I reminded myself that I'd had many months to mull all this over, and he was on his first day of shell-shock. *God must be trying to teach me patience again.*

On the way home, we didn't talk much. I could think of nothing to say. At church the next Sunday, though, I took the opportunity to tell my dear friend Margie about Jay. I felt safer now that I didn't have to live in fear of Rick finding out. As we drove home, though, he got angry when I mentioned it.

"What? Do I have to ask your permission about everything I tell my friends?" I was livid.

"I'm not ready to talk about it," he growled. "I don't want you telling the whole world."

My heart sank again. It was like nothing had really changed. Luckily, I'd told Margie not to tell anyone else yet. Almost four months passed before I got the chance, in a private moment, to tell my friend Jane, who I'd known since junior high.

When I asked Dr. B why Rick was acting like this, he explained that Rick was dealing with his feelings in a different way. "It's not better, just different. Try to respect where he is right now."

"Okay, but I sure wish Rick would respect where I am."

"That's unfortunate. All you can do is try to understand and accept him as he is."

"I know I need to do that." My eyes were beginning to tear-up. "Sometimes I feel like I'm getting the short end of the stick."

"You've spent many months adjusting to Jay's lifestyle. Rick needs time, too. Maybe even more than you. And he needs you."

"I guess I need him, too." I pulled a tissue from the box Dr. B always kept on the low table between our chairs. "The hardest part is how Jay has pulled away from us. I worry about his emotional state."

"Where did you say he went?"

"Phoenix. It's so far. He could have found a teaching job closer to us, I'm sure. I feel abandoned and empty."

"He must need space right now. It will take time. You still love him, I can tell."

I nodded through tears.

"Jay will realize that and gradually come around."

"I hope you're right."

Dr. B reached over and squeezed my hand. I was surprised how much this simple touch helped. *I need to reach out to Rick like this,* I thought.

"Why do I feel like God is far away, up in the sky, and too busy running the universe to deal with our problems?"

"We can't feel his touch physically," he said before he let go of my hand. "But He's still here. Don't give up on Him. I'm praying this whole situation will help you and Rick draw closer. Just rely on God to help you through it."

As that day's session ended, he let me give him another hug.

CHAPTER 15
Finding Bedrock Through the Years

A few weeks after the revelation of Jay's letter to Rick, I began to feel less fear about Rick's reaction. I could tell he wasn't angry with me. Perhaps Dr. B was right, and we were drawing closer.

Rick and I had met at Colorado State University, first crossing paths in a geology club, as I mentioned before. We had other things in common, too, such as our faith in God. It seemed we were meant for each other, and we got married a few months after graduation.

He soon found a job with a big oil company. I was more interested in the historic/paleontology side of geology, which meant looking for a college professorship and an advanced degree. With all our moving around in the oil fields of the Overthrust Belt east of the Rockies, I was left high and dry in this job market, especially in getting another degree. Back in the seventies there was no Internet or online college programs.

After the arrival of two children, I opted instead for teaching geology in high school. This was something I could do wherever we moved, and I already had the teaching certificate.

As our marriage entered its second decade, work pressures began to come between us. Rick kept late hours in the midst of big projects and often had to travel. I took refuge in my teaching. After all, there were always lessons to plan and papers to grade, and I enjoyed working with the students.

Still, a chronic lack of self-confidence made me anxious much of the time. I didn't know how to change, and this upset Rick. As Amy and Jay struggled with self-confidence, too, I was sad to think they'd inherited this from me.

It wasn't until years later, when I started going to counseling, that I realized the problem came from my childhood. Talking to Dr. B, I remembered how Dad was always quick to point out errors and what I needed to improve. Yet he seldom gave out compliments.

One event that still stood out in my mind occurred when I was looking at potential colleges my junior and senior years in high school. Living in Texas, of course I wanted to follow in Dad's footsteps and go to his alma mater, Rice University. Then one day, I overheard him say to Mom that he didn't think I was smart enough for Rice.

I must have buried this hurt by going to college at Colorado State. Our family had been to the Rockies on several vacations, and I really loved the mountains. When I met Rick at CSU, everything seemed to fall into place. I thought I was in the center of God's will for me.

They say girls often marry men like their fathers, and over the first years of life with Rick, I realized I had. Many times, Rick lost patience with my anxieties and lack of confidence. He couldn't help it, of course, but to me it felt like more of the judgment and correcting I'd gotten from Dad. *He doesn't mean to hurt me,* I told myself, though it still did. *I guess I'm the unstable one.* Often I prayed, "God, please help me change."

Going to a counselor was a big help, something I shouldn't have avoided for so long. From Dr. B, I learned that Rick couldn't help following his own nature—the need to fix things. But my husband couldn't fix me—any more than I could change him.

Instead, I began to work on accepting him—and myself—just as we were, warts and all, reminding myself that no one person could meet all of my needs. Deep down, I still believed God had brought us together all those years ago for a reason.

Dr. B helped shift my gaze from what I didn't like about Rick, to things I did. For example, my husband was a faithful Christian, who cared about other people's needs. Many days now, I tried to love Rick for who he was—overlooking the rest. We were both mellowing with age, and I began emerging from a long, dark tunnel.

Having a child with Jay's issues had put a huge strain on our marriage, though. Whenever I read books saying trials make people stronger, I often couldn't agree. Many times, the difficulties of raising Jay had made me hang on, but not because I was stronger. Instead, I was just afraid to rock the boat, cowering in the stern and holding on for dear life.

Another thing I learned from Dr. B was I'd been a conflict avoider most of my life. Arguments made me panicky, and I'd do anything to get away, such as clamming up and withdrawing when tempers flared. Perhaps that was why I shut down when I thought Rick was trying to change me.

All these character traits made it more difficult to talk about problems with my husband. If something bothered me, he gave advice, when what I needed was someone to just listen. Since Jay's coming out, I felt cut off from most of my friends, so for a while I talked only to the cats.

After we were on the far side of thirty years of marriage, Rick decided to move into our guest room. He liked to go to bed much earlier than I did, and fell right to sleep. On the other hand, I liked to read in bed for an hour or so, and even then I took another hour to fall asleep. With such different sleep patterns, we each got a better night's rest in separate rooms. When we'd built this retirement house, here in my old home town of Palestine, separate bedrooms and bathrooms were already in the plans. Actually, I had a couple of married friends who lived in separate houses from their spouse. I didn't think we needed to go to that extent.

***

After menopause I often awakened in a cold sweat, my head aching from another migraine. The doctor said it was a symptom of stress, which was frustrating. How was I supposed to know what triggered my migraines when I got them in my sleep?

Over the years, various doctors had tried all the usual meds that are supposed to help prevent migraines, but none of them worked for me. I also kept food journals looking for any triggers there, but patterns never emerged. Sometimes dreary weather correlated with them, but other times one came on a sunny day, which was really depressing because then I couldn't enjoy the sunshine—hiding in a dark room.

Some people told me to avoid caffeine, but it was one of the things that helped with the pain. The over-the-counter migraine meds only worked for a day or two, then quit, not to mention messing up my stomach. Often, I told my friends I knew how St. Paul felt about his 'thorn in the flesh.' God didn't heal him either. Paul learned to trust God though, saying, "I've learned that when I am weak, God helps me be strong."

If only I could do that.

Most of my mornings began with a cup of coffee while I sat in my favorite chair with a cat on my lap. I wanted to pray and ask God to forgive my negative attitude, but no words would come. Many days I hoped the Holy Spirit would "pray for us with groans too deep for words"—like it said in the Bible.

There were many days when that hope was all I had. Living with pain so long had taken all the starch out of me, left me with nothing to lean on but my memories of God's love. At least I still had those.

One pattern that emerged was how I often woke with these headaches after strange nightmares. I didn't always remember details, just vague images. Dr. B said my subconscious was working through problems this way.

In one nightmare, Rick was angry and went into another room and began throwing things and shouting. My dreams were usually hazy, but this one was almost as clear as reality. I wanted to follow him and say, "You never want me to vent like this, so why do you get to? I never get to say more than a sentence before you judge me for my feelings." The strangest part was that Rick was usually the calm and collected one, so this dream was completely out of character for him.

Where were the dreams coming from? Were my suppressed anxieties about Rick and Jay causing them? I wasn't sure what to think, so I asked Dr. B about it at my next appointment.

"I think I'm too negative and anxious," I told him. "I need to have a more positive attitude, don't I?"

"Positivity can be powerful," he replied. "I'll help you any way I can. But don't expect yourself to be perfect. None of us are. Nobody's happy all the time."

Feeling flustered, I changed the subject. "When my friends ask me how I'm doing, I want to be honest, but I feel guilty about telling them I'm still in pain. I'm sure they get tired of hearing about my troubles. I would, if I were in their shoes.

Often, I lie and say I'm doing better, but this is suppressing more stuff, I suppose. Is this leading to more of my pain?"

"That's very possible."

"You probably get tired of hearing me say the same things all the time."

"No, I don't. It's my job, you know."

One time, he shared that he originally was planning to be a researcher in brain chemistry, but decided to go into counseling instead, even though it wouldn't pay as well. "It was a way I could help more people," he said.

I was very thankful he did. Where would I be without him? He'd become like a port in the storm.

***

There also were days when I hated myself because of being clumsy. When I was 12 years old, I grew six inches, and ever since I'd been a klutz. I often tripped over things, had broken most of my toes and sprained both ankles multiple times. It was surprising that besides the toes and a finger, I had no other broken bones. Over the years, I'd banged up my knees so badly that when people saw the scars they'd ask if I'd had knee surgery. I hadn't.

When I was first attending college in Colorado, before I met Rick, I dated a guy who drove a little Datsun. One evening he got too bold and drove it off-road on a mountain trail, getting it stuck. Then he had me reach under to try to move a rock. The car shifted just enough to trap my left ring finger between the frame and the rock. *Ouch!* Thus, the broken finger.

The car was still stuck, so we had to walk back down the mountain road. Fortunately, there was moonlight. Sounds kind of romantic? It wasn't. We broke up soon after. It was four more years before a wedding ring went on that broken finger. Ironic.

I was still wearing that ring, except as years passed, I'd gained enough weight that I couldn't pull it off without applying lots of liquid soap.

Now that I was over 65, falling was a bigger worry because my balance was off. Some of my meds warned of dizziness as a side effect, so I tended to walk slower than I used to. Rick, on the other hand, was still very athletic for his age. The result was he often left me behind, though not intentionally.

Two years ago, when we were hiking in a nearby park, he was ahead of me on the trail—because of his faster pace and longer stride. Trying to catch up, I slipped on a loose rock, turned my ankle, and tumbled to the ground. I felt a sharp crack and feared it was broken. Rick was so far ahead that he didn't hear me call for help.

Fortunately, another hiker came along soon and helped me up. By then, Rick looked around and saw I wasn't behind him. He came back, apologizing and helped me hobble back to the car.

At first, he made excuses why this fall wasn't his fault, but then—to my surprise—he reached over and took my hand. "I'm so sorry, Honey," he murmured.

The ER X-rays showed no broken bones, thank goodness. Just a bad sprain, though the doctor reminded me that sprains often take longer to heal than breaks.

After that, Rick was better at waiting for me when hiking or walking. One day, after a more strenuous hike than usual, I thanked him for his patience, and he chuckled, "Well, if I don't wait, I may have to carry you home."

Thanks to Dr. B, I was learning to notice positive moments

like those—more than the negative. At one session I told my counselor, "That's my husband, the one with the quirky sense of humor. He's helped me learn to laugh more, including at myself."

"That's good," Dr. B smiled.

***

As time passed through 2019, I couldn't help wondering if Jay's bisexuality was my fault. He called it pansexuality, but I was too traditional in my thinking to wrap my head around that. He'd also told me, "Alex is non-binary, not a 'he' or a 'she'—and needs to be referred to as 'they'." This didn't come naturally to me, either.

One chilly early December day I took a walk on our gravel road. (Dr. B encouraged me to walk every day, if possible.) Above me, a skein of geese flew south, flexing and bending like a piece of yarn across the sky.

The sight drew me into the past when we lived in Wyoming, and I was pregnant with Jay. In my first trimester, I dreamed this baby was a boy. I didn't know whether to believe in dreams, and didn't tell anyone about it. All my friends, even the doctors and nurses, kept saying I was probably having a girl, based on the fast heartbeat and how low I was carrying. Ultrasounds were still rare back then.

People had so convinced me, that when I delivered a boy, I asked the doctor, "Are you sure?"

This was probably crazy, but I wondered if I caused Jay's sexual-orientation from the start. Or would it have helped if we'd encouraged sports with him? Gone out to toss a baseball or shoot hoops?

Jay preferred art and science activities like me, and wasn't athletic like Rick. He tried Little League and track, but they just didn't work for him.

Can nurture really overcome nature? I was never sure. Amy was always more athletic and competitive, which helped her bond with her dad. Early in that pregnancy, I dreamed I was having a girl.

I turned around in my walk, for I'd reached the end of the road, nestled in a woodlot left behind over a century ago when this area was cleared for farmland.

I'd reached a dead-end in my thoughts, too. There was nowhere else to go, so I trudged back toward home.

As soon as I walked in the back door, Muffin met me in the hall, meowing loudly. When I poured food into her bowl, she nibbled a little, then rubbed against my legs, almost tripping me. When I settled in a chair, Muffin jumped into my lap. Soon she began shoving her head under my hand, as if to say. "Pet me. Right now."

"You are such a selfish cat," I chuckled, as I rubbed Muffin's soft fur. A joke my brother Dan once told popped into my head:

"How many cats does it take to change a light bulb?"

I'd shrugged. "I don't know. How many?"

"Only one," he grinned. "It holds the lightbulb up to the socket, and the whole world revolves around it."

Whenever I thought of it, that memory made me smile. It was a cat trait for sure. Come to think of it, humans also acted this way—all too often.

CHAPTER 16
Holidays - 2019

As Christmas drew near, sadness descended as I realized it would be just the three of us in Palestine—Amy, Rick, and me. I enjoyed Texas for its warm winters, but there were times I missed having a white Christmas, like we did in Montana or Wyoming.

Another advantage to Texas had been extended family around, but my parents had died over the first years we were here. Rick's sisters still lived far away in the Midwest. Up until recently, my brothers were nearby. Besides moving to Alabama, John and his family decided to take a cruise that year for the holidays. It was a way for all of them to be together. I tried not to feel left out.

Dan was divorced and spending time with a new girlfriend and her family, so I didn't want to intrude. Jay hadn't indicated whether he was coming or not, and I was unsure what to say to him anyway. Some days, a huge wave of sorrow washed over me when I thought of him, leaving me nearly drowning.

I was grateful when Amy suggested opening gifts and having Christmas dinner at her house. We were blessed to have her living here in my old hometown.

It turned out to be a relaxing holiday with fewer distractions. I sat on my daughter's couch, admiring the ornaments on her tree—the old ones bringing back memories of her childhood, as well as the new ones that were gifts from her students and friends.

Like most Texas homes, there was no fireplace from which to hang the stockings. The last time we had one was when Amy was a little girl in Montana. She came up with an idea to hang the stockings from the drawer handles of the old buffet we gave her when she bought her house. That piece of furniture had started in my grandparents' house, then later moved to my parents'.

Looking at our three stockings, I thought, *Great-Grandma Parker would be pleased to see those stockings hanging there.*

Long ago, right after Dan was born, Grandma Parker had made us beautiful felt Christmas stockings that we used for the rest of our childhoods. I wished I still had mine, but it had been lost in one of my parents' moves. At least they saved the buffet cabinet, and when Dad died, Rick and I brought it to our house for safe-keeping. Mom had died two years ago, so it only seemed right to pass this piece of furniture along to the next generation. Amy was the fourth generation to use it.

As I gazed at all the lovely decorations our artistic Amy had made, I felt a quiet joy begin to bloom in my heart. *Old traditions can't last forever, so we must make new ones. That's what we're doing today.*

After opening presents, we arranged Christmas dinner on Amy's little kitchen table. We'd collaborated to make some Parker holiday favorites: baked ham, au gratin potatoes, and cranberry salad. Rick asked a blessing for the food and all our families. Then each of us took a turn reflecting on what Christmas was really about, the birth of Jesus so long ago.

When dinner was over and the dishes were in the washer, we sat again in Amy's living room, watching *How the Grinch Stole Christmas*. It reminded me that even if I felt grinchy sometimes, there were still things about the holidays to be thankful for.

Sadness rose when I thought of Christmas Eve service last night, though. The organist at the Methodist Church, where I went as a child, happened to play one of Jay's favorite Christmas carols, a very old one called *Of the Father's Love Begotten*. It was a Gregorian Chant, and I thought it interesting that my son liked something so ancient.

During the song, I happened to notice Rick wasn't singing and glanced over at him. Tears were streaming down his cheeks. I knew he was thinking of Jay, too. My heart sank, but I had no words to say. Instead, I reached over and patted his knee. There was nothing else to do. Maybe next Christmas would be better.

Those thoughts wakened memories of another transitional holiday in my life. When my parents moved our family out of Texas for a few years, I missed the pine trees and oil wells the most. People would have thought this strange, but those things meant home to me. We'd moved because Dad had changed jobs when I was almost twelve, becoming the manager of a fertilizer plant in Nebraska corn country. The seemingly endless fields of corn and soybeans made me homesick for the piney woods.

All these memories floated in and out of my mind as we sat and talked about our own family's holiday memories.

"The best place for Christmas trees was in Montana," said Rick.

I nodded. "For sure. The fir trees in the mountains were the nicest. I don't suppose you remember that, Amy."

"Not really."

"Well, you were only five when we left there," Rick added.

"I remember a funny happening there that I bet Amy doesn't," I said.

"What?" Amy asked.

"You were about three, I think. Most of our Christmas presents came in the mail from relatives who lived far away. You saw me open those boxes with a kitchen knife, and I guess that idea got fixed in your mind. On Christmas morning, when we started opening the brightly-wrapped gifts under the tree, you toddled into the living room carrying a large kitchen knife, saying 'Let me help, Mommy.' I nearly fainted and got the knife away from you as soon as I could."

"You're right," Amy grinned, "I don't remember that."

"Me neither," said Rick. "I was probably directing Jay to his presents so he wouldn't open the wrong ones."

"There were challenges back then, but mostly a lot of fond memories," I smiled. "I wouldn't change it for anything."

"Yeah, Mom. I remember a lot of good times, too," said Amy.

As we sat looking at Amy's ornaments, I was glad I'd done my best to save them over the years. Jay's too, but those were still in a box in our upstairs closet. Hopefully he'd want them someday. Some ornaments I'd made for my family in Nebraska never made it back to Texas. Mom must have gotten rid of them when we moved. *That's just the way she was,* I reminded myself. *There's no use regretting what I can't change, but I can still remember and smile.*

When Rick and I got home later that evening, he headed for bed in the guestroom, but I pulled my old childhood Bible off the shelf before turning in. Somehow, I needed to look back a little longer. It was the Bible I received in Sunday School when I was in fourth grade at the Palestine Methodist Church. It still had the messy gold leaf on the cover where I tried to write

"Holy Bible", not realizing the bumpy leather cover would totally mess up the writing.

As I flipped the pages to the section in Luke where I'd read the Christmas story, I thought of all the years I made my younger brothers dress up as shepherds to act it out. I got to be the angel because they didn't think that was a manly role.

Reading those familiar words, I heard my own young voice saying them aloud, along with echoes in my mind of ministers reading them, and even later, our own children saying them as part of their Christmas pageants. Yet it all felt different and strange now. Ever since Jay came out, nothing had the same depth of meaning—like someone or something in the back of my mind kept whispering, "You used to believe this, but do you anymore?"

I had no answer. I was trying to hang onto my faith, but some days it seemed to be slipping away. Tears streamed from my eyes while I crawled into bed and waited for sleep. Thoughts kept spooling out of my mind: *I'm hoping things will look up for the new year of 2020. At least Rick hasn't disowned Jay. Maybe each of them will find a way to accept the other. I know he loves his son as much as I do. Lord, we need you to hold us together. Amen.*

In 2019, however, something was looming on the horizon no one saw coming. Well, some may have seen it and chose to ignore it or lie about it. A few may have tried to tell the truth, but no one listened. There'd been a little talk in the fall of some new virus in China. Almost all of the respiratory viruses came from there—influenza, H1N1, SARS. It seemed like no big deal. Until 2020 rolled around. Then the whole world changed.

CHAPTER 17
Winter Breaks into My Spring, 2020

On a warm morning for early February, the singing of birds woke me before dawn. Sometimes, I wished they'd be quiet and let me sleep longer. Other days, I lay in bliss, enjoying the sounds of coming spring. If only I could take flight with those birds out there in the warming air.

Often, I wondered why they started to sing long before the sun rose. Could it be they instinctively knew the sunrise was near? When I was in darkness—whether physical, mental, or spiritual—I found it nearly impossible to sing. Perhaps I needed to learn a lesson from the birds, to sing in the dark. I knew the Bible said true hope looks forward to what it cannot see.

As I rose with the sun to meet this day, Rick headed out the door for his morning workout at the gym. I gave him a quick hug. I knew that Amy, across town in her own house, was getting ready for another day of teaching.

My mind touched on Jay, wondering how his teaching was going in Phoenix. Instead of letting myself dwell on him, I sent up a quick prayer for his safety, health, and happiness.

Looming in my mind, though, were thoughts of how often I prayed for that. Would those prayers ever be answered? When would the next trauma or crisis fall? Like the old saying I'd often heard from my dad, 'waiting for the other shoe to drop.'

Then the image of a huge pile of shoes popped into my mind, and I couldn't help but smile. Jay used to leave his shoes all over the house. Often, when he went to put them on, he couldn't find their mates. *How many shoes can one person have, or lose? How many have to drop before something pairs them back up? Before a life begins to come together?*

At least I still had a little sense of humor. I poured a cup of coffee and headed for my favorite chair in the sunroom. Muffin was stretched across it, so I moved her as she grumbled at me, but she began to purr once she was settled on my lap. This early morning coffee and cat-petting were my daily therapy.

***

Now that Rick knew about Jay, one weight was lifted off my shoulders, the paralyzing fear of his reaction. But there was another, what would my friends think?

In our church, homosexuality was seen as a terrible sin against the natural order of things. The more I read, and the more I mulled it over, the less certain I became. After all, the same church said "sin is sin" and "all fall short of God's laws." My own experiences and feelings didn't agree with some of those doctrines anymore. Why was homosexuality (if it was a sin) worse than all the others?

A few days later, my childhood friend Jane called and invited me over for coffee. It was unusual for her to call me. Either we saw each other at church functions, or I was the one looking for someone to spend time with.

Jane lived nearby so I walked to her house in the lovely sunshine. When she greeted me at the door, we embraced with big smiles. I felt more relaxed with Jane because she already knew about Jay.

The dining table was in a sunny nook, with a vase of fresh flowers in the center. Beside it, a tall white pillar-candle had been lit.

"I smell vanilla," I said.

"Must be the candle." Jane nodded as she poured the coffee.

"Mmm, that coffee smells good, too. Where did you get flowers this early?"

"At the florist."

"You didn't have to do that."

"I wanted you to feel welcome."

"Hey, we've been friends for years. You don't have to treat me like company."

"I like fresh flowers, too," she shrugged.

Soon we were seated at the table with steaming mugs of coffee in our hands. At first, talk was just about the weather, how warm and humid it was for this early in the year. I relaxed, enjoying the calm colors of Jane's home, beige and gray, with highlights of blue and green. My eyes were drawn to the texture of her homespun green and white tablecloth.

Then I heard Jane say, "What do you think of this Corona Virus we keep hearing about?"

"It's hard to say," I replied. "There have been a lot of viruses coming out of China. Seems like there's a new respiratory bug every year. It's probably just one of those."

"Yeah, right now doctors are saying to be more aware of washing hands often and staying away from others if you feel sick."

"That's nothing new to a teacher," I said. "We've been told all those things for years. I think it will blow over, like all the other viruses have."

Jane's next comment was a bolt from the blue. "I wonder if there's something you and Rick did to cause Jay's homosexuality."

My stomach dropped to my feet.

"What do you mean?" I managed to murmur.

"Well, you know. All the moving around in those early years for Rick's job must have been hard on you all. Maybe Jay just never got a sense of stability."

"We did our best. Other people move a lot, like those in the military. We built a good spiritual foundation. That's what matters most."

I glanced across the table at her face. Jane looked as open and friendly as she always had, except for a slight tightness around her lips.

"I know you tried, Honey."

Honey? She'd never called me that before. The one word changed everything. I stared at the patterns in the tablecloth as Jane's voice went on.

"All the experts say that being homosexual is caused by a distant father. Rick's work probably kept him from interacting enough."

"Now, wait a minute." I couldn't help interrupting in Rick's defense. "Rick was a great dad. He always took time for the kids, even changed diapers. He wasn't distant at all. You might as well say every father in the military is distant with his kids."

"Maybe you just didn't see it."

Tightness formed in my gut, like I was back in the high school principal's office the day Jay was accused of fighting in the boys' locker room. I took a deep breath to clear my mind.

There must be some misunderstanding, just like that day years ago. After all, Jane was one of my closest friends.

"I know you've never experienced what I have," I said as calmly as I could. "You've always had family close by. For us, the church became like our extended family, whenever and wherever we moved. Thank the Lord, we're closer to some of my family again. Well, Dan at least. I miss John since they've moved to Alabama. I confess I'm envious that most of their family has followed them there. Plus they're close to Emilia's family, too."

"I guess it can be hard."

"Well, I don't think you're in any place to judge, when you've never experienced what I have."

"Like that old song, *Walk a Mile in My Shoes*." Jane's voice grew tense.

"We don't live in a perfect world, you know," she continued. "Still, the experts say the responsibility for how children turn out lies with the parents."

"Wait. What experts? This sounds like the 'nature versus nurture' arguments I heard in child psychology classes. There's still no definite research that shows which is more important. Genetics has come a long way, and researchers are beginning to see how much does depend on our heredity. Studies of identical twins raised in different homes show they have many similarities, in spite of their completely different environments."

"Oh, you sound too secular, dear. You need to listen to what the *real* Christian experts say, like that family-based doctor."

"Some of their stuff is almost fifty years old, Jane. I *have* been reading up on it, for your information. New research hasn't supported those old theories."

"Well, of course not, Honey. The so-called new research is backed by the homosexual agenda."

"The what?"

"You know, the new Far Left. The ones trying to undermine all our morality and freedom."

"That's getting pretty simplistic. I don't recall anything in the Bible saying Jesus belonged to a particular political party. If politics was the answer, he would have overthrown the Romans. Even his disciples expected that, but he didn't. Besides, homosexual isn't an accurate description. Jay, for example, is bisexual not homosexual. LGBT is better."

"LG-what?"

"It means 'lesbian, gay, bisexual, and transgender'."

"So?"

"It's just more respectful and accurate."

"Well, forgive me if I'm not politically correct." There was a mean edge in Jane's voice now.

"I don't understand why you're getting angry with me."

Jane was staring at her tablecloth, not meeting my eyes. "I'm just trying to help you, Honey."

'There was that word again. Why did I feel like my strict Presbyterian grandmother was lecturing me?

"Like I said a minute ago, Jay isn't homosexual," I said into the stony silence. "He's bisexual and always has been. As I look back over his life, I can see it now."

"Oh, Mary Anna," she sighed. "They've already started to pull you away."

"Who?"

"Those gays, or whatever you want to call them."

"Pull me away, Jane?"

"Yes, from us true, Bible-believing Christians. They want you to believe it's okay for a person to get an operation to change their sex—the sex God gave them when they were born. They're saying God made a mistake, and they have to get it fixed."

"That's not Jay. He only wants the freedom to be himself, the way God made him." My hands began to tremble, along with my voice.

"Why would God make anyone gay?" she snapped.

"Not gay. Bisexual."

"Same thing."

No, it's not, I wanted to shout but swallowed hard instead. For some reason, my mind flew to memories of a day right after the move to Nebraska, when a bully was teasing John and me about our 'funny accents'.

"All right." I tried to keep my voice calm and even. "If God doesn't make mistakes, why do children have autism, or Down's syndrome, or even Tourette's like Jay does?"

"Well, we live in a fallen world," replied Jane.

"I agree, but is it God's true will for people to be disabled?"

"I don't know. Maybe it is. Maybe it's sent to test us and make us strong. I believe God permits it."

"I'm sorry, but I have trouble understanding why a loving God permits suffering. I guess it's just the way life is. God never answers my 'why questions'. I guess He didn't with Job in that story in the Bible, either. Besides, what if being LGBT is just another one of those results of this fallen world we're part of?"

"It's not the same thing as a physical or mental disability. It's wrong."

"So, is a child with autism 'wrong', too? People used to think so. They said it was the mother's fault for being too distant. Sound familiar?"

By now I was clenching my fists in my lap.

"No, that's different." Jane started to rise from her chair, then stopped.

"Because it doesn't involve sex? Why is our culture so hung-up on sex, anyway?"

"It's a sin."

"Sex is?" I squirmed in my chair, unable to hold still.

"Well, outside of marriage."

"What about all those Old Testament patriarchs and kings who had multiple wives and concubines, too? That involved sex outside of marriage, didn't it?" I was having trouble staying in my chair.

"I suppose God allowed it, because of a sinful world, and the culture of the times." I noticed her clenched fists on the table across from me.

"Oh, I see. So, God allows sin, if he chooses to." I waved a shaky hand toward the ceiling.

"Honey, you're twisting the truth." She stared hard into my eyes.

"Whose truth? What *is* the real truth?" I avoided her gaze by looking at where I'd pulled a loose thread in the tablecloth.

"You sound like Pontius Pilate at Jesus's trial."

"Speaking of Jesus. I wonder what he thinks about all this," I said.

Jane finally got up and grabbed a large, black-bound book from the kitchen counter behind her. "We just need to look at what His Word says."

"That's what I've been doing for over two years now—searching and asking questions. The answer I keep coming up with is that God loves us unconditionally." I finally met her gaze. "One night as I was falling asleep, I actually heard a voice inside my head, saying, 'When all is said and done, remember

Jesus loves you.' Jesus told us to 'love one another as I have loved you'. I think that's in the book of John."

"Like the Beatles song, 'All you need is love.' You don't really believe that leftist 'love everyone' drivel, do you?"

"Come on. You know me better than that. At least I thought you did."

"Okay, what about tough love?" Jane was back in her chair again, setting the Bible in front of her.

"What about it?"

"Sometimes it's necessary."

"Wait, are you saying we should disown Jay or something?"

"Well—"

"Who are you to judge something you don't even understand? I wonder if you'd feel the same if it was your child." Now my head was beginning to throb. I couldn't believe I was sitting in my good friend's dining room with a cup of cold coffee in my hand. "I wish I wasn't hearing this," I mumbled through gritted teeth.

"Sometimes friends have to use tough love," said Jane, her voice terse.

I couldn't calm the roaring in my ears.

"I know my Bible, too," I said, trying to ungrit my teeth. "The people Jesus paid the most attention to were what others called 'those tax collectors and sinners'. And the people he was most critical of were the religious leaders. He called them hypocrites." I couldn't stay in my chair any longer.

By this time, I gripped the edge of the thick wooden table. The soft tablecloth bunched between my fingers.

"I'm not a hypocrite, Mary Anna." Jane rose and moved toward me.

The buzzing and ringing in my head threatened to

drown out her words, as I said, "The ones who claimed not to be hypocrites were often the worst offenders." These words bounced against the inside of my head like a crashing gong. "I came to your house because I thought you were my friend. I thought you cared about me and what I've been going through, but you only preach at me. I don't need any more of your self-righteous judgmentalism."

The next thing I knew, I was out the door, stalking down the sidewalk, trying to catch my breath. My eyes were burning, but no tears were falling.

Words flew in and out of my mind, things I could have said instead. My brain was too fast for my mouth to keep up—like flashes of lightning, barely seen before they were already gone. Too often, as soon as I opened my mouth to speak, the next flash came and wiped away the words. Many things had gone unsaid, and some shouldn't have been said, but it was too late. The rumbling of the thunder had reached me.

CHAPTER 18
Hard Lessons

I never wanted to hurt like that again. How could Jane and I ever patch things up? The next few days were rainy and wet, with periodic thunderstorms, which was appropriate somehow.

The dark clouds began to break on the fifth day, and I sat on the deck with my morning coffee. The warm sun seeped into me, and the earth smelled fresh after the rain. But my heart still ached.

I looked across our yard where the grass was greening up. Listening to the birds, I saw a bright red cardinal flitting across the small woodland at the back of our lot. Cardinals were my favorite birds. Their color added a beautiful contrast to the greens, browns, and yellows of the rest of the world.

As I sipped the cooling coffee and stared into space after the cardinal disappeared, I could still hear its call, "pretty, pretty bird." That was how Dad always interpreted their sound. There was no other bird-call like it. All the years we lived away from Texas I missed it. Many birds are distributed widely over the U.S., but not the cardinal. They're mostly an eastern bird.

At last, the red bird's sound faded away. When I was small, Dad always called them that. I later learned their true name in school.

The next thing I heard was the sound of the wind in the pines, like a whisper in the gentle breeze. When the wind was stronger, it sounded like the distant roar of a waterfall or the tumult of a crowd applauding.

A childhood image peeped into my mind, of the treetops swaying in a strong wind. "Mama, how do the trees move to make the wind?" I'd asked.

"No, dear, the winds make the trees move. It's not the trees making the wind," my mother smiled.

I'd shaken my head and wondered aloud, "Then what starts the wind?" But now I don't remember Mama's answer.

Thinking of my parents brought a lump to my throat. *If only I could talk to one of them now, maybe I'd feel better.* The last time I remembered really crying hard was at Dad's funeral. I'd sobbed and sobbed—on Jane's shoulder—which added more to the ache now.

I whispered to the pines, *I want to be finished with pain like this. Never again will I let myself be so vulnerable.* The wind in their branches seemed to answer.

Was it a mistake to trust my best friend? Now I wondered if the only way to keep my feelings from getting crushed and stomped on was to keep them to myself.

Maybe I could be like one of those locusts that buried itself in the ground for seventeen years and only came out for a brief month at the end of its life to mate. Evidently, mating was a hazardous undertaking, since it needed so many years of preparation in the darkness of the earth.

At least I was done with the mating thing. Maybe I could retreat to darkness for the rest of my life, with no need to ever come out. But even as I thought that, I knew it was false hope. Once you're a parent, you will always be one—for the rest of your life.

I sat in the sun on the deck most of the morning and read a book which caught my eye at the library last week. It was called *The Dark Night of the Soul**. The idea of darkness had appealed to me. The book told the story of a monk named John of the Cross, who lived back in the days of the Spanish Inquisition and was put in solitary confinement for his beliefs. I could relate to that, since I often felt alone in the dark with my own doubts and fears.

The thing that surprised me most about this book was it didn't depict darkness as bad or evil. In fact, darkness became a refuge for this man John. In one place he described it as a place of hope, the very opposite of the way most religious people see it.

I'd been taught darkness represented evil, while light was good. I often said I was looking for the 'light at the end of the tunnel' or other such symbolism. Maybe I'd had it all wrong.

My eyes began smarting as the sun brightened on the page I was reading, and my head started to ache. Perhaps I'd been out in the sun too long.

I put a bookmark between the pages and closed the book. Picking it up along with the empty coffee cup, I headed back into the cool of the house.

***

The next morning, Rick surprised me by bringing me a cup of coffee in bed. It was still early morning, but I'd been lying awake for a while. I'd had a very strange dream last night, that Rick and I were trying to climb a mountain. The higher we got, the more snow there was, and I kept sinking to my waist in the powdery white. Just before I woke, Rick was trying to pull me out of a deep drift.

And there he was, standing beside the bed with a cup of steaming coffee. He'd even put in my favorite creamer.

"Whoa, you're like a dream come true, Hon."

"I like that idea," he said, handing me the mug. "I came to say I'm sorry about the other day."

"What day?"

"When I scolded you for dwelling on too much negative stuff."

"Oh, okay." At first, I wasn't sure what to say. "I'm trying not to let things bother me as much. It's hard, especially when I think of Jay."

"That bothers me, too—" His voice stopped in mid-sentence.

"Yeah, it's confusing. I'm leaving it in God's hands, because there's nothing I can do anyway, except pray. Most times that doesn't feel like it's helping."

He sat down beside me on the bed and nodded. "I feel that way, too." Then he really surprised me by taking my hand. "Mary Anna, I don't want to lose you."

My voice left me, and all I could do was squeeze his hand. "I love you, Rick. We don't always see things the same because we're two separate people. Yet I know the Lord is the one who brought us together all those years ago."

He interlaced his fingers with mine. This was a physical touch I didn't often have. "I believe that, too," he whispered. "I'm sorry that I can't always find the right words to say how much you mean to me."

After this, he brought me a mug of coffee more often. It dawned on me that he was showing his love through acts of service, his love language.

***

It had been two years since I told my brothers about Jay. John was the one still married, and I felt guilty that I hadn't told his wife Emilia. I knew I could ask John to tell her, but thought it should be my own task to tell her in person.

I had a trip planned to Huntsville in the spring of 2020, but now it looked like it wouldn't happen. As the Corona Virus ramped up, Rick said he was not comfortable with me flying, so we cancelled the trip.

Now I wasn't sure what to do. Thoughts of how to tell Emilia kept popping into my head. One evening I just called their number, and by 'coincidence' Emilia answered.

"Hello, Mary Anna," she said, seeing my name on their caller-ID.

"Hi. Are you busy?"

"Just washing up the dinner dishes," she replied. Over the phone, I heard the sound of running water.

"If you have time, there's something I need to tell you."

"Okay, sure." The sound of water stopped, and was replaced by dishes being moved and stacked.

"We need prayers for Jay," I continued. "We've been having a rough time with him." Now that I'd started, I rushed headlong into everything. "He's told us he thinks he's bisexual. And he's been dating another guy, named Alex."

As I said this, it occurred to me that we didn't even know Alex's last name. My heart pounded in my ears as I wondered what Emilia thought—maybe what a bad mother I was. In my heart, I prayed that my sister-in-law wouldn't react like Jane did.

"Our children can make life hard sometimes, can't they?" Emilia said through the throbbing in my head. The tone of her voice filled me with relief, and my thumping heart slowed.

"That's for sure," I sighed.

"You know we've had similar issues with Tim?"

"Just about a year ago, Tim contacted me," I said and wondered why I hadn't thought of it when I first called.

"Oh, I'm glad he did," Emilia sighed. "We were too hard on him at the start, and now he doesn't communicate with us much."

"Yeah, we don't hear much from Jay either, though he has started texting once in a while. All I can do is pray that God will take care of Jay. I'm really thankful he and Rick are communicating a little, even though Jay knows Rick doesn't approve of him and Alex."

"Have they talked about getting married?" Emilia asked.

"No. I guess I'm thankful for that. Recently, Jay has been looking into buying a house, but he's told us he's doing it on his own. I guess in my mind, there's still hope."

"I'm really happy for you, Mary Anna."

My eyes began to tear up as I heard the pain in Emilia's voice, so I added, "It's never too late to build bridges. You know, Tim told me he'd known he was gay ever since junior high."

"Yes, he told us, too, when he mentioned that he'd talked to you one morning in Palestine. He said that was when he finally realized he needed to reach out to us again."

"I'm glad to hear that. We did have a nice visit that day."

"Well, you must have been a good influence on him. Thanks. Tim's been a tough pill to swallow."

"It's probably harder because it happened fifteen years ago, when society's opinions were a lot different than now." I searched for something reassuring to say.

"For sure. I wanted to crawl into a dark cave and never come out." She took a deep breath and continued, "Don't you think our culture is just getting more corrupt by relaxing these morals, though?"

"In my heart of hearts, I guess I still do. But I've been doing a lot of reading. People, especially church people, can be too judgmental. Didn't Jesus say, 'Judge not, lest you be judged.'?"

"You know, Mary Anna, that reminds me of what Jesus said once about trying to take a speck out of your neighbor's eye, when there was a log in your own."

Like some so-called friends of mine, I thought to myself. Then I spoke aloud. "Some scientists think gender identity may be a genetic problem, more than a moral one."

"I've read that a distant father causes boys to become gay."

Uh oh. Here it comes.

But then Emilia added, "Other sources say this is an old theory, though."

I sighed with relief. "I've read that, too. It's like the old assumption that autism was caused by a distant mother."

"We know that's not true, Mary Anna."

"Yeah, autism made the child act distant, and the mothers had trouble relating to their child, not the other way around."

"We don't know what causes autism, even now," said Emilia.

"Maybe we don't understand what causes homosexuality either."

"But how about what the Bible says?"

"I'm still confused, Emilia. You know, Jay isn't the only person I've known who seems to be born different. One thought keeps coming to me. If being gay is a choice, why would anyone choose it?"

"What do you mean?"

"Why choose all the anger, disappointment, hurt, and persecution?"

"I suppose if it's just the way they are, they can't help it. Maybe there is no real choice," she said. "To be honest, I don't know what to think. I guess all we can do is trust God has a plan, even if we can't see or understand it. We all are imperfect, and it's unfortunate how the church has gotten fixated on just the one problem of homosexuality."

"I agree, Emilia. Remember when we were young and divorce was the big no-no? Now the church doesn't make a big deal about it at all. It's like some people have a one-track mind when it comes to gays, and call them the worst of the worst, when there are many other sins, too. Still, I'd appreciate your prayers for Jay."

"And yours for Tim."

"For sure. We still love our children, don't we? It's like the saying, 'hate the sin, but love the sinner,' right?" I hoped these words were encouraging to her.

"I'm glad you told me this, Mary Anna. Now I don't feel as lonely with our problems. I've lost some friends over it, which adds to the hurt."

I didn't say it to Emilia, but I wondered if that was part of the reason they moved away from Texas—to get a fresh start and leave those troubles behind.

"I'm sorry I didn't tell you sooner," I said. "I was nervous and afraid. About the same time Jay came out, Amy's boyfriend broke up with her. We liked Jeff so much that it was a double heartbreak. Now she's more distant and doesn't tell us what she's doing, or if she's dating anyone."

"Maybe she's trying to shield herself from more pain and disappointment. I've been there, Honey."

There was that word, but coming from Emilia, it didn't have the negative feel it did with Jane.

"I really wanted to tell you this face-to-face," I added. "My trip got cancelled by the pandemic. I couldn't wait another whole year to tell you."

"Who knows what next year will bring, anyway?"

"This is more like a bad dream, isn't it? Some days I wonder when I'll wake up, to find it was all a nightmare," I sighed.

"That's how I feel, too."

"I hope we can stay in better touch now, Emilia. I admit, I'm feeling hurt that Amy and Jay have both pulled away from me."

"Well, Amy knows that her breakup with Jeff hurt you, too. She probably doesn't want you to get your hopes up again."

"Wow, I hadn't thought of it that way before. Thanks."

"For sure. We need to keep the family ties strong. That's one thing this whole pandemic experience is teaching me, Mary Anna."

"Me, too. Thanks so much for listening."

"No problem. Anytime. Now I guess I'd better get back to those dishes."

"Okay, God bless you and all your family."

"You, too, Honey."

As I signed off the call, I was light-headed and sat in my chair for a long time, trying to get recollected. I was glad I'd called her. That weight was off my shoulders. I was glad Emilia and I were getting closer again like sisters, even though they'd moved.

***

A famous song says that some days are diamonds. Most of mine lately were more like rocks. The Covid pandemic continued wreaking havoc all over the world, and with my emotions. If my life was a rollercoaster before, it had become well beyond a thrill ride, almost to terror. What was going to happen next? Fear and uneasiness filled my mind most days. No one had any good answers about the pandemic. Everything was unraveling at the seams.

The Ides of March, the day associated with the assassination of Julius Caesar in the first century BC, now became my watershed day. Who'd have thought it would have such significance two thousand years later? That morning, we went to church with no idea it would be the last time we gathered for months. By the end of March 15th, everything was cancelled, including schools and churches. Most businesses and restaurants closed their doors.

The country was on lockdown. The whole world had changed, not for the better. I couldn't help wondering if things would ever be the same again. Every morning, it got harder to get out of bed and face another day.

One day, as I pulled an old favorite shirt out of the closet, I noticed how worn it was. The cloth was threadbare and almost see-through. *That's like hope,* I told myself. *All the troubles that piled up in my past have worn my hopes this thin. Will hope disappear like this fabric and dissipate into holes? There's no way to salvage this shirt.*

"Lord, help me," I prayed. "Strengthen the things in my life that are hanging by a thread. I don't want to lose the hope I've struggled so hard to find."

CHAPTER 19

Paranoia – Early Spring 2020

Fear was becoming the watchword of 2020. It was nothing but a black hole. Everyone became a germophobe, filled with uncertainty. No one could make plans for the future. My brother Dan reminded me to take one day at a time, but I wasn't very good at it. Sometimes I needed something to look forward to—something to make life still worth living.

Many days I asked God, *Will things ever work out? If you're still in control, why is the world so out of control?* I began keeping a journal, hoping it would help me work through my fears. One day's entry read:

What's the matter with me? Am I too focused on myself? The more I try to stay calm, the larger the waves of panic and depression that wash over me. How can I possibly go on, since Jay has come out of the closet and endangered my whole belief system? The close friends I could confide in are no longer there for me. Either they've begun to ignore me, or I don't feel comfortable talking to them anymore. Why did Covid come along to erode my faith?

It's my own fault I've crawled into this hole, I guess. I should lay it all at God's feet and let Him take care of it. I do try, but nothing seems to get better. Something in my mind says, 'Why bother?'

Perhaps these last words were from the Devil. Though I tried not to listen, the voice of doubt was always there. Sometimes, I felt like I needed to run away and hide somewhere. But where could I go?

I was more and more thankful for my counselor during those days. When I saw Dr. B, he reminded me that many other people were having these same problems due to the pandemic.

"It's called Covid Insanity," he said. He had also prescribed another antidepressant to try, and it would take time to kick in. I hoped I could hold on long enough. I really didn't want yet another medication, but it was necessary to keep the dark thoughts at bay.

At one session I told Dr. B, "I think my life is like a path along the edge of a deep canyon. Every so often, I slip and fall into the dark chasm below. I'm just thankful that you don't judge me for all the times I backslide. I make progress for a while, and then I slip again."

"God forgives us for our failures when we turn to Him, Mary Anna."

"I know. I just don't want to let you down."

"You're doing the right things. When things get too dark, reach out to me, okay?"

"I pray God will help me remember that, when my thoughts go down into the pit."

Trying to pray or meditate. Taking a walk in the sunshine. These were ideas Dr. B suggested, and sometimes they helped. Other days the depression was still there, like a dark shadow following me.

At the next session, he told me, "What you're hearing is the depression talking. If you can learn to let those thoughts go, let them be, you'll be able to get past them. Don't cling to them. Try not to fall back into old habits of negative thinking."

"I know I need to do something about my negativity. No one wants to be around me and my black hole. I think I'm a hopeless case."

"No, you're not hopeless. It takes time and hard work to change your thought patterns," he said.

"But I'm just a burden on my family and friends." Tears gathered in my eyes.

"Can you think of one thing positive about yourself?" He looked at me and smiled a bit.

I had to ponder that question for a while. "I guess I can be a good listener. I try to let people have their say, instead of arguing."

"That's good," he smiled. "Next time the feelings of worthlessness rise, find one good thing to tell yourself. Even if it's very small."

"Okay, I'll try."

At the end of this session, I asked Dr. B to pray with me. He agreed to right away. "Would you like to start, or should I?" he asked.

"You start, please. I'm not sure what to say right now."

We were seated in his big leather chairs, hands folded, as his voice began, "Dear Lord…"

Hearing the caring in his voice brought tears to my eyes again. When he paused and waited for me to speak, all I could manage to say was, "Amen."

***

Each morning, I started with a quiet time to read my Bible and pray. This habit was still with me, even though it seemed to be from a former life.

Throughout my life, I'd run across some big misconceptions about God. When I was a teenager, I was told the Bible said, "God helps those who help themselves." But that's not anywhere in the scriptures. Later I learned some ancient Greek philosopher had said it. What the Bible really says is that God helps those who can't help themselves. Which is all of us.

As I grew into adulthood, another common saying was: "God won't send you more than you can handle."

It took me many years to realize this was a misquote of First Corinthians 10:13, which actually says: "God is faithful; he will not let you be tempted beyond what you can bear. But when you are tempted, he will provide a way out so that you can stand up under it."

When I read this passage more carefully, I realized the emphasis wasn't on what I could do, but on what *God* would do. That original misquote needed to be reworded to say, "God won't send you more than you can handle *with His help*." Or better yet, "God won't send you more than *He* can handle."

"There must be a grain of faith deep in my heart that keeps me from giving up," I told Dr. B one day. "But sometimes, I want to tell God, 'I turned Jay and my other problems over to you, and you haven't done anything. You must be too busy taking care of others. Or looking after the Universe.'"

"I hope I won't offend you by saying this," he replied. "But perhaps you're trying to put your own expectations onto God, instead of letting Him be who He is."

The next morning in my quiet time, I found Romans 8:28 and read it aloud. "For we know that all things will work together for good for those who love the Lord."

"Okay, God," I sighed. "I'll try to keep believing this."

As I closed my Bible, Muffin jumped on my lap and began licking my hand, like she was saying: "You're my kitten and I'm your momma. I'll take care of you."

Maybe that's my answer for now.

***

Nature became my healer. On nice days, Rick and I took walks in our neighborhood, and he walked beside me. I tried to name the wildflowers or watched the birds, reassured now that Rick meant well and loved me. I could even smile at some of his personality quirks, for I knew I was learning to love him just the way he was. He was more mellow and accepting than before. Maybe he could see how I was accepting him and our situation with Jay. Or perhaps it was just that the cat was out of the bag, and I wasn't hiding things from him anymore.

Acceptance of the way things were had become key for me. One day I shared one of my journal entries with Dr. B:

What good is it to rail against things I can't change? It doesn't hurt anyone except myself. I can't change Jay or undo the decisions he's made, and preaching at him will just drive him away. The only thing to do is leave him in God's hands.

After we talked about it, I had an idea, and said, "When I was young, there was a popular saying, 'Let go, and let God.' To some this may sound like a copout, but I've learned the hard way that letting go is actually very hard to do. It takes faith and trust. Too many times I've handed a burden to God in prayer, only to pick it up again, trying to carry it myself."

"We all do that at times," he nodded. "You are starting to improve at processing your thoughts. Don't give up on yourself when the going is tough. You're stronger than you think, with God's help."

As the weeks of the Covid crisis went by, Jay didn't call as often as I wished he would. If I tried to call him, all I got was his voicemail. Sometimes, I'd send a short text, saying "Hi" or "Here's a virtual hug." Gradually he began to send replies like, "Thanks." Or "Love you too."

One day I realized God accepted *me* just as I was—not because He approved or overlooked my mistakes, but because He loved me, and His Son died for those sins. *While I'm learning to accept Jay, God must be teaching me to move deeper into His love and acceptance of me.*

Yet, Covid Insanity continued. John and Emilia, in Alabama, were sheltering in place and hadn't been able to see their grandchildren or other nearby relatives for about six weeks. Rick and I were thankful to live in a rural area instead of a big city, because we had more options to get out of the house. Now the simple things meant a lot, like taking a walk or going for a drive in the country.

On Sundays, Amy joined us for dinner, choosing to come because we were family, despite Covid restrictions. Often we worked on a jigsaw puzzle. She was much better at these than I was, so I really enjoyed working with her. Those evenings were a warm light cast over the chill uncertainty of the pandemic. Rick began joining in to help us. This was when I began to realize how much he also treasured family time. When I went to bed those nights, I prayed God would somehow bring Jay back into our family circle, too.

Still, the days of 'shelter in place' got long. I was even having trouble remembering what day of the week it was. One of my friends on Facebook said, "Every day is Blursday."

Gradually, Jay began to call more often to reassure us that he was all right. Both he and Amy were having to teach their students online. This was good for Jay because of his experience with computers. For Amy, it was more difficult because her kindergarten students were so young. We were thankful both our children were staying healthy. As Dr. B had suggested, I kept looking for positive things, though sometimes they were hard to find.

CHAPTER 20

Reality Crashes In

The day my phone woke me at seven a.m. was the day my world took the deepest plunge.

"Mary Anna?" said a low, raspy voice.

"I think you have the wrong number," I mumbled, still half asleep.

"No, it's me. Your brother Dan."

"What? You sound awful." This jerked me awake.

"I think I have Covid. Probably caught it from one of those kids I teach guitar to."

As he said this long sentence, his voice got weaker with each word, and his breath came in gasps.

"Stay in bed, Dan. I'll be right there."

"Okay." His voice was barely audible.

I threw on some clothes and rushed out the door, yelling to Rick that I was going to Dan's. He called out something from the guest room, but I didn't wait to hear it. The sound of the garage door opening drowned him out.

Dan's house was only a half hour away, but that morning even that felt too far. My heart pounded and my mind raced. I'd heard the news reports of how fast this virus hit some people. Even though Dan was younger than me at 62, and fairly healthy, he was at risk because of being overweight. Like me. A Parker family trait, unfortunately.

He taught music at Athens High School, in another East Texas town like Palestine. I was thankful when all the Texas schools required online learning. Dan had kept teaching his private lessons, but I wished he hadn't. I also wished he lived closer than thirty miles, as I topped the speed limit all the way, hoping it was too early for the Highway Patrol to be out.

When I finally arrived, I realized I'd forgotten to grab his house key and had to pound on the door for long minutes before the lock clicked open. He stood in the doorway, in a gray sweatshirt and sweatpants, pale and shivering.

"Quick, get in my car. I'll take you to the hospital."

"All we have here is a walk-in clinic," he rasped. "Better take me to the hospital in Palestine. If I die on the way, just take me to the morgue."

"What?" I hoped he was joking, but it was hard to tell. We didn't go back into his house for anything. Once he was in the passenger seat of my Honda, I stepped on the gas and sped back the thirty miles I'd just come. There was no point anymore in wishing he lived closer. Like Dad used to say, 'It is what it is.'

When I pulled up to the Emergency Room door of Mother Frances Hospital, an orderly in a face mask came to the car before I could even get out.

"He thinks he has Covid," I panted, trying to catch my breath after the harrowing drive.

Before I even finished talking, the orderly was taking Dan's temperature with one of those sensors they hold in front of your forehead. These always made me think of the sick bay in *Star Trek*. The future had arrived.

The orderly pressed a button on a pager attached to his arm. Two more people in scrubs, masks, and face shields joined him. "We're admitting him," he said. "Temp is 103."

"Can I come with him? He's my brother."

"Sorry, we're on lockdown for any visitors."

They helped Dan onto a gurney. My heart pounded, and tears sprang into my eyes. "Please?" I repeated. "What if I never get to see him again?"

A young blonde female patted my arm. "We'll take good care of him. I'm sorry," she whispered. "I wish you could come in, but it's policy statewide now."

"I love you, Dan," I called, but I wasn't sure he heard. They were already wheeling him through the big double doors into the ER.

***

The next ten days were some of the worst of my life. There was no word from the hospital. Even when I called, I didn't get answers. I went to the front lobby, but no one was allowed in except patients and employees.

Not knowing what was happening was the hardest part. Why did Dan have to be alone? Were they taking good care of him? What if he died, and I didn't even get to say good-bye?

I knew this was happening to many people across the country, but that didn't make it any easier to bear. Ironically, whenever our mother had been in the hospital, I didn't like visiting her. Hospitals had always made me uncomfortable, but now when I wasn't allowed in, I wanted nothing more than to be there.

As days wore on, I couldn't stay focused on the day-to-day chores of life. Rick ended up doing most of the cooking. Amy came to our house when she could spare time from preparing her online lessons, and joined us for dinner on Sunday. Churches were all closed, so their services were online.

As the days and nights passed, sleep became more and more elusive. Some nights, I stared out my bedroom window for hours. When the stars were visible, I even wished on them. I knew I should pray, but all I could manage was to hold Dan in my mind, and whisper, "Please, God, please."

One night, when it was warm enough, I opened the window and listened to the silent darkness. "God, are you there? Why can't I hear you?"

As I murmured this, an owl hooted from a tree across our grassy field. My mind traveled back to a night when I'd walked a long dusty road, praying for Jay and wondering what I could do to help him with his problems in school.

"Lord," I sighed to the night, "Are you reminding me how you've seen me through trials before?"

Then a verse I must have memorized long ago came into my mind, "Neither height nor depth, nor anything in all creation, will be able to separate us from the love of God in Christ."

Closing the window, I dug my Bible out from under the books that had covered it for the past few weeks. Opening it toward the back, I found the verse I was looking for, Romans 8:39.

Tears streamed down my cheeks, though this was nothing new. I cried a bucket of them almost every night. After a few moments, a strange sense of calm enveloped me. "Lord, what does this mean for Dan?"

"Love never fails," said my mind. Another verse I'd memorized somewhere.

As I held the Bible close to my chest, I began to pray, "Lord, if your love never fails, and nothing can separate us from it, then I pray you'll be with Dan like that—never failing, even though I can't be there myself."

One morning a couple of days later, the hospital called at last. A soft female voice said, "Mary Evans? Are you Dan Parker's sister?"

At the tone of that voice, my heart nearly stopped. Was this the end? Relief washed over me when the voice continued, "Dan is finally showing some improvement. We were able to take him off the ventilator last night."

"Ventilator? Why didn't I hear he was put on one?"

"I'm sorry. Everything is crazy around here. So many cases, and too few beds. The doctor will check on him today. If he's still improving, he should be able to go home in a couple of days. Does he live with you?"

I was about to tell her Dan lived in Athens, but then remembered the harrowing drive and said, "Yes. He can stay with us." Having him alone at his house, a half-hour from the hospital, was definitely not a good idea until I knew he was completely well.

Three more days dragged by. I focused on that night the owl—and perhaps God—spoke to me. But fears threatened to drown me again. Every night when I crawled into bed, terror grabbed me and wouldn't let go. It wasn't fear of getting the virus myself. Sometimes, I almost wished I would just catch it and die. Then my troubles would be over. I never mentioned this to Rick, though, and tried to keep it out of my mind.

Dr. B had been my lifesaver through the ordeal. When we couldn't meet in person, he called and did our session over the phone. With him, I had a place I felt safe to reveal all the dark thoughts I was ashamed of, the ones that would be too upsetting for the rest of my family to hear.

Mornings became worse than the nights. Once the sun finally peeked over the eastern horizon, I had to force myself to get out of bed because if I did, it meant facing another day of life, another day of unanswered questions and uncertainty.

The hospital called again on a Friday in April, telling me to come pick Dan up at the side door, where patients were discharged. What I saw when I arrived was a shadow of my brother's former self. He was thin and pale, sitting in a wheelchair. A nurse helped him into the passenger seat, and he smiled at me weakly.

"Love you, Sis," he murmured.

I grabbed his hand and squeezed it. "I love you forever, Dan."

***

It was a good thing we kept Dan at our house. He was so weak, he couldn't have managed alone. Since I had no job obligations anymore, I could devote myself to taking care of him. His school gave him sick leave for six weeks, too. After thirteen days in the hospital, he took another two weeks at our home before he felt strong enough to go back to Athens.

During Dan's stay, Rick was a blessing, helping me cook when I was too tired. He walked with me in the spring warmth, and did most of the grocery shopping, so I didn't have to expose myself to a lot of people. The grocery stores were still open, even though some of their shelves were empty. We hadn't been able to find yeast, flour, or powdered milk for over a month, not to mention toilet paper. That was something I'd never expected to experience in America. How did it happen?

With more time on my hands after Dan went home, I started mulling over my life. It hadn't turned out quite how I'd envisioned when Rick and I graduated from college and got married.

One day a memory from 2008 rose in my mind, as I sat and stared out the window at the trees in our yard here in Palestine. They were mostly southern pines, unlike what we'd had in Montana. But the memory they triggered that day was of one particular little green ash tree:

We had only a couple more weeks in our Eureka, Texas house, when there came an unexpected ring of the doorbell. Cautiously, I opened to see a worker in a Gas Company uniform.

"Sorry to bother you, ma'am. We have to remove some of your trees because of the gas line running across your property."

"What? After all these years? Why now?"

"Well, there have been some gas line fires and explosions, you know."

"Yes, I've seen it on the news," I nodded.

"We've been told to clear away any tree roots around the lines. Roots extend as far below the ground as the branches do above."

"I see. Which trees have to go?"

He led me outside and pointed to a large cottonwood down by the road, and a huge pine tree next to the driveway.

"Oh, dear. Those are so big. The lot will look bare without them. At least we're moving soon."

"Well, I guess that's good, ma'am. Be sure to let the new owners know they can't plant trees there."

"Uh, okay. If we get to talk to them."

"That little green ash over there is right over the line, too."

My eyes followed his pointing hand, and my heart sank. We'd planted that tree when Amy was young, soon after buying this house. It had grown up right along with her. After several years it was thriving, just beginning to get taller than Amy. What could I say? A large lump rose in my throat, and all I could do was nod and retreat into the house.

Soon the chainsaws revved. I watched through the window as the larger trees were limbed and dropped to the ground in pieces. Then like an afterthought, someone stepped to the little ash and sliced its trunk in one swoop. After that, I couldn't watch anymore.

As the tree fell to the ground, it felt like part of myself died with it. It had grown up with our children and was full of memories, which I now prayed wouldn't die, too. Back in 2008, Mom had been showing early signs of Alzheimer's. Though she'd never been able to go to college, she was always learning new things—reading books about science or art, researching places she and Dad traveled. Yet, she was losing that curiosity and all those memories. She'd been so intelligent, it was sad to see, and frightening to think this could someday happen to me.

Other trees in our neighborhood fell because of the gas line, too. Foremost in my memory, though, is the vibrant branches and leaves of that green ash lying limp on the ground, already in the first stages of dying. It was a good thing we moved away shortly after, so I didn't have to stare for long at an empty spot in the lawn where dear memories used to be.

As I looked back, I often took that tree for granted when it was alive. I'd hurry about life's activities, heading off to teach school, or arriving home just in time to pick up the mail and throw some dinner on the table. But the image seared in my mind wasn't of that tree alive and growing, standing in the sun, but rather the sight of it lying prone on the lawn. The same way the image of my dead mother, lying in her hospital bed, was what first came to mind whenever I thought of her.

Another of Dad's parental proverbs came into my mind, 'You don't know what you've got until it's gone.'

***

Those days of 2020 began to help me realize how often the old must be cut down to make way for something better. The people who bought that house planted a flower garden where the ash had been. But over ten years since it happened, that image of the fallen tree was still vivid in my mind. The new owners had flowers to enjoy.

One day I found a verse in Paul's first letter to the Corinthians where he said, "When I became a man, I put away childish things." Closing my eyes and thinking on this for a few minutes, I began to write in my journal:

Lately, I've been having to release a lot of childish things I used to cling to, things I was substituting for God in my life. These aren't just simple 'worldly' things, either. Some of them are religious practices and habits I've had for years—even images I had in my mind of what I thought God was like. I've come to realize my childish ideas of God as an old man up in the clouds must go. They're becoming crutches for me, substitutes for real faith. Excuses for my unbelief. I need to accept that God has His own way of doing things, and He doesn't need my advice.

It's been as painful as watching that tree fall, or like having branches lopped off me by a pruning saw. Ways of thinking I used to cling to—or thought I was supposed to believe—were pulled right from under me when Jay came out of the closet. I no longer know what God thinks of gays, lesbians, transsexuals, or bisexuals. I'm not sure anymore that the Bible condemns them. All I can do is trust God to take care of it. After all, He can see the whole picture, and I definitely can't from my human perspective.

I have no answers to my many questions. Maybe I never will. Everything is hazy, dark and obscure. But now it's not an evil or sinister darkness, just mysterious. I used to think I understood God and what He expected of me. Now I realize He's truly unknowable and unfathomable to my limited human mind. All I can do is lean back and rest in this darkness, trusting God to lead me somehow. Like the old song says, "leaning on the everlasting arms."

More and more, I wondered if looking for a light at the end of the tunnel was the wrong thing to do.

Once Dr. B said, "Maybe it's time to light a lantern."

That reminded me of the verse in Psalm 119:105 which says, "God's word is a lamp to my feet and a light for my path." Perhaps instead of waiting for God to turn on the light, I needed to search for it myself.

At that same session, I told Dr. B "Maybe the light comes in unexpected ways, instead of the ones we prescribe. I tend to tell God what I want Him to do, instead of waiting and watching for what He wants to show me. Oh boy, that means patience, doesn't it? My big problem."

In my bedroom stood an antique dresser which came from my great-grandmother's house. The old mirror mounted on top of it had deteriorated in places, so the image was getting fuzzy and distorted. As I looked into it each morning, I began to realize it represented many things I must say farewell to. That mirror would never clear up. My old ways of knowing and experiencing God had served their purpose in my youth, but they'd become hindrances to faith. They must go, to permit something new to rise in their place, a new relationship with God—a deeper one.

Again, Paul said it well in First Corinthians13:12, "For now we see but a poor reflection as in a mirror, but then we shall see face-to-face."

CHAPTER 21
A Freak Storm - 2021

The new year of 2021 dawned more hopeful than 2020, at least at first. One of the best things that happened was Jay called from Phoenix one Saturday morning in early January.

"Happy New Year, Mom," he said.

"Same to you," I replied.

"Guess what?"

"Uh—"

"I've bought a house. Just me. Alex doesn't have a good credit score, so it was better this way."

"That's good. Is Alex paying you rent then?"

"He will when he gets a job."

"Uh, huh." I decided it was better not to mention that they'd already been living in Arizona for almost two years.

"Mom, I was wondering if you and Dad would like to come out and see the place. And maybe bring the rest of the boxes in my closet?"

Ah, now I see.

By this time, Rick had gotten on the extension, once he figured out I was talking to Jay. I wasn't sure what to expect from my husband, so I was relieved when he said, "Sure, Jay. We can come. Do you want us to bring your couch, too?"

Jay had left a couch in the bedroom he'd used upstairs because when he and Alex came in 2019, his car was too small to haul it.

"Yeah, Dad. That'd be great. All we have right now is camping chairs to sit in. And a full-sized bed. Could you help me check on one of our bedroom lights that isn't working, too?"

"Sure," said Rick.

I was thankful Rick's Mr. Fixit was shining through. I saw that even though Rick didn't agree or approve of Jay's current situation, he still loved our son. Relief washed over me like a cooling rain.

"What weekend is a good time to come?" Rick asked.

"I have a four-day weekend for President's Day in February," said Jay. "Would that work?"

"Yes," I said. Rick echoed me.

When that weekend came, we set off on Wednesday because we were going to stop midway to Phoenix. If we were younger, we would have made the long haul in one day, but my aching knees couldn't handle those treks anymore. We got a motel reservation in El Paso, which was about halfway.

At first, things went well, but soon the temperature began to drop very low for Texas.

"Looks like we're in for some ice or snow," I told Rick, scanning the weather forecasts on my phone.

Sure enough, within the next hour, we began to see cars and semis that had slid into the ditch along the interstate. I began to tense up, afraid we would be next.

Rick's experience with Midwest weather as he was growing up came to the fore, though. He avoided going too fast, even as other vehicles zipped past us. Often, we saw them in the ditch a few miles on.

I kept my fears to myself as much as I could, knowing it

would only make Rick's task harder. "I can't believe we're in Texas," I said at one point.

"Yeah, it feels more like Wyoming. Don't worry, Hon," he patted my knee. "We'll be okay."

I squeezed his hand with mine. "I'm glad I'm with you, Rick." My pulse raced, but I took deep breaths in an effort to calm down. In my head, I prayed The Lord's Prayer over and over.

The sun had set long before we made it to El Paso, but the motel wasn't hard to find. When we pulled in, we were surprised to see three inches of snow in the parking lot.

"This is way more than the usual Texas snowfall," I mumbled. All my tension kept me feeling light-headed, so I stayed in our pickup while Rick checked us in.

"The manager apologized that he can't get anyone to plow the parking lot," said Rick, as he climbed back into the truck's cab.

"I'm glad we brought our four-wheel drive vehicle," I said.

"Me, too. We'll be okay now."

"I hope Jay's couch isn't getting too wet in this weather."

"I wrapped it as well as I could in tarps. Besides it's so cold, I doubt this snow is going to melt anytime soon."

"Gosh, it's been so long since we moved from Montana, I'm not used to this weather anymore, Rick."

"Hey, calm down. We're safely here." This time he patted my shoulder. It dawned on me that he was communicating in my love language—physical gestures.

"Thanks to you." I gave him a quick hug.

It turned out El Paso was the only major city in Texas that was prepared for winter weather. When we turned on the TV in our motel room, the news was filled with stories about snowbound roads and vehicles. Cities all across central and eastern Texas were without power.

"El Paso appears to be the only city that took fair warning from the big freeze of 2011," an announcer said. "They were prepared for snow and cold, while the rest of us were not."

"Wow," I said. "I think it's good we're here and not at home. I just hope our cat will be okay."

"I'm sure Muffin will manage to keep warm," Rick laughed. "She's chubby, and her fat is good insulation. Besides, Amy will check on her."

"If Amy's not snowed in."

"She'll be okay, too. Don't be such a worrier."

When Rick said things like that, I used to get angry, but I guess I was finally learning to take things in better stride. "Yes, you're right, of course," I murmured.

Rick was correct about the weather farther west, too. Once we got into New Mexico and Arizona, the roads were clearer, and we arrived in Phoenix on time Thursday evening. We'd reserved a motel there, too, since Jay only had one bed and no other furniture yet.

The weather was still colder than usual, so we spent most of our next three days indoors at Jay's. Alex, it turned out, liked to cook, too. He and Jay took turns making us some of their favorite dishes, such as fried rice with spam, and chicken tikka masala. They didn't have a dining table, so we sat in the camping chairs or on the couch, once it was unwrapped. Fortunately, when we'd packed our truck to head out, I'd convinced Rick to put in a couple of wooden chairs that I'd bought at a rummage sale.

It was easy to see what was important to Jay and Alex. Each had their own computer set up, in separate rooms, and there was a big-screen TV in the living room. We watched several movies while we were there, since there wasn't much else to do.

I was relieved to see Jay and Rick working together on several different projects around the house.

The second day, Jay took his dad into their laundry room. "I got this new washing machine," he smiled. "It was delivered the day before you got here."

Rick nodded and smiled back. "I had a feeling you might need a clothes dryer. That's why we brought our old one. It still works fine, but we got a new set last winter when the old washer broke down."

"I hope you don't mind helping me install them, Dad."

"Of course I'll help, Jay."

When I saw Jay and his dad working so well together, my spirits lifted in hope. There was a big change happening in Rick.

Because so much of Texas was frozen over, we stayed a day longer than we'd planned. The last evening, Jay treated us to sushi from his favorite Japanese restaurant, within walking distance of their house. Rick wasn't sure what to make of raw fish wrapped in rice and seaweed, but he managed. I enjoyed it.

By the time we headed back home, it was still unseasonably cold for Texas. Announcers on the radio were talking of record breaking lows all across the state. That cold snap and snowstorm was unlike anything I'd ever experienced in Texas. Yes, it snowed occasionally, but it quickly melted away in a day or two. The storm of 2021, however, was accompanied by bitter cold temperatures for almost a week afterwards, which put even more stress on the overwhelmed utilities. People complained that the power companies had been too careless about winterizing their equipment.

I remember hearing one spokesman from a power company talking on the radio, as we listened in our truck, "We don't get this kind of weather in Texas. It seemed too expensive to prepare for such a rare event."

"This is having ripple effects all the way into other states, even as far north as Montana," said the interviewer. "What about that?"

The company official hemmed and hawed.

"We should have been more prepared, like El Paso was," Rick said.

"Sometimes, it seems like everything in the world is falling apart," I sighed. "Especially since Covid came along."

"Mary Anna, you know all we can do is trust the Lord."

"I guess you're right." I said those words and wasn't sure I believed them completely. But I tried to.

As we continued on our way home, I was thankful the roads weren't as icy as on the trip to Phoenix, but the thing that gave me the most comfort was Rick's acceptance of the situation with Jay. Perhaps there would be a way to rebuild our relationship with our son—and with each other.

A few verses from the Bible kept coming to me as I watched the West Texas plains pass by us: "Love covers a multitude of sins," said one. And another: "Love bears all things, believes all things, endures all things, hopes all things. Love never fails."

God loves us so we can love others, my thoughts reminded me. *Love is the only way to overcome hatred. Anger and hate only breed more of themselves. Lord, help me be more loving.*

A scrap of the Prayer of St. Francis of Assisi popped into my mind: "Lord, make me an instrument of Thy peace."

CHAPTER 22
Pastor Mark

Most of the world was hoping that the worst of the pandemic was over, but it didn't turn out that way. Though some things resumed, there were still too many cases of Covid, and hospitals filled up again.

At sessions with Dr. B, I told him, "I don't think I should watch the news anymore."

"Why is that?"

"It gets me depressed, especially all the political arguing. I feel like I'm always on the edge of that knife-edged ridge I told you about."

"I like that metaphor. Believe me, I see many people who are feeling the same way you are. The pandemic has been hard on all of us. I'm getting more referrals than ever before."

"So, I shouldn't feel bad about trying to ignore the news?"

"No, of course not. You are the best judge of what gives you self-care, and what drags you down."

"Thanks for reassuring me."

"It's too bad we have to make such choices," he said.

"Yeah, I remember when I was a kid, people were happy for vaccines to protect us from diseases like polio and the measles. But now so many are refusing to get a Covid vaccine, insisting it violates their freedom. I just don't get it."

"It's unfortunate that politics has gotten messed up with

science. I work with all kinds of people, though, so I have to keep myself apolitical."

"To me everything seems insane. Like you once said, it's Covid Insanity."

"That's good," he laughed. "I do remember calling it that."

I liked the minister at our church in Palestine, Pastor Mark. At first, he was quieter than our former pastor, and harder to get to know. But as time went on, I found he had a skill for comforting people. Back in 2017 when Mom died, he was the one who dropped everything to meet us at the memory care to do a short service, commending her soul to heaven. I was very touched.

He'd also ministered to Mom before that, when she was living with us. When he came to the house to visit her, she would open up and talk more than usual, telling him about her childhood memories of the church where she'd been baptized.

One time in 2016, after Mom was in Memory Gardens, I went in to talk with Pastor Mark because I was feeling uneasy about my faith.

"What's the matter?" he'd asked.

"I feel guilty that I'm not visiting her more. There are even days when I wish she'd go ahead and die. Maybe I'm questioning God too much. Am I losing my faith?"

I'd been afraid he'd criticize me for saying that, but he didn't. "Having to watch a loved one gradually decline is very hard, Mary Anna. You're not the only one who's ever felt this way."

"Really? I think I must be a very bad Christian."

"Times of stress and grief can pull any of us down, but that doesn't mean your faith is weak."

"What should I do?"

"It's not really a matter of doing something differently. It's more like letting the Lord be with you in the dark. Someday, the light will return, but He's promised to be with us even in the valley of the shadow of death. He meets us where we are, instead of just telling us where we ought to be."

Something like a lightbulb flashed on in my mind. "You mean, He's not angry with my weakness?"

"No, He's not angry. He wants to come alongside you, hold your hand, and guide you with His love and power."

"Then it's not *my* strength that matters?"

"Right. He's the one with the strength, and He offers it to you whenever you need it. That's how He helps us through tough times like these."

"Even on the days when I can't feel His presence?"

"Especially on those days. We can't understand the whole picture the way He does. I know that's frustrating."

"For sure, Pastor."

"We humans want to be in charge, but the Lord keeps reminding us that He's the one in control."

"Sometimes that makes me angry," I sighed.

He continued, "This fallen world has troubles. Look at Job, in the Bible. Many bad things happened to him all at once—his children died, he lost his wealth, and almost lost his faith. But God came and reminded Job that He was the one in charge."

"I've always had a hard time with that book in the Bible, Pastor. God never answered Job's 'why' questions."

"That's right. Instead, He reminded Job that He was in control and could be trusted."

"Meaning God is all-powerful, and we can't fathom Him?"

"Yes, Mary Anna. He also scolded Job's friends for giving him bad advice—like saying his troubles were his own fault and punishment for sins."

"You know, when something goes wrong in my life, I do wonder if I caused it, or if God is punishing me."

"The book of Job is in the Bible to remind us that isn't true. God doesn't work that way."

During Covid, after Mom died, I still had questions for Pastor Mark. Since we couldn't meet in person, I called him on the phone. After he answered, I said, "Pastor, remember when Job's friends gave him bad advice? Now it feels like the whole world is full of bad advice.

"Yes, there is a lot of confusion right now, Mary Anna."

"So I guess you're telling me to listen to God instead of the world, aren't you?"

"That's right."

"It's really hard to keep from being anxious and depressed right now."

"No one ever said life would always be easy," he said. "But think back to the time two thousand years ago when Jesus was born. The world was in turmoil then, too. All kinds of wars and political intrigue were going on, but that's when God determined it was the right time in history to send His Son into this world. Times of strife and uncertainty show that God is on the move."

"Wow, I never thought of it that way, Pastor. I just hope I can keep my faith through all of this Covid Insanity."

"I believe you will, Mary Anna. You're braver and stronger than you think—with God's help, that is. Just keep reminding yourself how much God loves you. He sent His Son to save you, and He sees the big picture that we can't understand with our limited minds."

"Thanks for reminding me of that again, Pastor."

When I signed off that call, my heart was more peaceful that it had been in a long time.

***

A few days after this conversation, a flock of honking geese flying over our house woke me in the morning. As I lay in bed listening to the sound, an image of soaring high above the ground filled my head. I imagined viewing the land far below, and I realized that the hills and valleys, the great rises and falls, became of less significance than before.

Thoughts began to bloom in my mind. I grabbed my journal from the nightstand and began to write: *As our modern world has removed us more and more from the sources of all our needs, we forget to take care of our earth. Instead we use and often abuse her. If Covid has taught me anything, it's to not take the goods in the grocery store for granted. Even our technological lifestyles are more fragile than we thought.*

I realized I was feeling more at peace than I had in a long time. As I rose from bed that morning, it seemed I'd come down to the bottom of the well and found that God had been there all along. Now I was beginning to see that the darkness I'd been living in was only mysterious, instead of evil. I'd thought I needed to get out of the pit, but instead I found God there with me—even through the many things that came crashing down in 2017, from my mother's death to Jay's coming out.

That late spring morning, it was warm enough to sit on the porch with my coffee. I opened my Bible, something I'd stopped doing when I was in deep despair, but better days were beginning to dawn for me again.

Normally, I wasn't one of those people who randomly opened the Bible's pages to see where God might speak.

Today, as I searched for the beginning of the *Book of Acts*, the pages fell open to the sixteenth chapter of *John*. Words leaped off the page: "In this world you will have tribulations, but take heart; I have overcome the world."

Words Jesus said to his followers two thousand years ago. Now I know they're also true for me.

Not all the days ahead would be sunny. Some of our hot, dry summers had brought home the lesson that the earth needs both sunshine and rain. Maybe that was God's way of reminding me rain was vital in our lives at times, or as Dad often quoted, "Into every life some rain must fall."

I hoped and prayed I could keep this reassurance in my heart, no matter what surprises each bend in the road brought. A quote I'd read somewhere reminded me of this, "I don't know what tomorrow holds, but I know Who holds tomorrow."

EPILOGUE:

"Cast all your cares on him, for he cares for you."
—I Peter 5:7

One summer day, as the early sunshine woke me, I realized I believed this verse again. Gone was the negative voice in my mind saying, 'Yeah sure. So you say.' Or, 'Whatever.'

Where did that negativity go? Will it come back? I don't know, but I don't miss it.

There wasn't anything dramatic, no flash of light from heaven or thundering voice. Still, I felt more hopeful, like I'd been lifted out of my dark pit during the night while I slept. I hadn't done anything different, but a new day had dawned in my soul.

This was the day I finally realized it's okay to question God. He knows we humans can't help it. It's what we are. I was wrong to expect myself to always be upbeat and positive, to keep hiding my true feelings.

God wants to help us grieve. He even wants to grieve with us. We can't help asking, "Why, God?" He knows that, so He lets us ask, even though He doesn't always give the answer we want to hear. Now I see this is one way He shows his love for us.

He helps us move past the unanswered. Instead, He reassures us of His love and care—and continues to walk with us, even though He won't always answer our questions. For in place of endless explanations and words, He gives us a spiritual hug. Then somehow, we awake one morning to realize we are loved—beyond anything words can ever express.

APPENDIX TO
"Far from Magnolia Drive"

This book has been harder to write than all of my others. Probably because it is drawn more closely from my own life. I debated about whether to write a true memoir or fictionalize. Here is the factual side of my story, which was barely begun in the appendix to Journeys Saga Book I, *Voices in the Past.*

The thing about memoir is that in a sense it's still fictional. Everything I relate here, or in my fiction, has been seen through the filter of my own eyes and life. Even when I think I'm telling the "true story" this happens. Laura Ingalls Wilder said it well when she told an audience, "Everything I have written is the truth, but not the whole truth."

Feser kids (Robert Henry, Daniel Leroy, and Mary Frances) dressed up for Easter, Magnolia Drive, about 1961.

A NOTE ABOUT COUNSELING

The story of how I found my counselor, Richard, is very similar to Mary Anna's. I had to overcome my pride and admit I needed help, too. It took me years to get past the stigma I felt about having mental problems. Much of this came from attitudes in my own family, as well as those in society.

Richard has been helping me with something called Acceptance Commitment Therapy (ACT)*, first developed by Dr. Steven Hayes. With his help, I have learned to step back when I feel panicky or depressed—to 'expand' around those feelings, so they don't sweep me away. It is called 'defusing'—to mentally let something be and say to myself, *This is just the way things are. I can't change them, but that's okay.* Gradually, I'm learning to stop blaming myself for everything that happens. Migraines are one example. When I get one now, I don't ask myself, "What did I do to cause this one?" I treat myself with care instead of blaming.

This therapy is explained very well in a book by Russ Harris, titled *The Happiness Trap.** After Richard suggested it, I read it twice and bought copies for both my children. Changing my thought patterns, learning to 'defuse' and 'expand' as ACT suggested is not as easy as it sounds. It has taken a lot of time and practice, but it's beginning to make a difference in my emotional life.

One thing I've had to accept is that depression will always be part of me. Though new medications were helping, an unexpected wave of anxiety is all it takes for this dragon to rear its ugly head. I'm learning not to 'fuse' with that, but instead, to 'defuse' and let it be, not letting myself fall into a pity-party. (Most of the time, at least.) One of the things Harris suggests is to say to yourself, "Thanks mind, for reminding me of that. Now I'm going on to think about something else."

That's what ACT means by *acceptance*—not that I like or approve of something, but just let it be. This kind of accepting helps the depression pass sooner, so I'm not as overwhelmed.

Another thing I've learned is that it's all right to let myself grieve. In fact, trying not to grieve is dangerous. I know well the truth of this, because I've stuffed grief when it came over me—the grief of losing my parents, and especially grief over the loss of the son I thought I had. The longer I tried to avoid this grief, the more it festered and ate me from the inside out.

Learning to let pain be there, to accept it, is the hardest thing I've ever done. In many ways, ACT's teachings go against natural human ways of responding.

An image from Dr. Hayes* which helps me the most involves seeing myself standing on a railroad overpass, looking down on several trains passing underneath. Each car of the trains represents some problem, hurt, grief, anger, or poor self-image. Instead of jumping down and riding along with any of those train cars, I visualize staying on the bridge and letting them just go on by, passing away. This is how he illustrates 'acceptance'.

There are still times I don't succeed at this, still days when I catch myself riding on this "Mind Train". Those are the days when I remind myself of some of Richard's words of wisdom:

"Nobody is happy all the time. Don't dump on yourself. Be kind to yourself, instead. Think about how you would like others to treat you, and then give *yourself* this kind of acceptance."

One morning when I was writing in my journal, I thought of a new application for the acronym ACT. Yes, the **"A"** still stands for "Accept life as it is." **"C"** now reminds me to "Center myself in God." **"T"** has become "Trust that there is a plan and meaning to life, even if I can't see it."

This has been a decade-long journey so far, and I know I'm still learning. There are many days when I fall down into that dark chasm—like Mary Anna describes. But they don't come as often now.

***References from this section:**

Harris, Russ. *The Happiness Trap: How to Stop Struggling and Start Living,* 2007-08, Trumpeter Books, Boston, MA.

Hayes, Steven, Ph.D. *Get Out of Your Mind and Into Your Life: The New Acceptance and Commitment Therapy,* 2005, New Harbinger Publishing, Inc. Oakland, CA.

What follows in this appendix is the true story of my life, at least as I remember it.

CHAPTER 1
Distant Memories

The first things I remember are sketchy, as of course they would be for a preschool child.

I think my very earliest memory was an evening when I was sitting on the old brown rug of our rental house in Arkansas. I know it had to be there because that house had hardwood floors, and it was the only house we lived in that did.

Across the room, my dad and my grandmother are talking in upset-sounding voices. Someone has given me a cup of cold water to drink. (It may have been milk or juice, too. I don't remember that part.)

The next thing I remember is the cold drink spilling down my chest and my grandmother rushing over to scold me and try to clean up the mess. She picks me up, and that's all of the memory.

But I have figured out what was happening then. It has to be the night my sister Roberta Lee was born. I must have been under two-years old. That is the only reason my grandmother would have been there alone with my dad, and it explains the strong feelings in their voices. It also shows I was picking up on that tension when I spilled my cup. The feeling of the cold liquid running down my chest is the most vivid part of the memory.

I didn't know about my preemie sister who died, until I was about 9 years old, when my dad finally told us about her (much like I've related in the last chapter of my book, *Voices in the Past*.) Then things fell into place in my mind. It was her grave that we visited on Sunday afternoons. I remember walking on the tombstone and looking at the carved shapes that were most likely letters and numbers. It was one of those stones that lay flat on the ground, grey in color. Many times in my adulthood, I've wondered if I could ever find it, somewhere in the cemetery of El Dorado, Arkansas. But I've only returned to El Dorado once since I married, and I had other things on my mind then. I managed to find Roberta Lee's information on Find-a-Grave. She was born Feb. 10, 1954 and died on Feb. 11. That fits with what Dad told us, that she lived only a couple of hours. I even added my sister to my bedtime prayers after, "God bless Robby and Danny. And Roberta Lee, wherever she may be." Neither Dad or Mom ever commented about this.

One other early memory has to be before March 1955, when my brother Robert was born. I was in the bathtub, and Mom grabbed me out, wrapped me in a towel, and we went outside. There were firetrucks and sirens. Apparently, Mom had started some trash burning in the burn barrel (people used old oil drums back then), and it got away and started a grass fire. Maybe that's why I have a fear of house fires.

I have some other early memories in that rental house, like my mother reading to me, and my learning to recite poems by heart: like "There Once Was a Puffin" and "A Visit from St. Nicholas". There was a tiny record player that played the scratchy records we had. The only one I remember had songs from the Disney cartoon movie "Cinderella." I also remember looking at the covers of books on a shelf. Momma said they were from "the Book of the Month Club." I just remember the colors and the designs on the covers. None of them were paperback, and none of them had their dust jackets.

One day my favorite ragdoll had gotten wet somehow. Perhaps I tried to give her a bath. When Daddy got home, he teased me, saying, "Susie has fallen into the well." "No, she didn't!" I replied. To me a 'well' meant an oil well, because there were hundreds of the tall oil derricks and pumping stations all around our town.

I don't remember when my brother Robby was born, but I was still 2 because he was born in March, 1955, and I didn't turn 3 until July of that year. I do remember him sitting at the low baby table with a seat in the middle. Seems like he ate a lot. My mother called him her "eager eater."

Other memories I have are probably from photos of birthdays and Christmases in that house. I know we had a light green couch with scratchy tufted fabric—must have been popular then. And it was in two pieces, an early form of a sectional sofa.

I also remember when Daddy was drawing up the plans for our new house, and going with my parents to see the walls going up. It was across town in a nice subdivision in El Dorado, Arkansas called Magnolia Drive. True to its name, there were magnolia trees by almost every house. Our lot was a hillside, and much later I realized that was why there was so much terracing in the yard.

We moved into that house shortly after my 5th birthday, in 1957. Our neighbor across the street was a Chevrolet car salesman, and every year he had a new Impala to drive, so I always knew what each model-year looked like for the 6 years we lived in that house.

Six years isn't really such a long time, but it seemed to be a wonderful place of childhood to me—neighborhood kids to play with, walking to school once I started first grade. Lots of good memories. Two neighbors had boats parked in their yards, and we would pretend to be sailing in them.

My youngest brother Daniel was born while we lived in this house. I remember Mom waving at Daddy and me from her hospital window. Children weren't allowed to visit the maternity ward back then. I was in first grade, and was so excited about having a new baby brother. He was born just before Halloween, on October 25, and I remember him lying in his bassinette in the living room while we answered the door for trick-or-treaters.

Holidays were great in southern Arkansas. On Halloween we could wear just our costumes—no need for coats! Easter was warm with spring flowers. Again, no need to cover up the new clothes with jackets. It was popular back then to get little baby chicks for Easter, sometimes even dyed pink, green, or blue. I remember one time when our next-door neighbors had some and we saw them running around their fenced back yard. I wished we could get some. But a couple of years later I 'pet-sat' for a friend's chicks, who were getting about 8" tall by this time. When I found out what a job it was to clean out all the chicken poop, I decided having chicks wasn't such a good deal.

At Christmas we always wished for snow, but of course it never came. I remember snow falling twice that actually stuck and stayed on the ground for a few days. And there was a terrible ice storm when I was 5, that bent the pines laden with ice. Some even broke and one nearly hit our house.

Music began to be part of our lives. I learned many Christmas carols and other songs from singing in the children's choir at church. We also had a picture book about Christmas, and I can still visualize the illustrations for each carol in that book. As December counted slowly down, I'd lie in bed and sing myself to sleep with Christmas songs I knew by heart. One of the last Christmases in this house, we all sat around the tree and sang some carols. Mom even lit a candle that I'd made at school. It was mounted on a paper plate, with pine cones and gumballs (seed pods from the sweetgum trees) and all spray-painted gold. After that Christmas, it disappeared. Mom was always good at tossing things out.

The tree itself was our only Christmas decoration. Mom didn't want to fuss with anything else, I guess. We couldn't put the tree up until Dec. 21, and it came down shortly after the 25th. I think she was always worried about it starting a fire, and I know she hated the evergreen needles falling on the carpet. (The only room in our house that had carpet was the living room. The rest were that asphalt tile that everyone had back in the 50's. It had to be mopped and waxed.) She did let us put those silvery icicles on the tree, though. They were the good kind made of real foil. Once they were replaced with plastic ones that clung to everything, I didn't care for them. Now I'm not sure they make them anymore. Must have been a choking hazard.

Another thing I loved about Christmas was the huge candlelight service at First Methodist Church. There were dozens of choirs, from first and second graders up through adult, and all of us (except the very youngest) got to carry real candles. We'd process in to "Hark the Herald Angels Sing", choirs each following their designated route around the huge sanctuary, crossing each other's paths in a magnificent candlelight procession. Once we were in our designated places, each of us had a special part of the program to sing, and we got to keep the candles lit.

One year, when I was in fourth or fifth grade, I was fourth in line in my blue-robed choir. The three in front of me started

226

to walk down the aisle as the organ began to play, but I knew we weren't supposed to process until we began to sing the first verse. People behind me in line kept whispering and signaling to move, but I stood my ground. The three who had jumped the gun stood by our seats all alone. No other choir had started to move yet. Once the singing began, I led the rest of my choir down the aisle, across the front of the church, and to their places. I don't remember anyone making any comment one way or the other after the service, but I knew I'd done the right thing.

Of course, Mom always worried that the candlelight service would burn the church down. As far as I know, it never did. I'm sure the fire-marshals put an end to it soon after we moved from Arkansas. I've never seen anything like it since. Candlelight services now-a-days involve holding a burning candle for one song, "Silent Night." I was so disappointed when I found this out.

I still wish sometimes that my own children could have experienced that wonderful service of beautiful carols, done entirely in candlelight. At the end, we'd all walk out to "O Come, All Ye Faithful" and then we'd stand on the tall church steps, out in the usually balmy Arkansas December air, singing all the verses of "Silent Night" as a message to the whole world—the faithful had moved beyond the church and into the mission field. At least that's how it felt to me. I can't remember Mom ever attending this service, but I do remember when my Dad first took me. That must have been when I was in kindergarten and too young to participate yet.

One of Dad's favorite things to do was drive around to see the Christmas lights. My most vivid memory was the county courthouse. They had a four-story oil derrick on the lawn which was covered with lights, and at the top was a figure of

Santa in his sleigh, with all the reindeer. It was so high up, we could barely make out Santa's form, in fact. We thought it was amazing and beautiful. The idea of an oil derrick in the middle of town did not seem strange to us, because they were scattered all over the landscape around El Dorado, Arkansas.

True to its name, this place was one of the early "bonanza" oil fields of the post-war years. Dad worked for Lion Oil. The other big company in town was Murphy Oil, which later became the gasoline supplier for Walmart of northwest Arkansas. Because Walmart got so huge, Murphy Oil's name is on Walmart gas pumps all over the country.

But Lion Oil was bought out by Monsanto, so that's who Dad worked for most of my childhood. I wonder if this is why he held on to "the lion" plaster sculpture all his life. It graced our mantel or some other part of our house for most of my life. Before it came to our house, it was at my dad's parents' house in Houston. Family custom was to take pictures of toddlers sitting on the lion. Now it's been passed on to Robert's son, Adam, who has a son named Emery Matthew Robert Feser. (Dad's name was Robert Philip, my brother's was Robert Henry, his son's was Adam Matthew, so that's where Emery's names come from.) The tradition of the lion goes on, though I doubt many remember where it started.

Another thing I remember about Christmas in Arkansas was hanging the stockings our grandmother (Nana, Daddy's mother) had made for us. Mine was white with an angel on it, and Robby's was green with Santa. I wished mine was green because that was my favorite color. Daniel's was blue and just a little one since he was a baby the year we got them. Of course, the next year it was too small, so we had to buy him one of those felt ones. His was green, too! We didn't have a fireplace, so we hung them on the tall radio console that had a record player inside. It was a nice old piece of furniture, but it didn't come with us when we moved from Arkansas. The stockings did, but after I was out of high school they disappeared, too. I sure wish Mom had saved them for us, but she just wasn't like that.

Dad always had a way of making Christmas special, like when he'd make his delicious pecan pralines and divinity. Mom didn't seem to like the holidays as much as Dad did. At least we always got to have a real tree. I loved to sit and stare at the pretty colored lights and ornaments. In the early years of our family, all these ornaments were fragile glass, so we had to be careful. By the time Dan was born, I remember plastic ones we put on the lower branches where his little hands could reach.

Up until I was 13, we had no fireplace, but Santa still managed to get our presents in. One night, when I was maybe six or seven, I remember waking to a sound down the hall. I knew it must be Santa, and I couldn't resist creeping down the hall toward the living room where the tree was. I saw no lights, but there must have been moonlight coming in the windows, for I could make out dim shapes of strange new things that hadn't been around the tree before. I didn't want to scare Santa and maybe lose my gifts, so I dashed back to bed as fast as I could. In the morning, there was a new pink crib for my toy dolls to sleep in.

One year, Dad heard a new subdivision was going in behind our elementary school in El Dorado. I'll never know if he got permission, but we went up that hill and cut a six-foot loblolly pine he said was going to be chopped down anyway. When we set that fresh tree up in our living room, it smelled so wonderful that I lay down under it and pretended to have a picnic. Mom didn't mind the tree as much that year because it was fresher than the firs or spruces we got at the Lions' Club tree lot. Too bad we couldn't have cut our own tree every year.

The last real tree we had was in 1963, the year we moved to Illinois. That holiday season, Mom entered a raffle at a local pharmacy. She won first prize—an aluminum tree. Now we didn't have to worry about shed needles anymore.

Our record player must have broken when we moved to Magnolia Drive, because I remember hearing songs at other people's houses instead of at home. I heard The Chipmunks', "Hurry Christmas" on the screen porch of the neighbor across the street. They had a huge white oak tree in their back yard, and we collected a lot of acorns from it. Way up high in the top there were a couple of patches of mistletoe. I wished we could get some, but they were much too high to reach.

At the next-door neighbor's, I remember hearing "Frosty the Snowman" for the first time. And dancing to "Let's Do the Twist" by Chubby Checker. Some of my girlfriends were taking dance at the little studio I walked by on my way to school, but I didn't get to. I gathered somehow that my dad thought I was too clumsy to waste dance lessons on.

I loved to listen to other friends play the piano, and remember that I always wanted to learn to play. But we couldn't afford the cost of lessons or a piano. Later I learned that my dad had been forced to take 8 years of lessons as a boy and hated it. So I reaped the harvest of that, I guess.

Finally, when I was in high school, my parents bought a small Lowery organ from some friends, and I taught myself to play it. As an adult I never gave up on this dream, though. More later on this.

My dad wasn't mean or cruel, but he was a perfectionist, always ready to tell what you needed to improve and seldom giving out compliments. He came from the generation—or perhaps it was his family—that thought compliments would make you conceited. So, I learned that he'd told the church children's choir director, "I hope you can do something with her. She can't carry a tune in a bucket."

It didn't strike me until years later that I hadn't actually heard him say this. My mother told me, and I still wonder why she felt she needed to pass that along. It seemed I was always being told my inadequacies. No wonder I had such an inferiority complex.

I remember almost nothing of kindergarten, just playing on the playground and waiting what seemed like forever for my turn to paint on the easel. Kindergarten was at the First Baptist Church, as schools only started with first grade back them. We went to the First Methodist Church, though. In the South you were known by which church you went to—-Methodist or Baptist. Our next-door neighbors were Presbyterian, which was less common. I remember only one friend who was Catholic. There was a Jewish Synagogue in El Dorado, which our church group visited one Friday evening. Their Sabbath Service was very interesting.

Most children played outside in those days. Cowboys and Indians was one of my favorites. Or we'd ride bikes and roller-skate. Skates back then had metal wheels and a metal frame that you could attach to the bottom of your shoes. You had to have a skate key to do that though. It was actually an early form of a socket wrench. It must have rained sometimes, but mostly I remember sunny days. One time it did rain so hard that the cul-de-sac at the end of our street became a lake. We had a lot of fun splashing and wading in that warm water, and for some reason we didn't worry about how clean it was.

As my brothers and I got older, we were allowed to play anywhere on our side of Magnolia Drive. When it was time to come home, Mom would blow a loud police whistle as our signal. No one thought it strange back then.

This was also when Barbie dolls got started. I really would have liked one, but didn't ever get one. So, I played with my friends' dolls when I was at their houses. I remember a friend named Gail, who not only had Barbie dolls, but a Magic 8-Ball, and an Etch-a-sketch. She was an only child, so maybe that's why she got more of the neat toys. Much later, when I had children, I tried to get them some of the 'cool toys', but not spoil them. They didn't get any video games as early as most of their friends. But they didn't seem to feel deprived.

Saturday morning cartoons were a big thing then. There were no videos yet. You either watched what was on TV or nothing, and usually there were only two channels to choose from. My brothers and I would get up early to watch our favorites. But my absolute favorite wasn't a cartoon. It was reruns of old Flash Gordon programs, and they came on at 6 or 7 a.m. It was worth it to get up so early, so I guess I was already beginning to be a science fiction fan.

By the way, I think the two channels we got were NBC and CBS. I remember the NBC peacock, though ours was in black and white, not 'living color.' And I vaguely remember the CBS eye. I guess we watched NBC more. That was when the Today Show got started, and Captain Kangaroo. On Sunday evening we always looked forward to Disney's "Wonderful World of Color"—in black, white, and many shades of gray.

I don't think Mom watched TV much during the day when we were at school. But when I was sick, I was allowed to make a bed with blankets on the divan (what we called the sofa back then) and watch the game shows, like "Concentration" and "Truth or Consequences."

Mary Frances, Daniel Leroy, and Robert Henry at Feser grandparents' house in Houston, Texas. 1959

CHAPTER 2
A 1950s Childhood

Once I started first grade I could walk to school, only a couple of blocks away. My first-grade teacher, Mrs. Martin, read us the story of Noah's Ark, from the Bible. And I also heard "How the Grinch Stole Christmas" for the first time.

It seemed I was always one of the last ones to get my work finished. I don't know if I tended to daydream or was just slow. One time, we had an open house and our parents were looking at our work on the classroom bulletin boards. My dad pointed out some nice handwriting, but it was slanted, like cursive would be. I tried to explain to him that this wasn't correct. Printing was supposed to be straight up and down, like mine was. But he didn't believe me. Even though I was trying to do what the teacher said, I felt he told me I was wrong.

Another time I remember being scolded for getting a "B" in deportment (behavior). I was probably whispering to a friend, or not staying focused on my work. He was angry and said there was no excuse not to get an "A" in deportment. Once again, I wasn't measuring up to his high standards, so I tried harder, and I didn't get any more B's in deportment.

I distinctly remember the day in third grade when I finally finished my seatwork on time. What a sense of accomplishment I felt! Then we had to start learning math facts, getting through a sheet of addition or subtraction problems in a certain length of time. I just couldn't do them fast enough, even though I tried. I think the pressure of trying to do things fast made me too nervous.

My dad thought he'd help by drilling me on these facts. I remember one night in my bedroom, standing up against my closet door, trying to answer his shot-gun problems fast enough. But I must not have been doing it because he was getting angry. And the more he pressed me, the greater my panic became. I can feel myself leaning against the wooden closet door, wishing I could hide from him, or maybe even sink into the wood.

I think this is why I have a phobia with numbers. I still struggle to do math in my head, and a page full of numbers triggers a tiny wave of panic in me. One thing I've avoided all my life is being treasurer of anything. It wasn't until I was forced to, that I learned to balance a checkbook. I'm so glad my husband does our taxes. I really do have trouble dealing with long columns of numbers.

Most of my lifetime later, I went to a counselor for depression, and he helped me revisit some of this. With his help, and a technique he was trained in called EMDR, I began to re-shuffle some of these memories. I finally learned that my father did love me, and only wanted the best for me. I can't explain it, but the image of standing there with him towering above me, getting angry, has been replaced with him reaching down to hug me.

"Daddy, I'm doing the best I can," I say.

And he says, "I know, Kiddo. I understand."

But this didn't really happen, you say. I'm not sure. All I know is that there must have been sometime in my childhood that he did do this. And by re-sorting the memories, and accessing parts of my subconscious that ordinarily I can't (that's what EMDR is said to do), I replaced the frightened-child memory with a loved-child one. It's too bad it had to take until I was in my 60's.

Even when my father died in 2010, there was still an atmosphere of fear and distance sometimes. I never felt I was good enough in his eyes. Even when I was in my 50's and began teaching guitar lessons (with some pointers from my younger brother, Dan) my mother told me, "Dad is concerned that you don't know enough about guitar to teach." Why did she do this? I still don't know. And now that she has died of Alzheimer's, I never will.

Still, I do know my Daddy loved me. He always called me "Kiddo" —his pet name for me. My brothers didn't have those. For a lot of my preschool years I thought Kiddo was a real part of my name. My fondest memories of Dad are when he read to me. When I was still a preschooler, he read from *"The Hollow Tree Books"* favorites from his own childhood. I love these stories about "the Coon, the Possum, and the Old Black Crow." (Some might not think them 'politically correct' now, but I never saw them that way.) They were wonderfully imaginative tales, some from nature and others more about human nature. I still have these old books, and read them to my own children, but the books are beginning to fall apart. I'm sure they're over a century old now.

As I started into elementary school, he began to buy volumes of the "All About Books". These were too hard for me to read on my own at first, so he read them to me. They were scientific, like *All About Flowering Plants,* from which I learned the names of flower parts long before I took high school biology. Other favorites were *All About Whales, All About Glaciers, All About Prehistoric Cavemen, and All About Apes and Monkeys.* I remember re-reading some of these on my own when I was almost ten years older. I'm so grateful to Dad for reading this type of books to me, when others might have thought I was too young.

Some of my fondest memories of Magnolia Drive were playing games of hide-and-seek as dusk was falling. We pretty much had free rein of the neighborhood. Everyone knew us and we knew them. No one was worried about us being attacked or abducted. Life was simple and good. I learned to ride my first two-wheeler bicycle there, and my favorite trees to climb were some mimosas in the yard next door. They had low limbs that were easy to grab and pull yourself up onto. And the neighbors never seemed to mind that I was often perched in their trees.

When I was probably eight, the neighbor on the other side of us built a platform on tall stilts, which was a sort of tree house. This became the new favorite play-place. Another fond thing I remember is that my favorite things to carry in my pockets were a yo-yo and a harmonica.

The tree-house neighbor's mother was an artist, and as soon as I was old enough, I was enrolled in art classes. This was something my father liked to do. We often watched him painting in our living room. His favorite subjects were abstracts and the female body. Mom didn't let us look too closely at the latter.

So even though I didn't get piano or dance lessons, I did get to take art. In fourth grade, I worked in water-colors; fifth grade was tempera paint; and in sixth grade I finally graduated to oil paints. But I was deeply disappointed when we moved from Arkansas to Illinois in October of that year. I barely got started in oil painting. Although I tried to teach myself over the next few years, I didn't get very good at it. (Many years later in 2019, I took art classes at our community college. My teacher says I'm doing well with acrylic paints.)

As I mentioned before, Dad often read nonfiction science books to me. I began to learn junior high and high school level science while I was still in elementary school.

When I was nine, I asked for a chemistry set. Instead, Dad encouraged me to read library books and experiment with what could be found around the house, like vinegar and baking soda. He even brought surplus flasks and beakers from the lab where he worked as a chemical engineer.

I didn't stop with the basic vinegar-and-soda volcanoes, either. Instead, I read every book in the town library, experimenting with alcohol, oil, and water, baking powder, laundry borax, and many other things I convinced Mom to buy at the grocery store.

My next interest was building a weather station with home-made instruments. Again, I read every book the local library had on the subject. This time Dad provided me with a chart to calculate the Dew Point, based on the readings of the wet- and dry-bulb thermometers I'd made.

Big world events during my childhood were the Cold War and fears of nuclear war. Fallout shelters were labeled in many parts of town and once I found a bag of groceries in our linen closet. I guess that was our preparations to head for a shelter in the event of 'an actual emergency' as they would say on the tests of the emergency broadcast system on the radio. I didn't worry about this too much as a child; it was just part of life. It weighs on me now that these things have all come back to haunt us. All except the fallout shelters. Now I guess the authorities figure there's no point in trying to fool us into believing we'd survive a nuclear war.

Another tense time was the Cuban Missile Crisis in 1962. I do remember the TV and the adults talking about it, and

I think there was a sense of fear, and then great relief, when President Kennedy faced down the Russians and 'they blinked.'

A good event I remember is John Glenn's first orbit of the Earth. We were all really excited to have a man from America in space. The teachers even brought a TV to our school (a black and white one). We all gathered in one of the fourth or fifth grade rooms to watch the launch, counting down with the voice on the screen and gazing in awe as the rocket actually left the surface of earth. Watching the splash down was a big event, too. We even tried to learn a new trick on our yo-yos. Instead of just 'around the world' once, we'd do 'John Glenn' and go around three times.

It's interesting to think how much has changed in just my lifetime. We had no technology in our classrooms, no TV, except for these rare occasions. And now students have their own laptops or tablets and smart phones. We didn't have to put up with 24-hour news channels grinding the 'news' into the ground. We just got to watch the 6:00 o'clock news with Chet Huntley and David Brinkley. Or Walter Cronkite, the 'most trusted man' in the country, who'd gone to the same high school as Dad in Houston, San Jacinto High.

Christmas in Arkansas, 1960 or 61

Left to Right: Mary Feser (Nana), Frances Feser, Daniel Feser, Robert Henry Feser & George Henry Feser (Pop)

CHAPTER 3
Culture Shock & Cultural Learning

When I was 11, and just starting sixth grade, Dad took a new job. We had to leave Arkansas and move to northern Illinois, where he was to be the manager of a fertilizer plant, Illinois Nitrogen.

I still find it difficult remembering the trauma of this move to an entirely new culture—from the Deep South to the North. For one thing, I learned what we called "The War Between the States" was the "Civil War" in the North. And I learned that the South had lost. I was virtually a foreigner in my new school. I determined to try my best to fit in, teaching myself to talk with the Illinois accent—no more "Ya'll"; now it had to be "You gah-y-ez." In other words, I was learning Midwest diphthongs.

It would have been easier for me to adjust if I'd had better social skills. For example, if I'd learned to laugh at myself instead of getting hurt and overly embarrassed, I would have spared myself a lot of pain. Instead I became an easy target for teasing. My first school in Ottawa, Illinois was Washington School, on the East Side of town. This was a small school with only one class of each grade. Most of the students had known each other since kindergarten, and here I was the newcomer in sixth grade. I have very few happy memories of that school.

One of the things I really enjoyed our first winter in Illinois was the snow. I'd only seen it a couple of times in Arkansas.

I loved it so much that I was the one who went out in the morning to shovel the sidewalk before I went to school.

The house we rented our first 2 years in Ottawa (after that we bought a house a street over) had some interesting items left in the garage, among them some wooden Flexible Flyer sleds. Just from watching movies, I knew how to get on the sled and go zooming down the hill, about a block down the street from our house. It was amazing fun.

My brothers and I did find some unique places to play on the East Side. Instead of piney Arkansas woods, we had scattered remnants of land that hadn't been cleared by the corn farmers. Ottawa was surrounded by remnants of strip mines, mostly silica sand pits. We thought of them as great places to run up and down what we called 'the clay hills.' To us, they weren't mining waste at all, but adventures waiting for us.

Just a couple of miles from our house were the remains of the old Illinois-Michigan Canal. Like the more famous Erie Canal, which was a shortcut from Lake Erie to the Hudson River, this canal provided a direct route from Lake Michigan to the Illinois River, a tributary of the Mississippi. In its time, it cut days off the route from Chicago to New Orleans.

Now there is a site where the canal has been restored as a historical monument. But back then it was nothing but an overgrown ditch, full of trash, scrub brush, and spindly trees. The most wonderful part to us was 'The Aqueduct', the remains of the structure that took the water of the canal over the Fox River. (The Fox River and the Illinois were the two rivers that bounded the peninsula that was Ottawa's East Side.)

We took almost weekly walks to the Aqueduct, standing at its edge and gazing across the Fox River. But we never dared to cross it. Big sections of the wooden tow path, where the mules had walked pulling barges, were rotten. We knew it was off limits by the barrier and signs before us. The waterway portion of the Aqueduct was rusting metal, and Dad kept warning us we could fall through.

"You don't want to fall in the Fox River," he said. "It's full of sewer effluent from Chicago. Ever since they reversed the flow of the Chicago River, it's been getting worse."

We knew that, of course. You could smell it if you went down to the riverbank. My brother Robert couldn't resist fishing, though. He never caught anything except carp and bullhead, and we never cleaned or ate them. We knew better. There were probably some daring kids who crossed that aqueduct, but I never knew any of them personally.

Ironically, it was while we lived in the barely-rolling, hyper-cultivated cornfields of Illinois that Dad turned into a rock-hound. Maybe, like me, he was missing the rolling hills and piney woods of East Texas. Anyway, he started taking all three of us kids trekking through gravel pits and along streambeds, where the cornfields ended in little remnants of nature.

After two or three hours, we'd come trooping home with our rocky treasures, washing them in the kitchen sink. When I thought about it later, I was surprised Mom didn't object. She probably slipped in and scrubbed it well with cleanser after we'd left. Maybe it helped that Dad bought a diamond saw and grinding wheel, to make jewelry for her from some of the semi-precious stones he found.

The part I liked best about this rock-hound stage of our lives was the vacations to the mountains. Before Daniel was six, we didn't go on any vacations. Once he was school-aged, Mom seemed ready to try longer trips than just to Houston, where

Dad's family lived. We actually got to stay in motels. People called then Tourist Courts in those days.

We got to see all kinds of geologic wonders—the Great Salt Lake, the Colorado Rockies, Yellowstone Park with its geysers and waterfalls, the Grand Tetons, Glacier National Park, Crater Lake, Mount Rainier, and other volcanic peaks of the Cascades.

This was like heaven. On every trip, we'd stop at each rock shop we passed, and my rock collection kept growing. I still have a lot of those specimens.

There are special memories of my mother, too, though Mom was more distant than Dad. One of the main things that comes to mind is how she made almost all my clothes. She was a really fine seamstress, but I couldn't seem to sew a straight line to save my life.

Back in my earliest years, there were snapshot-like memories of Mom reading to me and helping me recite favorite poems. I can still say *A Visit from Saint Nicholas* from memory. Mom must have spent a lot of time helping me learn that one. Other shorter favorites were by Robert Louis Stevenson and other poets in *The Golden Book of Poetry*. This was a book I held onto through the years, and when my children were young, I read special favorites to them.

On nice days, Mom would walk me to the park that was near our rental house in El Dorado. Dad probably had our only car at work. In my memory I can see a lot of green trees and grass there. I liked the swings best but was afraid of the slide because it seemed so high. At my fifth birthday party, which was held in this park, I finally got up the courage to go down it.

Years later, I remember playing on the slide at the elementary school in Illinois with my brothers. We'd pretend it was the conning tower of a submarine, and when 'firing' torpedoes, we slid down, shouting, "Dive! Dive!"

This was probably after watching the movie *Run Silent, Run Deep.* In seventh grade I was totally absorbed with reading every book in the library about World War II. Not sure how I got into that. Maybe it had to do with the upcoming 20th anniversary of D-Day in 1964.

Now I realize this interest showed what a tomboy I was throughout childhood. I usually preferred playing 'boys' games like cowboys and army, though I sometimes played with dolls, especially when a girlfriend was visiting. When I was seven, I asked for a toy doctor kit for Christmas, and my parents got one. Later, a friend told me that I should have asked for a nurse kit because I was a girl. I'm thankful my parents honored my individuality, though. As I grew and asked for toy pistols, rifles, and cap-guns for Christmas, they got them for me, too.

When I was thirteen, I wanted more than anything to be a boy. The girly stuff of life didn't appeal to me. I wanted to wear slacks instead of dresses, to play baseball and football, to be friends with the boys, not to flirt with them. I didn't want to wear make-up or have to worry about my skinny figure. The boys called me "bean pole" and "giraffe." Sometimes I wondered if I really was a boy inside. Had there been some mistake?

When I moved on to Junior High the next year, I had the opportunity to meet many other students from all over our new town, population 20,000. There were ten classes of seventh graders, and nine of eighth. But I still didn't know how to make friends, and so I blew the opportunities I could've had. Instead I gravitated toward the other 'outcasts' in the school, since I could identify better with them.

The one good thing about junior high was getting to join the band. This was another activity Dad had enjoyed when he was growing up, and so we were encouraged to do it. I really wanted to play the saxophone like Dad did, but he was old fashioned in his thinking. The saxophone, in his generation, was associated with honky-tonks and jazz, and therefore not appropriate as a starting instrument in his mind. My brother Robert was told to start on the clarinet, and I decided my second choice was flute. I have a feeling I didn't want to directly compete with Robert (he wasn't 'Robby' anymore).

I guess my feelings had some basis, because Robert did get the "Improvement Award" in band his very first year, and he was only in fourth grade. Again, like his green Christmas stocking, he got what I wanted. Later, when he was in junior high, he got awards for art, too. I felt second best to him.

The band director, Mr. Kinnison, said my lips weren't right for a flute player, so he talked me into playing the oboe. I was already 2 or 3 years behind my peers, who had all started band in 4th or 5th grade. Mr. Kinnison did give me free private lessons, but the oboe is a difficult instrument to learn. I'm grateful to Mr. K, though. He always called me "Francoise" and said I played the "Hautbois", which is French for oboe. (It's pronounced "ah-bwa"—I didn't learn how it was spelled until I took French in college.) The oboe is a Medieval instrument in a modern world, so it's harder to play than the flute or clarinet, and the double reeds are a nightmare. Still, I stuck with it all through junior and senior high school, and by 12th grade, I was actually pretty good at it. My friend Diane, who

I really admired, said that if there had been an "Improvement Award" in high school, I would have gotten it. This made me feel good, because she was a whiz on the clarinet, and she won the highest award for music in our school her senior year, the "Arion Award."

As I look back, I know the hardest part of the move to Illinois was my age—just moving into adolescence. It's a difficult time for almost everyone, and mine was compounded by having to start all over again in a new and strange place, where I didn't feel I fit at all.

But not everything was bad. Joining band proved to be a place I could make some new friends, and I gradually began to find a niche, though it took a few years. I also think that playing the oboe was good for me in another way—I had to really work at it. In high school I practiced an hour every night. By this time, many of my school subjects (except math) were coming easily for me. But playing oboe taught me to persevere and not give up when the going was tough. That probably flowed into my personal/social life eventually. In Ottawa High School Band, I began to grow musically, and my fondness for Mr. Makeever, the band director, helped me work even harder. He became a kind of 'father figure' for me. He, like Dad, was demanding and exacting in his expectations, but he also showed his approval a little more.

Ironically, as my parents gradually stopped going to church over the first three years we were in Illinois, I began wanting to learn more about God. I'm not sure how it got started, but every Christmas Eve, I'd get the family to gather around the tree, and I'd read the Christmas story from the Bible. At certain key places, I'd have them sing an appropriate carol with me. Gradually things got added to this little pageant, like Santa Claus (after all, we still had to keep up the 'story' for 6-year-old Daniel). Many years later, when I was planning and presenting Christmas programs at church and in the school where I worked, I remember how I'd gotten my start in my parents' living room, directing my brothers.

At the end of our little program, we'd sing "Here We Come a-Wassailing" and Dad would make his extra-rich eggnog. He and Mom would have bourbon in theirs, but we liked it better with just whipped cream. Dad was a really good cook. He'd make the Sunday pot roast and the Thanksgiving turkey and dressing. Some of my favorites were his candy, pecan pralines and divinity.

When I think of Illinois Christmases, I picture the living room of the house we bought when I was going into eighth grade. It had a fireplace, a great novelty for us. We usually only lit a fire on Christmas. Dad always made us wait until he'd started a fire on Christmas morning. Then he'd put the Firestone Christmas Album on the stereo. (We finally got this when I was 12, I think). Once we heard the music, we'd know it was okay to come downstairs to see the tree all lit up and our filled stockings hanging from the mantle. I hope my children will have some precious memories like this when they get to be my age.

One of the most important events of my life happened because we moved to Illinois. The first summer we were there, the mother of a girl I'd met in sixth grade asked my mother if I could go to summer camp with Nan. Nan and I weren't what you'd call best friends, but I think our parents had met at the Elks Club. Anyway, I was really surprised when my parents said I could go. This camp, Honey Rock, was in northern Wisconsin and run by Wheaton College. I had a lot of fun doing things for the first time, like swimming in a lake, paddling a canoe, shooting a bow and arrow, and jumping on a trampoline.

But the most important part was I learned that Jesus wanted a personal relationship with me, and all I had to do was ask Him into my heart. I didn't have to keep trying to be good enough and earn my way to Heaven. When I heard this at a chapel service near the end of the two-week camp, something inside me said, "This is what you've been looking for. This is what you need." And so, I stood up at the invitation and asked Jesus to be my Savior. This was only the first step on a long journey, but I was on the right track at last. I began to try to read my Bible every day, even though I didn't always understand it. It helped that my cabin counselor followed up and sent me a devotional book that fall.

Another thing I started when we moved was writing. I'd written a couple of poems and short stories in elementary school in Arkansas. My first short story was called "The Adventures of the Mouse on the Mayflower." Dad continued to encourage my interest in science by getting me a microscope. He showed me how to make slides of all kinds of things from onion skins to tiny insects and seeds—even my own red blood cells.

So now that I think about it, Dad did really give us some rich hobbies in those early years. He got us involved in things he loved. And I still think of him every time I pick up an interesting-looking rock.

Back to the writing. I began keeping journals in 7th grade. By 12th grade I was editor of our school newspaper, a job I really enjoyed. And I started to write stories about places I'd like to live, and people I'd like to meet or be. One of my first ones was about a girl who lived on a mountain in Montana. No, I hadn't been to Montana yet; it just seemed fascinating. Maybe I'd read a story or seen a TV show about it.

I read voraciously, too, but not many of the typical books early teen girls read. I knew about "Little House on the Prairie" but I don't think I read much of it until I was an adult. And I rarely jumped from one subject to another. First, I had to read every single book the library had on a subject I was interested in. In fact, I was totally engrossed—first it was weather, then geology, then (for some reason) World War II. Later, Dad got me interested in Thor Heyerdahl's "Kon Tiki", so then I had to read everything he'd written.

By 9th grade I was beginning to steep my mind in science fiction, like Isaac Asimov. That's when I first discovered C.S. Lewis, when I read "Out of the Silent Planet." It was an amazing spiritual experience! A girl friend also got me to read "The Hobbit" by J.R.R. Tolkien, and I thought it was an interesting little fantasy. But it wasn't until my freshman year of college that I discovered "The Chronicles of Narnia" and "The Lord of the Rings," and I fell totally in love with Tolkien and Lewis. (I was amazed to see in the back of one of their books that they were good friends.) Now the world of spiritual fantasy began to engulf me. But most of my writing at this time was poetry, about unrequited love—a first-hand experience in my life.

Anyway, high school flew by, and I began to make friends who are still a part of my life, like my 'sister' Gay Heffley (now Hanson). We met in 9th grade, and have been fast friends ever since. I know Gay and her consistent letter-writing are a big factor in our staying in touch. We also had a lot of the same tastes in reading, but not entirely. She finally got me interested in British mystery writers like Dorothy Sayers and Agatha Christie, but I didn't have the same luck getting her into Tolkien.

My freshman year in college, I was only a couple of hours from home, and from University of Illinois, where Gay was, so we got together often. After the first Earth Day in 1970, which was my senior year in high school, I was determined to save the environment. So after my freshman year, I transferred from Illinois Wesleyan to Colorado State University to study forestry. (I knew about CSU because our high school band tour had stopped there the summer of 1970.) This is also when I discovered "Dune" by Frank Herbert. The first attraction for me in this book was the ecology themes, but of course the sci-fi appealed to me, too.

My ecology interest was further deepened by a 10-day canoe trip in the Boundary Waters of northern Minnesota. The youth group I had joined at Trinity Lutheran Church in Ottawa paid for any of us who wanted to go, and there were five of us who went the summer of 1970, right after I graduated from high school. This was my first time ever in the 'wilds' and I loved the adventure. It set the stage for my future adventures in the Rockies, and probably had a lot to do with my desire to go west for college after my freshman year at Illinois Wesleyan. The fellowship and Bible studies at Wilderness Canoe Base were good for me, too.

It's interesting that 25+ years later our son would follow in some of my footsteps. He worked 5 summers as a camp counselor at a sister camp of Wilderness Canoe Base—Fortune Lake Lutheran Camp in Upper Michigan. In high school, he'd go with the Michigan Lions All-state Band to Scotland, staying in dorms that were within view of the B&B where *I* stayed during *my* semester abroad at University of Edinburgh—25 years before. And later still, he'd work at Flathead Lutheran Bible Camp, a sister to Sky Ranch in Colorado, which was barely a stone's throw from CSU's forestry camp at Pingree Park, where his future father got his first glimpse of me. The intertwining of lives like this is amazing, and some would say, 'stranger than fiction.'

So, as I continued through college, science fiction, religion, and ecology began to simmer away in my brain. Sometimes one would pop out of the mix, and then another, and other times they'd just be there bubbling away. I kept writing poetry, journals, and a few short stories. Some of these have worked their way into my *Peaks at the Edge of the World Saga* in one way or another. It's only logical that peaks should play such an important part in my life—after all, I've always been fascinated by mountains. It seemed most of my best writing was done while I was living in the shadow of mountains—in Colorado, Idaho, and Montana.

Robert P. Feser (center front) and his children- (L to R) Frances, Daniel, and Robert (c. 2003). My brothers, who were my first 'pageant actors.'

***

I realize now as I'm writing this that I'm leaving out a lot of the negative and painful parts of my adolescence. But I guess I'd better at least try to give a balanced account here.

As I've hinted, I had trouble making friends all through my teenage years. I thought about things my peers considered 'kooky'—like my fascination with World War II. Given a choice, I'd rather spend time having intellectual conversations with my teachers than hanging about talking with teenage girls about boys. I have a feeling my parents had been like this, too, but they always avoided talking about their youth. Now I think I know why.

Sometimes I liked to pretend I was a boy instead of a girl. Many of my interests were rather boyish, anyway. I was what was called a Tomboy. In 6th grade I identified with the boy in the Black Stallion books by Walter Farley—I read them all, too. I liked to dress in slacks and even my brother's shirts and ties. This was in a time when girls were expected to wear skirts all the time. If I were living in this day and age, when homosexuality is not only accepted but even encouraged, it's a possibility that I would have been convinced I was gay, too.

Though maybe not. After all, I was much more interested in reading all the Nancy Drew books, instead of the Hardy Boys. And I *was* interested in boys as the opposite sex. I had crushes on a few in high school, but they never asked me out. Back in those days, girls had to wait for the guys to ask them. I went on one blind date in high school, and that was the extent of my dating. The only dances I went to were the open ones where people just came and danced with their friends, and my friends were all girls.

College got a little better, and I dated a few guys, but nothing ever seemed to click. Most of them were just one-time things. There was a short-lived summer romance with Pat C. He was a high school friend of my first roommate at CSU, from Evergreen, Colorado. I was attracted to him because he was tall, handsome, musical, and he'd read "Lord of the Rings"—I still have trouble finding people who have read all of Tolkien's books. Pat seemed to like me, too, and we spent a lot of weekends together because my roommate Mary either went home to Evergreen, or he came to see us.

I didn't find out, until after he'd jilted me at the end of the summer, that he was on the rebound from a break-up with his high school sweetheart. At the end of that summer, he decided to hitch-hike around Europe, which was a popular thing back in the early 70's. I got a few postcards from him, but then it all just died. When he got back from Europe, and I saw him about a year later, I didn't even want to speak to him. He was sitting in the lounge room of my dormitory, and I just noted his now-longer hair, nodded, and said "Hi, Pat." That's all. And I have rarely even thought of him since. I have no idea if he went to college or became a ski bum—his main interests were skiing and rock climbing. One thing I did learn from him is that the feelings of first love only happen once.

There were a few other boyfriends after Pat, and I let myself get too involved physically with some of them. Now I wonder if I was subconsciously trying to get back at Pat—somehow 'showing him' that I could be valued by other guys besides him. The problem was most of them didn't really value me, just my body. I had to learn some hard lessons from these mistakes.

Fortunately, it was about this time that I got the opportunity to study for a semester abroad at the University of

Edinburgh, in Scotland. This is still one of the most amazing experiences of my life.

***

While I was in Scotland, I met two Christian girls who were also participating in the Outdoor Education program I was part of. Cate and Nikki were the ones who hitch-hiked around Europe with me on the 3-week Spring Break we got at University of Edinburgh. Cate wanted to go to L'Abri in Switzerland, so we managed to get there. I'd never heard of the Schaeffers and their ministry to wandering youth, but I was definitely one of those wanderers at this time in my life. I really had strayed from my faith.

Dr. and Mrs. Schaeffer weren't at L'Abri when we were there, but I still heard some speakers who really helped me begin to get back on the right spiritual track. And Cate and Nikki were great witnesses to me, also. Nikki and I are still in touch at Christmas, but I've lost track of Cate. I took a lot of pictures of the countries we visited, and the whole experience of being in Europe was amazing. There was so much history and depth to their culture. What they called 'New' in Europe was older than the whole United States.

Scotland was my favorite place, but I also liked what I saw of England, Ireland, Holland, West Germany, France, and Switzerland. I think we crossed a bit of Austria, but it was at night on a train. We didn't always hitch-hike, but a lot. The world was a much safer place back in 1973.

I carried a full-sized *Living Bible* with me on all those trips. I'd learned about the *Living Bible Paraphrase* at Honey Rock Camp back in junior high. I wasn't worried about the weight, and felt it was an important part of my belongings, all of which fit into a backpack. (Pat had given me that backpack, ironically.) The notes I made in that Bible during 1973 still mean a lot to me.

The summer after we got home from Scotland, I made it to Long Beach, California to visit Nikki. This was the first leg of my trip up to the Society of American Foresters Convention in Portland, Oregon—which would turn out to be another big event in my life, but I'll go into that later. I've often wondered what happened to Cate. She was very charismatic in her faith, and I hope it stayed with her as the inevitable storms of life must have come. Her older sister was married to the Olympic runner Jim Ryun, who had broken the 4-minute mile a year or so before. She insisted we go to see the site of the Munich Olympics, even though that was where Jim had lost to a Kenyan runner in the Olympic mile. I'm ashamed to say that I didn't actually see the Olympic Village where the Israeli athletes were killed by Palestinian terrorists in 1972. (Yes, terrorists have been around longer than most of us realize.)

I was in the backseat of the rental car in the parking lot because I'd drunk too much beer at the Hofbrau House. But that was when I finally learned my lesson to keep away from drinking so much.

Okay, back to the story about Portland. Actually, it goes much farther back. The first summer I was enrolled in CSU (1971 - the summer of Pat), a friend and I in the dorm were just wondering what to do on a Friday night, when these two guys wandered in. They said they'd hitch-hiked down from Pingree Park, CSU's forestry camp up in the Colorado mountains. They wanted to explore Ft. Collins, they said. So, Barb and I went with them. We walked downtown to a 3.2 bar, and had a few beers (legal for 18 and over). Then we walked back to the dorm and just talked in the parking lot. Barb was with the guy named Joe, and I talked mostly to the shorter one, Pierre.

The rest of this story, I found out almost 3 years later. Joe had been work partners that summer with Paul Erler, and kept telling Paul about the 'really nice girls' he and Pierre had met in Ft. Collins. Pierre came to see me a couple of times the following fall, and we even wrote a few letters over the next couple of years. I think he'd joined the Air Force. Anyway, he faded from my life.

The following summer, 1972, I was enrolled in CSU's forestry camp for five weeks of classes. This was required for all students in the College of Forestry. I loved the idea of classes outdoors in the mountains, and had a great time. There were about 100 guys there and only 10 girls. The U.S. Forest Service Timber Inventory Crew (which Paul worked with for several summers) also had their training the first week of our session. Apparently, as I learned later, Joe remembered me and pointed me out to Paul that year. I do remember seeing Joe and saying hello to him, but I don't remember meeting Paul.

So, another year went by, I went to Scotland, came back in May 1973, worked for Youth Conservation Corps, a government program for getting high school students working in the outdoors. I was a counselor of the camp that lived in a dormitory on CSU's campus. After that, I went to Pioneer Girls Camp in Ward, Colorado, to be their Nature Guide. From there I caught a ride with a counselor who was from southern California. That's when I visited Nikki.

For some reason I'd signed up to be a student representative at the SAF convention, so I flew standby up to Portland for the Convention in early September. Classes didn't start at CSU until mid-September back then because they were on quarters instead of semesters. I met two people at that convention who had a huge impact on my life. The first was Dr. Denny Lynch, a forestry professor from CSU who gave a speech at the convention. I introduced myself to him as also being from CSU and noticed he had a fish-shaped pin on his tie. I knew that was a Christian symbol and told him I liked it. He invited me to look him up when I got back to campus. I didn't know it then, but Denny felt called to witness and minister to students, and I was one of the people he discipled through his Christian Foresters' Fellowship (CFF).

The other person I met was Paul Erler. He and another forestry friend, Gene, had come to the convention in hopes of making connections for forestry jobs, which were very hard to get back then. Paul came up to me and introduced himself and said what some would call a line: "I think I've seen you somewhere before." But he truly had—we figured out he'd seen me the previous summer at Pingree Park, but that was about all that happened then. He asked if I wanted to drive back to Ft. Collins with him and Gene, but I declined. Not because I didn't want to, but I already had a plane ticket and I had a job and classes to get back for by a certain date.

So, it wasn't until the following February that Paul and I really got acquainted. The circumstances leading up to it are worth mentioning. First of all, my best friend Kris Anderson was responsible (though I didn't know it then) for making sure I came to the Forestry Banquet for CSU's annual event, Foresters' Days. It seems I was to get an award and I wasn't to know about it beforehand, but she'd been ordered to be sure I was there. So she convinced me to sign up for the banquet, but I told her I really would like to be going with a date. She said, "I'm going to pray that you'll find a Christian guy to go with." I just shrugged. The odds of that seemed pretty slim.

Another thing that had just happened, was CFF had gone on a cross-country ski weekend up in the Roosevelt National Forest, and slept over at Red Feather Lakes Ranger Station. But I'd missed it because I had a bad cold. I really wanted to learn to cross-country ski, so I was very disappointed.

Early in February 1974, I went to CFF's Thursday morning breakfast at the Student Union, and there at the table across from me was a familiar face. He said, "Do you remember me? We met in Portland."

I nodded, and it felt like the Lord was tapping me on the shoulder and whispering, "There's the one I've planned for you, Frances." I know this sounds all mushy and romantic, but this is how it really happened.

From that day on, Paul and I started dating, and it wasn't long before we were talking marriage. But a lot of things had needed to happen from 1971 to 1974 before I was ready for this relationship. The Lord really does move in mysterious ways.

And yes, as he will tell you, I was the one who asked Paul on the first date. I just knew, because of what the Lord had 'told' me that this was right, and I didn't want to mess it up. So, when he mentioned cross-country skiing, I asked him to take me and teach me how, the next weekend. This was not the way things were done back in the 70's! Guys were supposed to be the ones to ask girls on dates. And I also gave him my phone number first—another aggressive move for a girl to make. Paul has told me he was surprised at this, but it made him feel less shy about calling me and asking me out for coffee the next week.

So that's how the Lord brought Paul and me together through Christian Forester's Fellowship, Denny Lynch, and Kris Anderson.

CHAPTER 4

Paul

Paul and I dated steadily for the next year or so. We'd get together on Friday evening to have dinner. Sometimes we'd eat out in Ft. Collins, where there were many choices of restaurants or fast-food places. We both had to be thrifty because I was a student, and he was only seasonally employed with the Forest Service. Actually, Paul was a good cook, and yes—I admit it was one of the things that attracted me to him. I think it was because my dad liked to cook, and they say girls tend to be attracted to men like their fathers.

Paul was also like Dad in his German descent. When I met his family at our first Christmas, eight months later, I felt at home with them right away. We were engaged by then. (Paul proposed to me at Midnight on Christmas Eve, 1974.) The Erler family was huge compared to what I was used to. My dad was an only child and didn't stay in much contact with his other relatives. Mom had one sister, Bonnie, that we visited only occasionally. I remember only three other short visits from members of her family. Once her Grandmother Harrison came to our house in Arkansas—she was from Arkansas, too, but this was the only time we ever saw her. There was also a visit from one of Mom's uncles, and another time an aunt, but again it was just the one time.

So, being initiated into a large and close family like Paul's was a bit overwhelming, but also exciting. Now I would have four sets of sisters-and-brothers-in-law, plus 13 nieces and nephews. His parents were great, too, especially his mom. When he first introduced me to her, she grabbed me into a big hug. This was something that was rare with the Fesers. Apparently, Esther Erler wasn't one of those unemotional Germans. And she told me I was an answer to her prayers for a Christian girl for her youngest son. Well, as I've already mentioned, Paul was an answer to prayers by Kris and me. God does work in mysterious ways sometimes.

Back to the dating phase. I was in my last three quarters of college when Paul and I dated, and I was working hard to get finished only one quarter late—I'd transferred schools and changed my major three times. Anyway, after spending Friday evening, most of Saturday and Sunday church together, we parted after Sunday lunch so I could concentrate on homework. And since there weren't things like cell phones, personal computers, email, or texting back then (sounds amazing, doesn't it?) we didn't have much contact until the next Friday rolled around.

So, I completed winter and spring quarters of 1974, and Denny Lynch helped me find a YCC job in Colorado Springs, where I was going to be student teaching in the fall. He also found a couple in a pastor-friend's church who had a guestroom they were willing to let me live in. So, there I was living with Colonel Jackson and his family of six, not far from the U.S. Air Force Academy, where he worked.

The summer of YCC was similar to the one before, except that this wasn't a residential camp, so I had my evenings free. I remember doing a lot of backpacking in the southern Colorado Rockies, and since Pioneers Girls Camp had also relocated to this area, I was able to work with them at the end of the summer, again as a nature guide. Paul and I got together about every other weekend. He was working out of the Vail area in central Colorado most of that summer. He had the car, so he was the one who drove over to see me.

He was really proud of that little car, a 1971 Opel Rallye Sport, yellow with black trim, with a stick shift. He'd bought it new in Indiana, right after he graduated from Purdue. So, this makes it all the more amazing that he offered to loan me Samantha—that was the car's name—while I was student teaching. I had managed to get from Jackson's house to my summer job by riding my 10-speed bicycle or getting rides from campers who lived nearby. But Coronado High School, where I was to student-teach biology and ecology, was too far for bicycle commuting, especially when the summer weather ended. I'd moved from the Jackson's to Sally Meadows' house, all the way on the south side of town and even farther from the high school. Sally had been the project/education coordinator for our YCC camp that summer, and she and I had hit it off as friends. Again, I could see the Lord working here, because when the trials and tribulations of student teaching mounted, it was good to have Sally to talk to.

I'd been contemplating buying a used car when Paul suggested I use Samantha. Fortunately, I'd learned to drive a stick-shift by this time. His intentions for marriage showed when he said it would be better to start out with one car that we owned, rather than being saddled with my car payment. His ever-present practicality came through because he said he wouldn't need the car when his Forest Service job moved out of the woods and into town for the fall. And so, I drove Samantha across Colorado Springs from Sally's neighborhood up to the northwest end of town where Coronado High School was located. This also meant I was the one who drove over to the Aspen/Glenwood Springs area to see Paul about twice a month. I got to know those mountain passes pretty well.

Student teaching was a rough experience for me. For one thing I didn't have one supervising teacher to mentor me; I had three. And each of them seemed to think the others would take on the job. The one I remember the best was Mr. Powell, who also got me involved in helping with a Young Life Group—this was a Christian outreach for high school students, held in the evening once a week. This was the first place I began to play guitar to lead singing by myself, rather than following along with another more experienced guitar player.

Coronado was a largely Hispanic school, and these were racially turbulent times, especially for Hispanics in Colorado and other Southwestern states. (That still hasn't changed much in 50 years, has it?) Some of my classes were people just filling a credit—seniors who didn't really care about their grades or the subject. One biology class I had was 38 sophomores spread out across a huge laboratory, where it was impossible to see what was going on in the back of the room. One day there was a girl in the back who was definitely high on something.

The only class I really enjoyed teaching was the senior advanced biology class, one of Mr. Powell's classes. They were using the same textbook I'd had in high school advanced biology and in my first college biology class, too. The students were interested in actually learning something, so that helped a lot. I felt like I accomplished something with that class. Fortunately, this was the class my university supervisor came to observe.

Again, some of the bad things are a blur, and I still wasn't sure if classroom teaching was for me by the time my semester was completed. I even remember talking to Dad about it once on the phone from Sally's. I was afraid he'd be disappointed in me, but he seemed to understand that I was still searching. What I really wanted to teach was outdoor education. And believe it or not, our son Jon also leans this way.

Paul and I drove Samantha back from Colorado to the greater Chicago area for Christmas 1974, our first Christmas. This was when we met each other's families, as I've described before. Right after we got there, he went on a trip he'd planned to visit his sister, Doris, and her family in Hong Kong. They'd been teaching there at Hong Kong International School for only two years, and the trip had already been planned before Paul and I started dating.

CHAPTER 5
Marriage

Between Thanksgiving and Christmas that year, I had the strange situation of beginning to plan a wedding to a man I wasn't officially engaged to yet. I talked to Pastor Swenson, at the church I'd attended in high school, about marrying us, and I got information on where to get flowers and a cake. Mom and I picked out a pattern for my dress and for my best friend Gay's brides' maid dress. Fortunately, we kept the wedding simple—just two attendants (Paul's older brother John was asked to be Best Man). A simple church wedding. My brother Dan was the photographer and provided the rock band that played in our basement—the reception was just punch, coffee and cake at my parents' house—and that was almost more than my mother could handle, even as simple as it was, but I didn't realize this until much later.

But I'm getting ahead of myself here. Paul was still in Hong Kong, and when he got back, we picked him up at O'Hare Airport on Dec. 21. He had gotten a little cross necklace with a small diamond in the center while he was in Hong Kong. In fact, it was specially made for him by a jeweler there. He officially proposed and gave it to me on Christmas Eve, 1974. It was a quiet, but touching moment in my parents' living room after the Midnight service at Trinity Lutheran, Ottawa, Illinois. Everyone else in the house was asleep.

We went back to Ft. Collins, Colorado at the end of Christmas vacation so Paul could keep looking for work. He'd been collecting unemployment benefits since November when his job and my student-teaching both ended. I remember Dad coming to me one evening in my room to talk about Paul. "I think he's a fine young man," he said, "But the employment situation bothers me." I assured Dad that Paul and I would both find jobs for the summer in Colorado, and hopefully also some to carry into the fall.

We didn't have a lot of luck, though from January to March. I did a bit of clerical work for the Colorado State Forest Service, as I recall. Paul kept sending applications to lots of state and federal forestry agencies, but none came up with offers. We each were living in separate apartments at this time, but fortunately the rents were low. Co-habitation was still rare then, and in Paul's family especially, not acceptable. I felt the same.

Our wedding was planned for April 5, 1975, and when it was time to drive back to Ottawa, there came a huge blizzard that closed Interstate 80 across Nebraska. We had no choice but to take the long way around on I-70—down to Denver, across Kansas and Missouri, then up I-55 from St. Louis to the Chicago area. We made it, though, and had a week before the wedding to get all the last-minute things done, like applying for a marriage license.

As I look back now, I see we were quite naïve in some ways, but also very practical. Weddings weren't the big productions back then that they are now, so we were fortunate. Besides, we couldn't afford all that extra stuff. There were no bachelor or bachelorette parties, and no limo, either. Paul's brother John's nice Oldsmobile served as our transportation the four blocks from the church to my parents' house for the reception. But we didn't mind at all. I think we enjoyed the homey nature of our wedding. Our wedding gifts to each other were very practical, too. Paul got me cross-country ski boots, and I got him a trailer hitch so we could pull a trailer when we moved to wherever a job presented itself.

Our honeymoon was six days long. The first two nights we stayed in Holiday Inns, but the rest of the trip we camped in Paul's little blue backpack tent. We went to Kentucky to The Land Between the Lakes. It was early spring and most of the trees were barely beginning to bud, but at least we didn't get one of those April blizzards that sometimes occur in the Ohio Valley. Oh, I must mention that we stopped by Paul's alma mater, Purdue, on our way back from Kentucky. He's a faithful Purdue fan, and I still like to tease him that he took me there on our honeymoon. Then we went back to my folks', opened the presents, loaded them up and drove Samantha back to Colorado.

I moved into the basement apartment Paul had been renting from an elderly lady named Marie. It was furnished, fortunately, because the only furniture we had was a card table and four chairs, a wedding present from Paul's siblings. This was the place where we entertained our first dinner guests— Kris Anderson and Nancy Olson, my closest friends who had driven all the way out to the wedding in Kris's little VW Beetle. With them, they brought the gift of a Guest Book, which we're still using now, 47+ years later. If that sounds like we haven't had many guests, that's not it. It has lots of pages, and we didn't have people sign twice, unless we'd moved to a new place. So, it contains the visitors of two apartments in Ft. Collins, two houses in Ashton, ID, the house in Rexford, MT, the house in

Tawas City, MI, and now the house in Kalispell, MT. That's seven homes so far in 47 years.

Paul and I were living frugally that first year of marriage. From April through June, we tried to figure out work and living arrangements. For a while it looked like we'd be relocating to western Colorado, Paul to resume his timber inventory job, and me to be a YCC counselor at yet another camp. But then Denny Lynch (and the Lord) came through again. He connected Paul with a job in the Colorado State Forest Service right there in Ft. Collins. It was a wildfire hazard mapping project. (Little did we know our firstborn would become a geographer and mapping expert, too.) Paul got the job because he'd been on the unemployment rolls for several months—another interesting 'coincidence'.

Then Denny clued me in on a science teaching job at Heritage Christian School there in Ft. Collins. His two children attended there, and I guess he gave me a good recommendation because I became the middle school and high school science teacher. Seven different classes to prepare for was a big load for a first-year teacher, but the Lord helped me through. There were many emotional ups and downs in that first year of teaching and some 'political' issues within the school that affected me, though they weren't my fault. At the end of the school year I didn't sign up for the next fall. But, as it turned out, I wouldn't have been able to stay anyway, because Paul was finally picked up off a Federal Job Roster to work as a Forestry Technician on the Targhee National Forest in southeast Idaho.

First, I'd better mention that we'd finally found a nicer apartment than Marie's basement. It was unfurnished, so we began to add a little furniture—a bedroom set and a dining table we still have, a second-hand desk I still use, and a couch.

We had been trying to get into the apartments on Peterson Street, that Paul had lived in when I was dating him, but there never seemed to be an opening. Then one day, we were riding by on our bikes and saw a "For Rent" sign. We went up to talk to the manager right away, and because Paul knew some people who lived there, we had good references and we got the place we'd wanted for several months. God's timing is always right. This was just before I started teaching school that fall of 1975.

Ed, one of the friends at Peterson Street that Paul knew, was going to Europe for a vacation shortly after we moved in, so we offered to watch his cat, Max. When Ed got back, Max had gotten so used to coming to our side of the building that he kept doing it. Ed asked if we'd just like to adopt him, and we said we could if he was sure he wanted to give up his pet. Apparently, he had his reasons, and so Max became our cat, and a member of our family for the next 15 years.

Max moved with us to Ashton, Idaho. This was a farming town of about 1000 people in the Mormon country and potato fields of southeast Idaho. We were in a very large valley but could see the west slope of the Teton Mountains in the distance. Paul's job was actually 30 miles up the road in Island Park, which was just over the state line from West Yellowstone, Montana. It was also snow country. Down in Ashton the snow would pile up so deep over the winter that you could drive a snowmobile across a 4-foot-high chain-link fence without even grazing it. The snow didn't all melt until April. But up in Island Park, it reached the eaves of the roofs and didn't all melt until June. I was glad we lived in Ashton! And it also worked that I got a job with the Ashton Ranger District. Back then, the Forest Service frowned on couples working in the same office.

Before I got my Forest Service job, I got involved in the Lutheran Church there. We were really lucky that there had been many German settlers there among the Mormons because this was the only Lutheran church for 60 miles. Another of those God things. I became a Sunday School teacher and helped with an after-school program, too. Paul and I joined the choir. I'd convinced him to join the choir with me back in our Lutheran church in Ft. Collins. It was the first time he'd sung in a group since he was in Gary Lutheran School through 8th grade. He had more musical talent than he knew. He's quite a good tenor with a very good ear, even though he doesn't read music. It seems like almost everywhere we've moved, there's been a choir for us to join, and a fellow-forester for Paul to sing with. In Ashton there were three—Greg, Gene, and Phil, all on various districts of the Targhee. We're still in touch with these guys. In fact, Phil is our son Jon's godfather.

Anyway, I started work on the Ashton District as a tree-wrapper. This meant standing out in a cold tent with snow still on the ground, putting baby pine trees into burlap bags that had to be filled with vermiculite slurry. It was a messy, cold job. I was happy when I was promoted to cleaning toilets in the campgrounds. Not long after that, the District Receptionist job opened, and I applied. The idea of being indoors after the cold Idaho spring sounded appealing.

Oddly enough, this clerical job also brought some unique opportunities my way. Joyce, the District Clerk and my supervisor, knew I was interested in environmental education so she let me get involved in training and teaching opportunities. This was especially nice of her because it meant more work on her when I was out 'doing my thing'. This office was extra busy, too, because hundreds of people a week came for firewood permits. There had been a huge bark-beetle epidemic and thousands of dead lodgepole pine needed to be cleared away. Offering free firewood was one way the forest did this.

I really enjoyed my opportunities to go to elementary school classes (right across the road) and tell the students about Smoky Bear and all the uses of wood. I also brought in the concepts of cycles in nature, recycling, and ecology. In one talk, I mentioned the relationship between forest fires and wildlife, and one example I gave was a little bird in eastern Michigan called the Kirtland's Warbler. Little did I know then that someday I would be living and working in that very forest, the Huron National Forest, and teaching students *there* about the Kirtland's Warbler!

The bark beetle epidemic also gave me an opportunity to take over updating a publication called *Targhee Lodgepole, Tragedy or Opportunity?* I loved the writing and learned a bit about illustration and photography. Back then there were no digital cameras, and computers were rare. I still did all my work on a typewriter. At least it was electric. Speaking of writing, I also was doing some on my own, trying my hand at fiction prose writing. And I kept up with poetry, as I'd done before.

About 18 months after we moved to Ashton, Paul and I bought our first house for about $30,000. Now-a-days you can barely buy a car for that. It was a cute little 2-bedroom, one-bath place. But it was bigger and nicer than the old drafty cabin we'd been renting on the other side of town. I turned the extra bedroom into my writing space.

Also about this same time, Joyce suggested me for a special project in Salt Lake City, which was the Regional Office for the forests in southern Idaho, Nevada, and Utah—Region 4. Apparently, the Forest Service was doing a nationwide survey of all the roadless areas on national forests, to determine which could be developed and which should be kept as wilderness. This was the second time the agency had done this "Roadless Area Review and Evaluation" so it was dubbed RARE II. There had to be a public comment period, open to anyone in the nation who wanted to express their opinion about any particular parcel or area. No one had any idea how much mail they might get, but it had been decided to have a centrally-located coding center where all the input could be coded and put into a database for computer access. Computers were just beginning to be used in the government agencies by this time in 1978.

So, I was one of four people who were to be the Coding Team for Region 4. Because she knew me personally, Joyce could tell I had the drive and intelligence to do this job—that I was no ordinary clerical worker. I was lucky—but I also know, it was just another one of the mysterious ways God works.

It was at this coding center that I met Steve Harper, who was the director of the whole operation. He'd been selected, I think, because he was a darned good manager of both people and resources. Also, he was Deputy-Forest Supervisor of the forest based there in Salt Lake, the Wasatch. And besides that, there was an old Federal Building right there in downtown Salt Lake that was being under-utilized (because it lacked handicapped access, another new thing in the late 70's).

So there we all were, people from all over the ten regions of the U.S. Forest Service, ready to read input letters and codify them according to the directions in our coding manual. And I seemed to be in charge of the Region 4 team. Even though I was only a clerk-typist, I had a full-time job, so I outranked the others on our team. It turned out Region 4 had not really taken this as seriously as other regions, which had sent more high-ranking officials for their coding teams.

It didn't faze me, though. I knew what was expected of me, felt more than capable of doing it, and so I did. When the mail started coming in by the thousands, rather than the hundreds of letters expected, we just worked all the harder. In fact, Region 4 got our input finished first, so we also got to help some other regions with theirs.

Steve Harper noticed me, which I found surprising. After all, he was a GS-13 Deputy Forest Supervisor. I was a lowly GS-3 Clerk-typist. But he seemed to think I had a lot on the ball, and it was a big boost to my confidence. By the end of this RARE II job, which took the better part of five months, I had been back and forth from Ashton to Salt Lake on two-week details several times. Each time I got back Steve seemed happy to see me. Finally at the end, as we were finishing up the final reports on the outcomes of all this public input, I ended up being the chief writer of the Region 4 Results. Normally a Forest Public Information Officer (PIO) would have this type of job. And that was a job I would have dearly loved to have. Unfortunately, however, I'd been passed over for just such a job on the Targhee, despite all my experience on these special projects. This had been a bitter pill.

Still I worked diligently on the report, even though the Forest Service was getting a bargain by having to pay me less than half the wage a PIO would get. Steve went out of his way to let me know he recognized and appreciated my talents, and often assured me that my time would come to get the job I really deserved. A career in the Forest Service wasn't to be, however. Doors kept closing that I hoped would open.

CHAPTER 6
Speaking of Seeds

Early on in our marriage I loved to cook and experiment with new recipes. I had quite a collection of cookbooks and recipe cards. In our apartment in Ft. Collins, a teacher I worked with offered a small plot in her yard for us to plant a garden. I think we raised some carrots, lettuce and radishes. I cooked my first Thanksgiving turkey in 1975, feeling a great sense of accomplishment. It was done in our tiny apartment kitchen which was about the size of a closet.

After a year, we moved to Ashton, Idaho so Paul could finally get a job with the Forest Service. Here we had a huge garden at our little rental house. We didn't know, because it was covered with asbestos shingles, that it was a log cabin. We got to use one bedroom, but the only other one was full of the owner's stuff. We were young, and we didn't mind, except on really cold mornings (like seventeen below zero) with no central heat. After one winter of having to buy No. 1 Fuel Oil (the expensive one) we got a wood stove.

The garden was the best part of that place. We raised tomatoes, lettuce, squash, carrots, peas, beans, potatoes (Idaho, of course), and believe it or not we even got a couple of soccer-ball sized watermelons to ripen. The neighbors couldn't believe it. We later found out the weather that first year in Ashton was unusually warm.

After about a year and a half, we found a little two-bedroom house for sale on the other side of town. We were comfortable since we didn't have much furniture, and the garden was fair. But typical Ashton weather returned. Paul had to shovel snow off our roof, and it was piled so high we could barely see out our front window. As the snow continued to fall and settle, it packed to over four feet on the level.

When the Targhee Forest Supervisor decided it was time for the GS-9 foresters to move on for more experience, no one could argue. You had to find an acceptable place to go, or he'd send you to the most remote place in the region. Luckily, Paul heard from a former co-worker about some openings on the Kootenai National Forest in far northwest Montana. They were about as isolated as Ashton, but not as bad as places like Powell and Avery, Idaho, which were in the middle of nowhere.

So far, we'd lived 60 miles north of Denver and sixty miles north of Idaho Falls, so 60 miles north of Kalispell, Montana couldn't be any worse could it? We took the job in Eureka, Montana. When we went on a house-hunting trip, we cried at first. The choices seemed to be trailers or shacks. Some of the houses had bowed-in foundations, some had bowed-out walls. But as last we found one in Rexford, a tiny town of maybe 100 people, about six miles away. It had been relocated when Libby Dam was built in the early 70s. Some of the houses had been moved, some were newbuilt (relatively). And we were even able to negotiate with the owner for a contract of sale at 10% interest. They had been forced to move by the closure of a logging camp in Rexford and really needed to sell.

Now 10% interest on a mortgage may sound way too high right now, but back then interest rates were around 15%+. Inflation was terrible.

We lived in that house for nearly ten years. It was perfect for raising our children, since it was on a cul de sac.

We moved in just before Christmas 1979. Jon was born, Nov. 4, 1980, the day Reagan was elected president. With a nice view of the Rockies in Canada, which was about 5 miles away as the crow flies, and a huge garden, we had plenty to do. The only problem was the hospital was 60 miles away, but at my last appointment, the doctor advised staying in town (Whitefish). Luckily, we did because Jon was born at 10:12 that evening.

As Jon grew through infancy and toddlerhood, I kept occupied with Christian Women's Club and selling Tupperware. And lots of canning and freezing of garden produce. Some we grew ourselves, some we bought, and some we picked up in the mountains—the famous Rocky Mountain Huckleberries. I even learned to make decent jam from the more prolific Serviceberries, also called June Berries. Old timers teased me for making jam out of "Junk Berries." But we liked it, just had to do all the work to strain the seeds out.

The ten years in Rexford were very good. I even earned a couple of ribbons for my jam at the Lincoln County Fair in Eureka.

Emilie was born August 25, 1983. This time my labor was long enough to make it to the hospital. She arrived at 11:50 p.m. Later her Dad and others teased her that if we'd been living in Eastern Time then, she would have been born on Aug. 26. Later, when we moved to Michigan (Eastern Time) she had a girlfriend who was born before she was, around 10:15 p.m. Mountain Time, but on August 26 in Eastern Time. So her birthdate was after Emilie's, even though in actuality she was older.

Both our children spent their early years in Rexford, and it was a good place to be a child. It was a small town with a lot of children, and they could roam and wander some, without my having to worry about them every minute. In the summer, it wasn't a long walk to Rexford Beach on a reservoir called Lake Koocanusa. We even bought a boat so we could travel up and down this 70-mile long lake. The fishing for Kokanee Salmon was good then, too.

Jon started school just before he turned six. The tiny Rexford School had closed the year before, so he had to ride the school bus to Eureka. At first that was hard for him, being the youngest student, but in a week or so things got better.

When I asked why, he said, "Now Ricky sits with me. He doesn't let the kids bother me anymore."

Ricky was a neighbor boy about ten years old. We'd been taking him and his little sister to Sunday School for several months by this time. It wasn't always easy having two extra lively children to take to church, but God used this little incident to show me how being a good witness for Him pays off, often in unexpected ways.

Emilie lived in Rexford for almost six years, but her memories aren't as distinct as Jon's, because she was younger. She says some of her fondest ones are of times I was at Christian Women's Club and she was at the babysitter's house. This woman didn't have a TV, so the children got to use their own imaginations in their play. What a gift my daughter received there! I see this now bearing fruit in her life as she teaches kindergarten.

Maybe partly because of this, Emilie has always been my artistic and creative child. Through the years, she got lots of sets of crayons, paints, and colored pencils for Christmas and birthday gifts. When she went to high school, she took every art class the school had available.

When the time came for her to choose a possible career,

she narrowed it down to art or elementary teaching. I remember talking with her about this.

"I love art and making crafts," she said. "I could be an art teacher, but I think I'd rather be a kindergarten teacher, because then I can do lots of arts and crafts with the kids. And there are more openings for kindergarten teachers than for art teachers."

This showed our daughter's practical thinking, too. After she turned 12, she began babysitting often and later worked as a helper at a local daycare. All these things added to her repertoire of working with young children. When I see her in her kindergarten classroom now, I swell with pride. Not just because she set her goal and reached it, but because she's such a talented teacher. And I'm not the only one who notices. Parents and grandparents of her students tell me the same.

When I was working on my Master's degree at Concordia River Forest, she came to stay with me for a week, and I'd arranged for her to help at the daycare there on campus. She was almost fourteen that summer, I think. After that week, the daycare director told me, "It was so wonderful to have Emilie help us. She's a natural. She adapted right away and did a better job than many of the college students who work with us in the school year."

So, it seems that seeds were planted for Emilie in Rexford, that took root and grew much later in her life.

The same was true for Jon. He also loved to draw, but his sketches were often of maps. Whenever we took road trips, which was usually annually, he kept occupied with the Rand McNally Atlas, pencil and paper. Of course, when he went to college, he studied geography. Interestingly, he and Emilie both went to the same college, Central Michigan University. But each had their own reasons. They chose this school because its strengths were in each of their areas of interest, early childhood education, and geography—seeds that had been planted in Rexford.

Okay, back to the garden. I was actually canning tomatoes on the day Emilie was born. We had friends with apple trees, who gave us bushels of them to make into applesauce. Jon and Emilie got so used to home preserved veggies and fruit that they refused to eat the stuff from the store. That kept me busy, but back then I enjoyed it. Those were the good years of my life.

It's hard to believe now that we spent almost ten years in Rexford. But besides the garden, many other 'seeds' were planted there, as I've already mentioned. Another one was that of directing church choir and learning to play the piano. This would blossom in very unexpected ways. The other was writing, which I continued to do on my own. And it was further encouraged when I took a part-time job at the local weekly newspaper, *The Tobacco Valley News.* I even got to do a few things with environmental education. But mostly, I was raising kids and volunteering at Christian Women's Clubs and church.

This is where the seeds of teaching music were planted, but I didn't realize it until much later. (More detail on this to come.)

Paul, Jonathan, and Max – all sound asleep in the chair. 1980 in Rexford, Montana

CHAPTER 7
Memories of Our Cats – The Real-life Ones Who Taught Us All

Over the years of our family, we have been blessed with the company of several special cats. It is just too bad they all cannot still be with us.

Max, Jonathan, and me. October 1981, Rexford, Montana

Max was a big brown tiger-striped Tabby. We got him when we were first married in Ft. Collins, Colorado from Ed Day, a friend of Paul's. Ed had gotten Max from the animal shelter—they thought he was around four years old. He lived in the same apartment complex we did, and so when Ed went on a trip to Europe, we fed Max for him. When Ed came back, Max kept coming to us, and he said we should just keep him. Max had some interesting experiences in the apartment complex. Once a girl down the hall threw him in the swimming pool because he chewed on her spider plant.

We took him on lots of trips with us, across the U.S., to Texas, Illinois, Canada, and many places in between. On one trip, he almost got left in Salmon, Idaho, though. We had stopped for gas, and he must have slipped out of the car. Just as we were about to pull away, Paul happened to glance out and saw a cat. "Boy that cat looks just like Max," he said. Then we realized it *was* Max! And we retrieved him.

Sometimes we would even take him camping. It was a great conversation starter, walking a big brown striped cat on a leash. People would even ask it he was a bobcat, because he was so big.

He moved with us to Idaho, and then on to Montana. He had to adjust to two new members of the family, Jon and Emilie. There were ups and downs for him because he was used to being the "only child."

After almost fifteen years, Max finally succumbed to old age and we had to have him put to sleep. He could not breathe very well anymore, and it was hard to see him suffer. It seems appropriate that we left Max in Montana, burying him shortly before we left there for Michigan.

When we moved to Michigan in May 1989, it was again because of the pressure of Paul's job. He hadn't gotten a promotion in almost 12 years, though he had been applying all over the West. At last we looked farther east and applied for a couple of jobs on the Huron-Manistee National Forest in Michigan. (Ironically, this was one of the forests Steve Harper, my RARE II friend, had worked on in his FS career.) The chances were still slim, but District Ranger Cal hired the guy he thought better suited for the job—Paul.

To try to make us feel more at home, we got **Tigger,** who was also a brown-striped Tabby. We got her from friends across the road as a kitten, shortly after we moved to Monument Road, probably because she reminded us of Max. She liked to hunt mice in our yard. Unfortunately, we only had her a year before she fell victim to the traffic on Monument Road.

Emilie and Tigger in her bed. Sleepers are so cute! 1990

I wasn't happy leaving the mountains and the West. But there was nothing I could do. It turned out to be very difficult for Jon, too. Shortly after the move, he was diagnosed with Tourette's Syndrome, a brain chemical imbalance which causes involuntary noises and muscular tics. So now he wasn't only uprooted from all the childhood friends he'd known, he was labeled as an oddball by his peers, and some of the teachers thought of him as a trouble-maker.

When he was in high school, he also began to show signs of Obsessive-Compulsive behavior (OCD). We didn't realize the full impact of this until his adulthood when we began to see signs of Negative Personality Disorder (NPD). Jon has never had it easy. They say trials are supposed to make us stronger, but the trials I've gone through with Jon have definitely made me weaker—I know I'm too emotional, plagued by depression, and occasionally even suicidal. All I can do is hope that Jon will come through somehow. My life is nearing the end. I'm already past 70. Jon has a lot of times and trials to come. Friends and relationships are very important to him, but he is also vulnerable in this area because of his disability.

I have asked God for over 40 years why He made Jon the way He did, but there seem to be no answers. Well-meaning pastors talk about blessings in disguise, and how our world is marred by sin and nothing is perfect. But I've often wondered, couldn't God just give us a break once in a while? Is there anyone out there who can help Jon be more stable? A friend? A mate? A counselor? We forced him to try counseling a couple of times, but we probably shouldn't have because now he is hesitant to consider it.

There are some medications that have helped, but Jon refuses to take them anymore. Maybe because we forced him to when he was in his teens. Refusal to accept help is part of the Negative Personality (NPD), I've read. It's human nature to look for someone else to blame for our troubles, especially for NPD. I suppose I do the same thing, but I tend to blame it on God. (I'm guilty as charged.) So, here is the Catch 22: if I suggest Jon try something, his first reaction is to refuse, though now he is gradually becoming more open to counseling

Not much else I can say, except I wonder if things would have been different if we'd stayed in Rexford. The mystery of the road not taken. (As you can see, much of the material in *Magnolia Drive* is based in large part on my experiences from this part of my life, but I have fictionalized it to help protect the innocent—and maybe the guilty, too.) I'm probably being too honest here, but sometimes I think this child of mine is more than I can bear. It has certainly caused the many stress-induced maladies I suffer from, such as migraines, irritable bowels, panic attacks, and many others. But I won't name them all.

Like Mary Anna, in this book, I have been fortunate to be led to a wonderful Christian Counselor. He has guided me in learning tools that help me cope better than I used to. One of them is **ACT, Acceptance Commitment Therapy**, described earlier in this Appendix. I hope that if no one bothers to read this long litany of my life, they will at least look at that short section on ***Notes About Counseling (p. 219).***

CHAPTER 8
The Cats of Our Children's Childhoods

So, I'm going to shift gears and tell the story from the viewpoint of our cats. I think they have been some of my best therapists, anyway.

Emilie playing 'dolls' with Fluffy and Garfield, 1991

Garfield - He came from the barn across the road, a beautiful silver-grey shorthair. He was Jon's cat. At the same time, we got **Fluffy**, Emilie's cat. They had the same mother, but were from consecutive litters that year. We thought Fluffy was a female, but he turned out to be a male. He was long-haired and grey striped. Garfield was our first little kitten. It was cute how he'd curl up on your shoulder. They loved to play together and would even cuddle up together to sleep. These were our only two cats who were really friendly with each other. But, sadly, they also fell prey to the traffic on the road, first Garfield, and about a year later, Fluffy. We had to bury Fluffy under the compost pile because the ground was frozen everywhere else. And we decided that if we got another cat, this one would be an indoor cat. We couldn't bear the thought of finding another dead cat on the road.

Tiffany - In April of 1992, I saw a picture of two kittens at the old Perry Drugs in East Tawas that said "Free to a Good Home." So we called and found Tiffany, a long-haired, white and buff colored three-month old kitten. (This was the first kitty since Max who already came with a name.) We learned she was half Himalayan. She did not have the Siamese coloring of a Himalayan, but she certainly had the body shape, long fur, and temperament. Tiffany would let us pick her up and she liked to play, though sometimes she would nip a little too hard. But she did not jump on beds or climb in laps. She did leave a lot of fur around the house. But the thing we liked best was the way she "talked" to us. She would answer with Meows whenever you addressed her.

Kitten Marbles, trying to make friends with Tiffany, 2000

While we had Tiffany, in September 2000, we also got **Marbles**, another male brown tiger with white paws. But his stripes were really swirls, hence his name. We had surprised Emilie by saying yes, when she asked if she could have one of the kittens that her friend Emily's cat had borne. So Marbles was really her cat, though he lived with us most of the time.

Tiffany did not like having a kitten in the house at first. After all she had ruled the roost for nearly nine years by then. But by Christmas, they were playing together, though they still kept their distance when it came to sleeping. Marbles was the one who liked to snuggle in bed with you, usually at the foot of the bed, but he did not like being under the covers. This is ironic because when we changed sheets on a bed, he would jump in right away and didn't seem to mind being covered by the sheets and blankets then. Tiffany would sometimes crawl up under the covers of a bed if no one was in it. You would walk in and see a strange lump in the bed that meowed or purred.

We had Tiffany for 12 years, long enough for both our children to graduate high school and go on to college. As I've mentioned, both Jon & Emilie went to the same college, CMU, but not because Emilie wanted to follow in Jon's footsteps. They were definitely their own persons, especially as they got older. Jon's love was music, especially marching band. He went to CMU in part because of their marching band's reputation. Also, in high school, he was chosen to participate in the Lions' Club All-State Marching Band, which went to Europe one year, and Southern California the next. Great opportunities for him. (That's how he was in Scotland so near to where I'd been 25 years before.)

Besides loving art, Emilie also was more athletic, like her dad. While Jon's sport was marching band, hers was running, especially Cross Country. At first, she had no interest in distance races, but the coach persisted in recruiting her. Once she got started in Cross Country, she actually liked it. The team aspect of this sport was a great thing for her, and the friends she made there were special. Her persistence in pursuing a goal served her well, too. In her senior year, she placed eighth at the state meet, out of field of hundreds. We were so proud of her! And this race put her on the school record board, which hung in the Tawas Area High School gym. She was in second place, just a few seconds behind another girl named Emily. (As of 2023, our daughter's name is still on the Cross Country record board, along with two other girls named Emily!)

People sometimes ask why we spelled her name with an 'ie' instead of a 'y' on the end. This is how her Grandma Erler's middle name was spelled. Even though Emilie never met her paternal grandmother, because Esther Emilie Erler died nearly a year before she was born, this name has helped her feel she has a connection to her. The 'ie' spelling is common for German and French names. She seems to like the uniqueness it gives her, and she also likes having her initials be E.E.E, like her grandma Erler's.

When I started teaching music classes to preschoolers, both my children had the opportunity to flex their wings, and I think this fed their teaching talents. Emilie came right across the street from her school to the church where my classes were. She was always a big help to me, and definitely had a knack for teaching.

Jon would come every so often to demonstrate his trombone to my classes. I was always amazed at how he blossomed when put in front of a group of children. It was like it came naturally to him to teach—just like his sister. Although he didn't set out to be a teacher initially, I think it was in the back of his mind.

Most of his summer jobs were at a camp in Upper Michigan, where he served as a counselor, games director, lifeguard, and waterfront director. He also did a lot of substitute teaching in Michigan after he finished college. God was planting seeds in him, still.

After deciding a desk job as a cartographer in Huntsville, Alabama didn't suit him, Jon joined us in Montana and pursued that teaching certificate. He also begin working at a Lutheran Bible camp on Flathead Lake, again counseling and lifeguarding. I still find it interesting that the little boy I had to force down his first waterslide became a lifeguard and high ropes instructor. God does work in mysterious ways.

Now both our children are teachers. I admire their abilities and am very proud of them. Emilie teaches kindergarten in Montana, and Jon teaches middle school social studies in Washington state.

Then came **Callie:**

Callie was a tortoise-shell female. We started by calling her "that calico cat" and the name stuck. She first showed up scrounging in our garbage or looking for handouts the winter of 2001-02. After we got back from our trip to Disney World in March, though, she was not around. Then

Tiffany "looking down" on Callie. 2003

Jonathan Paul Erler,
Class of 1999

Emilie Elizabeth Erler,
Class of 2002

she appeared again the following November, looking even scruffier and with a big belly.

In January of 2003, it was bitterly cold and I took pity on her and let her begin to spend the night in the bath room with her own litter box. Finally, we just showed her where the other cats' litter box was.

She and Tiffany did not get on really well, but Callie didn't let it phase her. She just took over one chair and gradually worked her way up to Beta Cat. Marbles, being the youngest didn't stand up to the older ladies, so he became Gamma Cat. Tiffany was still Alpha. After Tiffany was gone, Callie took over as Alpha. Marbles missed Tiffany because she would play with him, and Callie just growled at him.

In Fall 2005, almost all the piano students asked about Callie, and I had to tell them she got sick and died. Marbles became a lot more friendly, coming out to sniff music bags or students' shoes. He especially liked guitar cases. Once a student found Marbles in his case at the end of his lesson. This guitar student occasionally brought a pen laser, and Marbles loved that. He was soon climbing in our laps and became the one who crept up between us in the bed.

Meanwhile, Jon tried two career paths (as of 2020). After majoring in geography at Central Michigan University, he did various summer camp jobs (including lifeguard and waterfront director, which he did very well, we're told), substitute teaching, and swim instructor at a community pool. Then he got a job doing cartography (map-making) for a Defense Department contractor in Huntsville, Alabama. But the climate and a desk job didn't agree with him. After four years, he decided to go back to college and get a secondary-level social studies teaching certificate. I think this was partly so he could get back to the Pacific Northwest, too. Anyway, he has now accomplished this—with schooling at University of Montana. Now he's teaching middle school social studies in the Seattle/Tacoma area of Washington State. He just bought a house in Tumwater, south of Olympia.

Oh, yeah, the garden. Back when we moved to Michigan in 1989, we had about an acre of land in a semi-rural area three miles from Tawas City. But it was all clay—hard as rock when dry and impossibly gooey when wet. Besides that, our well didn't have enough water pressure to run a sprinkler, and the deer and rabbits ate everything that managed to push its way through the clay. No more garden. I think that's when I began to lose interest in cooking.

Fortunately, Paul liked to cook, too, so he was a big help. When I started teaching five days a week at Holy Family School, and 30-40 piano students a week in the evenings, Paul had to cook if he wanted to eat before 9 or 10 p.m.

CHAPTER 9
The Cats of the Return to Montana

In 2008 we returned to retire in Montana, finally fulfilling our dream.

Marbles came with us and lived until 2014. He got to spend six years as a free-roaming Montana cat, and even tried to make friends with my mom when she moved in with us in 2010.

Tiger Lily came to live with us after living at our dear friend Lorraine "Larry" Calvert's house for about five years. She'd come from the Humane Society. In the spring of 2014, Larry sold her house and moved into an assisted living facility. She was sad that she couldn't bring her kitty, so we said we'd take her. Her name came with her, but we usually called her "Lily" for short. She died of natural causes in 2017.

Tiger Lily helping with the laundry. 2015

Winter, 2020

After we finished a trip to Houston in 2018, to reconnect with my Feser cousins, we went to the animal shelter and adopted another brown tiger-tabby. This one is quite large, a female. She came with the name "Jersey", but we changed it to **Josie**, the name of one of my great-grandmothers. Even though she'd been brought into the shelter as a stray, she seemed quite well-fed. We've had her on a diet ever since we got her, but she's still heavy. She loves to be petted, especially by piano students.

I find that petting Josie is a good way to relax. Almost like meditating. I guess she's my guru. She usually sleeps on my bed, too. In the morning she licks my hand, like I'm her kitten. She's special, like all the rest.

None of our cats have learned to shake paws on command like Max did. He was unique. So far, we've had nine cats in

Josie sunning after playing with her toy mice. 2019

48 years of marriage. Each one of them has been special in his or her own way. I'm glad that I married a cat-person. A house without a cat isn't really a home.

Some people who aren't cat-people are probably wondering why I'm spending so much time talking about them. For me, their individual unique qualities are a microcosm of our human lives. Each of them has their own personality, talents, and faults. Just like people. Just like children. Over 30 years of teaching, I've worked with well over 500 students in various settings, and every one of them is one-of-a-kind. Each had their own skills and abilities, each learned in their own special way. That's why I enjoyed individual private teaching because I could work with each one where they were. We also tried to do this with our own children, of course.

As my faith has grown through ups and downs, trials and triumphs, I see that this is how God works with us, too. We're not mere numbers or parts of groups—or even denominations. Each of us is specifically created by our Lord to fill a unique place in His plan. There is no one like me—or you—anywhere else in the world.

As of this writing, I have been teaching music in one form or another for over 30 years. My student load here in Montana has fluctuated between 2 and 14. I'm glad that it's nowhere near what I had in Michigan—sometimes as high as 50 a week. I'm older now, and have less energy. I'm thankful for the opportunity to touch so many lives with the gift of music, but once I turned 70, I knew it was time to retire. I loved having students of all ages, from preschoolers through senior citizens over the past 30 years. Maybe old music teachers never die... they're too "sharp." Without music, life would B-flat. (Music teacher jokes—sorry!)

So, these are some of the memories I want to pass on to the next generation. My children's world is as different from mine as the world my parents and grandparents knew. This must be part of getting older, the need to leave something behind. That's why I attached a factual appendix to my *Journeys Saga* books. I find it more comfortable to tell my stories in fictional form. It seems to be the gift the Lord has given me.

On the other hand, there are many things in life that don't change much as the years roll by. Loves and losses continue. Values change, or seem to. The older I get, the more I cling to this promise Jesus gave, "Heaven and earth will pass away, but my words will not pass away."

One more thought, the idea of home can be elusive for some of us. To the best of my knowledge, I've lived in 25 domiciles over the course of my life so far. From Arkansas, to Illinois, to Colorado, with a side trip to Scotland for a semester, then Idaho, Montana, Michigan, and back to Montana. They say "Home is where the heart is." I believe I can say, "I'm just a stranger here; heaven is my home."

And I've learned that where you live isn't what makes you happy. All the time we were in Michigan, I longed to move back to Montana, but now that I'm here I miss Michigan more than I thought I would. I think too many things in the world started falling apart with the Covid pandemic, and the future looks pretty bleak now, from wherever you are trying to see it.

$$\overline{}$$

CHAPTER 10

So, How Did I Morph into a Music Teacher?

In many ways, I'm like my fictional alter-ego, Mary Anna. Earth Day 1970 instilled a desire in me to change the world and save the environment, so I started in forestry and natural resources at Colorado State. But the Lord had other plans for me, which took a while to unfold.

Music had always been a big part of my life. Dad liked music, and once we got a record player, we listened to a lot of recordings, especially jazz and classical. Dad liked to play his old 78s, too.

One of the first things I convinced Paul to do when we got married was to join the choir at St. John's Lutheran Church in Ft. Collins. He discovered that he liked singing. I had been in church choirs in Ottawa and El Dorado while I was growing up, and it was important to me.

Each place we moved, we joined the choir. And when our children were old enough, they were in the children's choirs in Eureka. When we moved to Tawas City, Michigan, Jon was eight years old. He missed the Eureka children's choir and convinced me to start one at Zion-Tawas. So I did. I had directed an adult choir in Eureka, so it wasn't totally foreign to me. I wasn't a music major, but I had a love for the music and wanted to serve the Lord. As it turned out, God had plans for me.

As time went on in Tawas, I started substitute teaching in the local public schools. One year I did a long-term sub for the lower elementary music teacher and discovered how much I liked it. So, I applied to get into a Master's of Music Ed. Program I heard of at Concordia-River Forest, a Lutheran college in Illinois. The classes were offered in the summer, so I could do it and still keep my job of teaching music (and also art and PE) at Holy Family Catholic School, where I was hired in 1994, about the same time I started the Master's program. And I was already teaching piano by this time.

How did I become a piano teacher? I always wanted to learn to play the piano, as I've related before, but my parents could never afford the lessons or a piano. When we were living in Rexford, though, I convinced Paul to buy a piano and started with a teacher right there in town. Later I changed to a young teacher who went to our church in Eureka. Jon started lessons, too. When we moved to Tawas, I contacted a teacher recommended to me, Kaye Phelps. And she became much more than my teacher—a dear friend and a mentor, too. She encouraged me to start teaching beginners, especially children. And for the next 16 years, I taught close to 250 students in the Tawas Area—not all at once, though.

At my peak load, I had up to 50 students in my home studio per week. I also branched out into teaching classes for preschoolers, first Kindermusik and later Musikgarten. It was all a lot of fun. When she could, Emilie helped me, starting when she was in fifth grade. I think this is where her natural talent for teaching came out. She knew when she went to college at Central Michigan University that she wanted to be a teacher. Now she's been teaching kindergarten here for 15 years so far (2022). And it was her ticket back to Montana besides.

I did get a Master's Degree in Music Education in 1998. My thesis was a curriculum for teaching music to preschoolers and kindergarteners, with a Christian emphasis. Paul and I 'retired' for the first time in 2006, him from the Forest Service and me from Holy Family. When we moved back to Montana in 2008, I continued my private teaching, and for the first two years, I also taught music at Helena Flats, a small rural school east of Kalispell. Paul took a part-time job delivering the local newspaper and servicing their vending machines all around the Flathead Valley, and even up into Glacier National Park. So I guess you can say we were only 'semi-retired'.

After I had to leave Helena Flats to care for my mother who had Alzheimer's, I did work very part-time teaching music at Trinity Lutheran School in Kalispell. It was sometimes fun and sometimes challenging. But I now realize that this was the plan God had for me all along. I'm not a virtuoso, or even very confident in my playing. But I love sharing the joy of music with others, and use it as a ministry whenever the Lord leads.

So now I've been full-circle, and I'm over 70. I have reached Erikson's * Reflective Stage, seeking the answer to the prime question, "Has my life been meaningful and worthwhile?" What follows are my thoughts and conclusions.

CHAPTER 11
A Meaningful Life?

Like many of my peers in the 1960s, I wanted to change our world for the better. I wanted to leave my mark and do great things. But it didn't turn out the way I expected. Instead of making me a leader and famous author, God morphed me into a music teacher.

Teachers in general, and especially teachers in the arts fields, are often seen as superfluous in our culture. Something nice to have, if the school can afford it, but usually the first thing cut when budgets are tight. The result for me has been a marginal income and very few "benefits" as the world describes them.

But for me personally, the benefits have been awesome, even though in our culture they aren't often recognized. I am not a greatly talented musician. My dad said I couldn't carry a tune in a bucket. I taught myself to play guitar so I could sing on key and not stray from the correct tune. I worked hard to gain the skills that came naturally to many of my friends and relatives. All my life I'd wanted to learn to play piano, and I finally got to take formal lessons after age 30.

I was completely surprised when my piano teacher, Kaye, urged me to teach some beginning piano students she couldn't fit into her schedule. She told me I didn't have to be a virtuoso to teach, that it was a different set of skills, and she saw them in me. What a wonderful door she opened for me!

Here I am 31 year later, and just retired from teaching music. I loved the opportunity to focus on each one's particular interests and learning styles. They are all unique. I also enjoyed the relationships that were built as I shared my love of music with them.

I have been fortunate to have had a positive impact on numerous young lives, but the greatest joy is that they will always hold a special place in my heart.

I am still in touch with some of my former students via social media. (It's not all bad.) They knew me when they were children, and now many of them are married and having children of their own. Some of them are even music teachers who can now play much better than I do.

I'm touched and humbled to have been given this opportunity to teach. Now I see that it was a calling from God, a ministry he had planned for me. What natural talents I lacked, He provided, in order that He might have the glory, not me.

A meaningful life? Perhaps not in the eyes of the world. But it has been precious, indeed!

CHAPTER 12
Final Thoughts and Metaphors

Since this book is technically fiction, I feel obligated to provide some closure (read "happy endings") which is what fiction readers expect. In order to do this, I had to manufacture closure for Mary Anna's story.

Most of us realists are forced to admit, however, that real life isn't like this. It has its ups and downs, and we never know what is around the next bend in the road. I've been told it's a cliché to call life a rollercoaster, but it is—whether we want to admit it or not. Some people thrive on the adrenalin surge of life's rollercoaster, but I'm not one of them.

Maybe a good metaphor for life is a yo-yo. As a child playing with yo-yos, I often had the problem of it not returning up the string to my hand. I'd have to wind it up manually. Now I find my life is often like that. Instead of downs followed by ups, it just stays down there at the end of the string—or another cliché 'the end of my rope'.

Too many days I doubt that my life will have any of the closure I depicted for Mary Anna. My son still gets suicidal at time, and whenever he does, I fall into the same black hole all over again—and I admit I sometimes feel suicidal, too.

At the very beginning of this book, I've put a poem my father wrote, comparing life to a poker game—another apt metaphor. "You win some, you lose some," is something Dad often told me. I would add, "If you can't play with the cards you're dealt, all you can do is fold."

Some days I feel the hope I've depicted for Mary Anna at the end of *Magnolia Drive*, but it comes and goes. The **"T"** part of **ACT** (trust) is the hardest one to hold on to. I remember believing, back in the idealistic days of my youth, that all the pieces of life's puzzle would fall into place someday—that my life would have meaning.

The years have taken a heavy toll, though, and that feeling of hope waxes and wanes like the phases of the moon. "Oh, the inconstant moon!" Shakespeare has Juliet cry this in his tragedy *Romeo and Juliet*. I guess I need to look to the sun instead of the moon, but it often hides behind clouds, especially here in northwest Montana. Hmm…I suppose that's enough metaphors for one short piece.

However, I must add that as I look back where my life has been, I'm beginning to see more of a pattern. And the key to it all is love—God's love for us, which never fails, so that we can pass it on to others. I just hope I'll be able to do this for a few people before I die.

ABOUT THE AUTHOR

M.F. (Mary Frances) Erler is a music teacher, outdoor educator, and author of fantasy fiction and non-fiction. Her teaching career has spanned over 30 years, and she has been writing most of her life. Her first Christian-based science-fiction book, *"The Peaks at the Edge of the World"* was re-written and revised in 2017, followed by six other books in the series.

Erler has been writing most of her life. In fact, some of the characters in *The Peaks Saga* were initially conceived in her youth. Her lifelong goal has been to bring spiritual ideas into fantasy-fiction, in the spirit of writers like J.R.R. Tolkien and C.S. Lewis. She enjoys public speaking and sharing her faith journey. She is an approved speaker for Women's Connections, a Stonecroft Ministry.

Now that she has published *The Peaks Saga,* she is embarking on a new venture in fiction, first with *"Voices in the Past,"* a historical fiction, and now *"Lauren's Dark Passage,"* which is contemporary fiction. These books are stand-alones, not part of a series, like the Peaks books.

Her books are designed to appeal to young adults and all who are young at heart. Among her many hobbies, Erler especially enjoys travel. She has been to several countries, including China, New Zealand, the British Isles, and Western Europe, as well as Canada, Mexico, Jamaica, and 45 of the 50

States. Her favorite mode of travel is cruising, but her current favorite place is her home in Montana.

Along with fantasy, true science, and science fiction, she is also a student of history, comparative religion, ecology, and music. Previous publications include non-fiction articles in *Today's Christian Parent*, and *Social Studies and the Young Learner*, as well as poems and short sketches in Standard Publishing Program Books. In addition, she has produced *Music in God's World*, a music curriculum for preschools, and *Wonders of Creation, an Environmental Education Curricula* for use in schools and camp settings. She has worked as a newspaper reporter and columnist, and was writer for various U.S. Forest Service publications, including being in charge of producing the book, *Targhee Lodgepole-Tragedy or Opportunity?*

She has a Bachelor of Science in Environmental Education and Biology from Colorado State University, and a Masters of Music Education from Concordia University-Chicago. In her senior year of high school, she was awarded a prize for her writing by the National Council of Teachers of English, the Quill and Scroll Award for Journalism, and a National Merit Scholarship.

Her love of singing has led to participation in many choirs and acapella groups, which enabled her to perform at two International Sweet Adelines conventions in Nashville and Houston. She sang with these women's barbershop groups for 18 years. Hobbies include reading, singing, playing several musical instruments, and acrylic painting. She and her husband, Paul, have two adult children who are also teachers. All make their home in the northwest. You are invited to connect with her at mferler@peaksandbeyond.com or on her blog at MFErler. blogspot.com.